**PEOPLE SAID THAT
IN PLEASANT HILLS,**
EVERYONE GOT THEIR SCANDAL.
FIFTEEN MINUTES OF INFAMY.

**THIS WAS
MINE.**

THE TRUTH ABOUT KEEPING SECRETS

savannah brown

sourcebooks
fire

Published by Sourcebooks Fire, an imprint of Sourcebooks
P.O. Box 4410, Naperville, Illinois 60567-4410
(630) 961-3900
sourcebooks.com

Originally published in 2019 in the United Kingdom by Penguin
Books, an imprint of Penguin Random House UK.

Library of Congress Cataloging-in-Publication Data

Names: Brown, Savannah (Young adult author), author.
Title: The truth about keeping secrets / Savannah Brown.
Description: Naperville, Illinois : Sourcebooks Fire, [2020] | Originally
   published in the United Kingdom by Penguin Books in 2019. | Audience:
   Ages 14-18. | Audience: Grades 10-12.
Identifiers: LCCN 2019033740 | (trade paperback)
Subjects: CYAC: Grief--Fiction. | Friendship--Fiction. | Lesbians--Fiction.
   | Mystery and detective stories. | Youths' writings.
Classification: LCC PZ7.1.B7972 Tr 2020 | DDC [Fic]--dc23
LC record available at https://lccn.loc.gov/2019033740

Printed and bound in the United States of America.
WOZ 10 9 8 7 6 5 4 3 2 1

1

SEEING THE BODY WAS SUPPOSED to be cathartic, but the man in the lipstick wasn't my dad.

I mean, he was. But he wasn't. There was so little Dad left in him that the emotional experience wasn't too dissimilar from gazing upon a giant steak in a suit: there was discomfort, and a sick sort of a fascination, but mainly a desire for the moment to end. That sounds callous. Maybe it was. Maybe it was a symptom of overresearching; the night before I had spent hours reading about embalming to prepare myself for what this would be like, and now all I could focus on were his glued-together eyelids, his sewn-shut mouth, and his bloated limbs stuffed into clothes tailored well enough to distract everyone from the fact that he looked like a Jim Henson fever dream.

Benjamin Whitaker, the artist formerly known as Dad, had hugged a telephone pole while traveling at approximately sixty miles an hour. Swerve, smash, gone. Well, not really, but *swerve, smash, unconscious* doesn't have quite the same punch. The lungs were the problem. The lack thereof. They'd popped like balloons, which isn't super-conducive to living; even so, he'd managed to survive long enough to get to the hospital, but not much longer. And when there was no one left to keep alive, the town officials and police officers were left to figure out *why*—but the investigation only led to more uncertainty. The front of the car had practically melted, and there was no way to tell if the accident had been caused by faulty brakes or steering or whatever, so the best they could come up with was that maybe he had fallen asleep, or been texting, or suicidal, or maybe there was a deer or a person, or maybe he simply wasn't paying attention.

And I'm sure, to the outside observer, any of those possibilities might have seemed realistic. But the outside observer didn't know Dad.

I'm exaggerating about how he looked. He looked fine. Enough to be recognizable, and underneath the pale foundation and pink lip tint, there was still the time-locked stubble and the square jaw and the pulled-taffy limbs. But the sight of his chest was jarring. A mountain range, all slopes and concavities where the newspaper balled up underneath his shirt had flattened. Then something occurred to me.

"Why the hell is he wearing his glasses?"

Mom turned to me, the outside of her cheek puckering as she

gnawed the inside. She was all red: red lips, red blush, reddish hair wound into a bun. Rushing red blood. Practically taunting him. "Language, please."

"Why the *heck* is he wearing he glasses?"

She sighed. "It's a symbolic thing, Sydney." I knew it was a symbolic thing. I just sometimes liked to fill the air with stuff that didn't actually matter to distract from my more pressing thoughts: at that moment, the corpse of my dad being lowered from the ceiling on a swing, singing a soulful rendition of "Rainbow Connection" with Miss Piggy.

Mom looked me up and down. She was just as stoic as I was; she wouldn't cry here either. "Straighten your skirt, honey. You're all crooked."

I didn't know where I was crooked, but I believed her—she knew more about skirts than me—so I did some miscellaneous smoothing until she seemed satisfied. I wasn't sure why she cared. ("Well, yes, the service was lovely, but that girl's lower half was a bit off-center, don't you think?")

"I'm going to fix myself up before everyone gets here," she said. "Do you want to come?" She wasn't asking me to come so much as she was suggesting I should.

"I don't need to fix myself up."

Mom was about to protest but seemed to be informed by Dad's ghost that she should drop it. She walked off alone, the ugly carpet dulling the tap of her stilettos.

Crawford Funeral Home was completely bleak—not that I was expecting anything else. Because of the light, I think. It was a sickly yellow, leaking on to stiff-looking armchairs and fake potted plants and paintings of places more beautiful. The paintings were the only indication that a world existed outside that place; there were windows, but they were the approximate size and shape of keyholes, and something about the awful baroque pattern on the walls made it seem as if they were slowly closing in on you. I wasn't claustrophobic often, but in here, each breath felt itchy and earned. That might've been the intention, though—to make you feel like you were the one about to be buried.

But Rick Crawford seemed right at home. He was the undertaker, well-groomed and stout, and spoke with a drawl. The Crawfords had owned the place for generations, and the guy looked like he hadn't been born, but had crawled out of a vat of formaldehyde. I wondered if he grew into the death business or the death business grew into him. Anyway, it couldn't have been an easy job. Especially not here, since I was sure he would have recognized at least half the people he had to drag onto the slab every morning. Sort of like Dad. Dad was the only therapist in Pleasant Hills, and I bet, collectively, he and Rick Crawford knew most of the place's dirty secrets, living and dead.

Our family was small—Dad's parents had died young, and Mom wasn't close to hers—so the people who started to trickle in were only faintly familiar. Old family friends. (*Your hair's so long now, wow, straw-berry blond, you have your mom's freckles, wow, junior year already? Wow, wow, wow.*) Teachers I'd had who felt some sense of obligation to me. Bible-thumpers. Tongue-chewers. The women Mom knew from the gym, from her Tupperware parties, who said things like *It was his time* over and over again. And there were a lot of strangers—patients—who thanked us for everything Dad had done for them. I knew none of them, which meant Dad had succeeded; he'd always made a point of keeping me away from that part of his life, from the cars pulling up before school and after school and on Sundays, from the murmurs and more-than-murmurs from behind the office door, from the weights fastened one by one to the heavy, rolling skin underneath his eyes.

But now they were all here, staring me in the face, and any one of them could have done it.

Olivia and I were best friends—mostly because we were supposed to be. We had barely anything in common besides the fact that fate had dictated we were to live on the same cul-de-sac, but she let me talk about movies, and I let her talk about everything else. She was the high school's head theatre tech, a social butterfly, had lots of friends. Me, not so much. Either way, we'd made an unspoken agreement to see out the rest of our years in formal education together; I don't think either of us had anticipated the agreement would include funeral attendance, but she was here, and although I wouldn't tell her, I was grateful.

"Oh, God," she said when she noticed I was staring. She looked pretty; her dark hair hung in unnatural curls and her cheekbones shimmered even in the dull light. She had single eyelids, and the glittery purple liner she wore kind of looked like it was part of the anatomy of her eye, swirling upward and narrowing to a point. The shape reminded me of a robin. Pretty. Not really funeral pretty. "I knew I shouldn't have come like this. I wanted to get ready first thing this morning, so, you know, I could stay as long as you needed without having to rush back or anything, but Miles's mom wanted us to be ready for pictures at four. Which is so early, right? That's early. And I tried to say it was too early, but they already made the dinner reservations, and I realize that seems not important compared to—"

"Hey." I envisioned us standing there until we began to decompose, Olivia still talking while chunks of flesh fell from her skull. I patted her on the cheek. "Don't worry about it. Deep breaths."

Olivia squished her mouth into an *O* and sucked, backward whistle, and it looked stupid as hell, so I laughed, but someone I didn't know shot me a glance and I folded in on myself. Lowered my voice. "I don't want to meet and greet anymore." Mom was talking to someone, which meant I could make my escape. "Let's go hide."

We managed to sneak away to an inconspicuous hallway near the entrance. I slumped against the wallpaper as Olivia wrung her wrist in her other hand, searching for something to say—unusual for her. "Do you want to, like, talk?" she asked. "I read that it's good to talk. You're supposed to express yourself because if you don't, you'll end up spontaneously combusting. Not really, but, you know. Metaphorically. With emotions."

"I appreciate the fact that you did research, but, no. Not right now." I shut my eyes, rested the back of my head against the wall, wished to be anywhere else. "Regular programming. Just...talk."

"All right. Oh! We missed you last night."

It took me a second to remember: the game. Right. It was the homecoming game, and a *very big deal*, and she'd invited me along, but to be completely honest, school spirit was at the bottom of my priorities list, besides eating food and behaving like a normal human being.

"How was it?" I asked, even though I wasn't particularly interested. Anything to keep her talking.

"Yeah, good. We won, obviously. Hooray, go Panthers, go football, so on, so forth. But honestly, it was probably for the best you didn't go, because it was freezing, firstly, and it went on forever. Like, overtime. I thought I was gonna have to get some toes amputated. Oh, and they did the homecoming court stuff. Heath Alderman and June Copeland won king and queen, obviously." Olivia had a tendency to insist upon the obviousness of nonobvious things, but she wasn't exaggerating this time; Heath Alderman and June Copeland might have actually been bred to be homecoming royalty, like some sort of champion line of miniature schnauzers. "I have no idea how June did it," Olivia continued, "but she was standing out in the field in this beautiful dress that had no sleeves. *Zero* sleeves. The wind chill was, like, minus three, but she didn't even have a single freaking goose bump. Oh, and speaking of homecoming things, are you *sure* you're okay with me going tonight? For real. I don't have to. Miles will get over it. We can stay in"—she nudged me with her elbow—"watch a movie or something. Even one of your weird ones."

Honestly, I didn't want her to go. It was nice to have access to *sound*, some sort of stimulation, but I would have felt guilty asking her to stay. "Don't worry," I said. "Bring me back, uh, a cupcake that looks like a fish, or something. That's the theme, right?"

"Oh, all right, let me tell you about the *theme*." Apparently, it was a whole thing that student council was split between Roaring Twenties (event coordinator extraordinaire Olivia's idea) and Under the Sea (not Olivia's idea; also, apparently, a horrible idea), and they ended up going with Under the Sea, and Olivia went on an admittedly well-constructed tirade about how democracy doesn't work because most people are too stupid to pick the right answer. Fine. Maybe we did have something in common.

Eventually, Rick called out from the main room that the ceremony was starting. Olivia went back to her parents, *plural*, and I sat with Mom in the front row, which was reserved for us. Phew. I was worried we'd be stuck in the cheap seats. I said this to Mom, who told me under her breath to stop it.

"Er, hello, everyone, thank you for coming," Rick began, standing at the podium, clearing his throat in between words. The casket was closed now, so I had to find something else to think about: the way the saliva in Rick's mouth went stringy as he talked would do. "My name is Rick Crawford, I'm a civil celebrant, and it's truly a privilege to welcome you all to this celebration of Benjamin Whitaker's forty-six years of life. He was, er, first and foremost, a husband to Rebecca and a father to Sydney." He gestured to Mom and me. I felt like I should wave. "But he was also a hero to many in our community, and it is with great sadness that we see him off here today." Rick was a nice-enough guy, but as he went on for a bit about the fragility of life and the human experience, it was obvious every other poor wretch had been given the same nonspecific speech. It was canned. Scripted. Insert cause of death, familial relations, and religious affiliations here.

And then it was me at the microphone. Plucked out of the ether, like this was someone else's funeral I'd accidentally stumbled into, but they were looking at me all blank-faced and brow-furrowed, so I had to say something. "My—"

The microphone screeched. I stepped back while the collective face of the audience curled into a wince. Apologized. "Uh, Dad is—well, was. Was." They stared. Mom ground her teeth. I apologized again. This was awful. "Um, so… Dad really cared about people. About everyone, really. His whole job was listening and empathizing, and that's, you know. That's something."

Mercifully, a few heads nodded, as if I had said something very important. I knew I hadn't. I had nothing to say. But that wasn't true. I did—but not to these people. If it'd been me alone talking into a void, oh, I would've had all kinds of things to say. I would have told the void the one when I'm six, and Dad and I are hiking at the River Styx, the place where I learned to love the world as much as he did, and we're on the secluded path that runs parallel to the stream, and I go to explore by the swampy pools along the riverbank—looking for tadpoles, or something—and my feet have already disappeared up to my ankles by the time I realize I'm sinking. But Dad hauls me out by my arms, the mud sucking and popping beneath me like I'm a loose tooth. We wash our feet in the stream, watch the mud get swept away with the current, and Dad says he didn't think anyone has ever been so calm in quicksand. I could have told the one when I'm eight and he lets me watch episodes of *The Twilight Zone* with him after Mom goes to sleep; when I'm eleven and we ride the bumper cars at the county carnival over and over even though he has a bad back; when I'm fourteen and he holds me after the girl breaks my heart; when I'm seventeen and he's sitting in a box to my right and everyone is expecting something of me, and I can't stand it, I really can't, because he shouldn't be dead.

He shouldn't be dead.

I fiddled with the microphone stand, my fingers slipping. "But why doesn't anybody know what happened? The...the car people. The coroner. Whatever. This sort of thing can't just happen."

At this point, the audience was still on my side—besides Mom, whose spine had got noticeably straighter. They were waiting for me to throw in the twist, the *but*, to share some glorious epiphany about how that was simply the way the world is, that sometimes we don't have all the answers, that life is unfair.

"Dad did care about people. But, I don't know. Maybe people didn't extend that same care to him."

Mom mouthed my name.

"He was told people's most personal stuff on a daily basis. Secrets upon secrets. Dark stuff. And maybe..."

At first, I thought maybe I'd been in a highly suggestive state and was experiencing grief-induced hallucinations, because I could have sworn that, near the back of the room, was the homecoming queen.

June Copeland stood with the posture of someone trying not to be noticed, but hunched shoulders don't hide much when you stand six feet in heels and look like her. She had these curls that cascaded down her back and around her shoulders, a foamy waterfall of ringlets so dark that the darkness seemed to fold in on itself like a black hole. In some places, the spirals were uniform, but around the top they burst forth like a halo, cumulus, cotton candy.

She met my gaze and gave me the saddest little smile I'd ever seen. Her cheeks rose as she did; they were a warm brown, the color of clay, like every terra-cotta pot in the world had gotten together and discussed all the reds and the browns until they arrived at the most harmonious combination, then bathed her in the result. But the smile disappeared as quickly as it had arrived, and I didn't know what to do besides stare.

Mom's hand on my bicep drew me away. "Come on, sweetie." I wasn't sure how long I'd been standing there. Maybe a second. Maybe an eternity. I let her drag me off the platform, watched my feet as I stepped down, but when I looked back toward the entrance, there was only the black hem of June's dress swaying through the closing door.

I sat. Folded my hands. Collected myself.

As the moment dissolved, I became increasingly aware of the eyes aimed at the back of my skull, like worms boring through the marrow. I didn't dare turn to meet them. I felt ridiculous. Thoroughly embarrassed. What had I done? What had I even been trying to say? If I had been watching myself from where June was standing, I decided, I would have thought something was seriously wrong with me.

Clearly everyone else agreed, because they took Dad to the cemetery without any requests for further autopsies or an impromptu search for clues. They had the decency to wait for me, at least; I opted to travel via bike instead of car behind the procession. And while they lowered him down with the awful creaking straps, I imagined him waking up inside the coffin, clawing at the polished mahogany until his fingernails wore away, and I wanted desperately for them to open it, just to check, just to see. The website had said Pleasant Hills Cemetery was eighteen rolling acres, and I had no idea where these walls were coming from, closing in, crushing, *crushing*, and I sucked air into my throat like it might be for the last time.

But that was it. They dropped him in, and that was it.

We lingered for a while longer. Olivia was noticeably gentler with me as she said goodbye, and Mom talked to people who thought I couldn't hear them. Hushed: *Sydney seems like she's taking it badly.* Oblivious: *I think Sydney should see a therapist.* Of course. There would be books in Dad's office that accused me of *projection*, of being so averse to the reality of the situation that I had made up some fanciful hypotheses about all the things that could have happened that didn't include the word "accident."

And when I pedaled away behind Mom, her trunk full of bouquets that would wilt and food we wouldn't eat, I swore I saw June Copeland at the curve where the hill met the horizon, her black dress playing between the stones.

That night, I replayed the funeral in my head once, twice, again. Again.

Dad laid out on the slab. Dad underground.

It all felt so strange. If someone had told me it hadn't actually happened, I probably would have believed them. When I tried to summon up the memory of it, it felt flimsy, like I couldn't actually hold on to it, like my brain knew it was something too deleterious to keep.

But June Copeland. She was there.

What the *hell* had she been doing? National Honor Society president. The likely salutatorian to Heath's likely valedictorian. I had never even spoken to her. Just admired from afar. Which makes me sound creepy, but we all did it. We were almost expected to. They were paraded around as Pleasant Hills' golden children, as some sort of goal for us, the commoners, to aspire to. Made even more impressive by the fact that June had only moved to Pleasant Hills freshman year from somewhere in California. Originally an outsider, she'd assimilated so successfully that she hadn't only become an insider, but now ruled over them herself. Actually, Heath *was* the school president— maybe June was there as some sort of fucked-up First Lady? But why had she…looked at me like that? Half like I was pathetic, half like I was pitiable, as if I'd been an ant she'd accidentally stepped on but at least respected enough to flick off her shoe.

But maybe it was more than that. The strangers, quiet, with their heads down—maybe it was a thank-you.

Most importantly, though: Why did I care?

That's when I got the text.

Hi Sydney.

My nerves stood to attention. There was no name. There wasn't even a number; it was only listed as *restricted*. And it was nearly three in the morning. Who was texting me at three in the morning?

I typed back with heavy fingers.

Me: Uh hello

Me: Sorry

Me: Who is this?

The ellipses that meant the person was typing appeared below my texts almost instantly. Like the sender had been sitting there. Waiting for my response.

You really think someone killed him?

It was an odd sensation. I still hadn't processed what exactly was going on—generally, but also in that exact moment—and it was as though my blood wanted to run cold but wasn't sure of it, and had instead opted for lukewarm.

You really think someone killed him?

I didn't know what to say. Wasn't even sure I should say anything.

So I didn't. I turned my phone off, rolled over in bed, willed myself to sleep until the light outside turned pink.

2

SUNDAY MORNING, I'D CONVINCED MYSELF everyone on the planet had disappeared. It was agonizingly quiet, only the hiss of my own breath slipping past my lips and the dry rustle of my sheets. Sunday. If everything had been normal, Dad would have been awake by now. Watching the news. Making coffee. I lobbed the thought of him around my mind for a moment, a little bit of self-mutilation, but I felt nothing. I could hear the news. Smell the coffee. Numb, numb, numb.

I smacked my head lightly, as if I were a faulty vending machine, and then harder, then scratched the back of my left hand until the scrapes blossomed and swelled. Breathe. *Breathe.*

I changed out of the hoodie I'd gone to bed in, put on another, splashed water on my face, and left without leaving a note. Mom would see my bike was gone and figure out the rest.

Outside wasn't much better. Of course it wasn't—what sort of life did I expect at seven in the morning in Pleasant Hills? There was an eerie, post-apocalyptic pall over the place; most stores in town didn't open until noon on Sundays, if they opened at all. Comfort came in the form of cars whooshing past and lingering church bells from somewhere in the distance. *I am okay. I am not alone.*

But every landmark served as a reminder of what I was running from. Past the city library where Dad and I photocopied my bug encyclopedia (in color!) for five cents a page; Frankie's, where he'd take Olivia and me to get ice cream after little league; the square at the center of town, all early-twentieth-century lampposts and hedges and sidewalks where we'd set out linen chairs with pops in the cup holders and watch the fireworks on the Fourth of July. The whole place reeked of Dad. I couldn't look anywhere without seeing his silhouette; his ghost crawled from the sewer drains. But in a town covered in residue, how could there have been such a *lack*? Outrage. Sound. Where were the sirens? The panic? Benjamin Whitaker was dead! Dad was dead!

There should have been chaos in the streets. The town should have been engulfed in flames.

It was cold. Freezing. I'd hardly been outside the week before, and in that time, the seasons had changed. It was only the end of September, but the maples were already going yellow and orange and crimson, the earliest sacrificial leaves bunched at the side of the road, making way for the inevitable first snowfall of the year. Due any day.

Fall didn't last long here. Since we were so close to Lake Erie, any cold air that arrived ricocheted off the bank and shot straight at us. You could already smell winter: frozen iron and fireplace smoke and car exhaust. On the long stretches of empty road, I rode with one hand clutching the handlebar, the other lapping up heat from my breath. I had never liked the cold, but today, it made me especially angry. I wanted to bite back at it.

I could *leave*, I realized, road stretching ahead of me like an invitation. Pedal and pedal until my legs screamed, until I forgot how to pedal. But where would I go? California? Dad had always wanted to take me so I could see the giant redwoods. ("You wouldn't believe how small they make you feel, Syd!" I hadn't understood why that was something that excited him.) But we'd never gotten the chance to go. We'd wanted to go to Yosemite the following spring, maybe. Obviously that wasn't in the cards anymore. But I could've gone. Lived in the forest. Hollowed out a redwood, sat still for days and weeks and months, waited for nature to reclaim my body. Maybe I'd have felt something with branches curling through my guts.

Two hours of aimless wandering had passed, and the cold had become entirely unbearable. I turned toward home—but I had to pass the cemetery anyway.

Twelve graves across, four rows down.

Even if I hadn't counted, the grave wasn't hard to find; his was the freshest, the dirt powdered with a thin layer of ice crystals. This place felt more like home than home did. It definitely hadn't the day before, with the mourners and the whispers and the gawking, but now, with just him and me, I felt the urge to scoop out a me-shaped hole, plant myself like a seed.

But I would have had to move the roses first.

Three of them in the bunch—white, like the sort Dad kept in his office. These were new. The flowers we'd left yesterday were clustered around the headstone, stiff with frost, but these were untouched. They must have been put there that morning. Had Mom come? She couldn't have—I would have heard her leave.

This unexpected thing tripped my brain, made me aware of the other unexpected things that I must have filed away as dreams. That text.

You really think someone killed him?

I pulled the message up on my phone to confirm it was real. Read it again. How could someone have known what I'd said at the funeral unless they were there? But then it occurred to me: freaking Olivia. She must have told somebody at the dance. Right. Couldn't keep her damn mouth shut. And now, I was sure, the information was already doing the rounds among the student body, a pack of ravenous sadists gossiping that good old Whitaker was at it again, and someone thought it'd be funny to mess with me. Ha, ha. Great work, everyone.

But this rumor wasn't untrue. I had said it. Implied it, anyway. And the scraps of lucidity I had left were telling me I was probably full of shit—but the rest of me was saying that maybe I wasn't.

The other unexpected thing was June. Weird, flowy, sad-smiling June.

Banal June. Shallow June.

I didn't care about June. Actually, no: I was sort of pissed off at June. Why did she think she had the right?

I grew angry at unexpected things. The unfairness of it all. I wasn't even grieving correctly, still unable to feel anything after he'd settled in for the Big Sleep, and all these unforeseen spines jutting from the angst weren't even supposed to *be there*. Only grief. That's all there should have been, locked around me like an iron maiden. Straightforward. Instead, the universe had opted for horse dismemberment, the horses Angst and Murder and Weird Girls all tearing me limb from limb—and I wished they'd get it over with.

Frostbite was becoming a genuine possibility, so I left and navigated along brick-paved side streets to the cul-de-sac. The act of stepping through the front door felt like willingly condemning myself to hell. Satan, I'm home.

Mom was awake, shuffling papers at the kitchen table. The scratching made the hairs on the back of my neck stand up. She grinned when she saw me, wide and careless. "Were you out?"

I thought the fact that I'd entered from outside implied I had been out, but I nodded anyway.

Mom looked down at the papers, then looked back to me, startled, like she'd been reminded of her own consciousness. "Are you hungry? I can make you a sandwich, or..." She stopped, chewed her thumb, presumably because Dad had enjoyed a sandwich or two in his time. I wasn't entirely sure. But I couldn't stand the thought of staying in this situation.

"I'm okay." I took the stairs to my room two at a time, aware of a new sensation: a terrible, dizzy lurching in my stomach. I savored it for a moment—feeling! It was back!—but after five seconds of nausea, numbness didn't sound half bad.

I lay in bed facedown, but that didn't help anything, so I rolled onto my side and hugged my knees to my chest, but that didn't help either, so I rushed to the bathroom and knelt, let the bile escape my body like a cooperative parasite. Made my nose run and my eyes water. And I was there for a while, gagging and gagging, until my heart began to skip beats.

The terror of it all was almost funny. Truly. The pain was ludicrous, completely unreasonable, completely alien. I found it impossible to believe this sort of feeling could even exist, that the boundaries of human suffering extended this far. As I collapsed back into bed, I realized that if good and bad feelings lived together on a scale, I'd never experience the good equivalent of the badness I was feeling. Ecstasy lives somewhere in the clouds, but misery tunnels, deep, deep, to the center of the Earth and out the other side.

Cockroach flesh. Itchy insides, fingernail-peeling. Pins and needles, but everywhere, inside, outside, upside down.

I took to self-inflicting; smaller bouts of sharp pain distracted me momentarily from the dull, all-encompassing one, so I pinched my arms, bit my tongue, punched my thighs, screamed into my pillow.

Dad was dead. Dad was dead. Dead was Dad and Dad was dead.

Perhaps the most selfish thought I'd ever had: maybe it would have been better if I'd never known Dad at all.

Eventually, "Dad is dead" turned into "I will die," which was my introduction to the fear. The fear of *gone*. The fear of nothing at all, of what happens to me, of *I am the main character, and the story will crumble if I'm not there to see it through*. This wasn't fair. It wasn't *fair*. I didn't ask to be born; I didn't ask to be hurt; I didn't ask to feel anything at all!

I screwed my thumbs into my eyes, watched as the black went pitch-black and the pitch-black went spotty, little neon stars convulsing and pulsing and dying. Pretended the stars were rushing past me, behind me. I was in a spaceship, maybe, or maybe piloting through the cosmos in my human body, and I was heading back to where I'd come from, wherever I was a week ago, the world before.

More than anything, I was trapped. I wanted out, because everything was awful, but there was no way out; the way out was what terrified me.

So I didn't move a muscle.

Monday. Mom's snooty friends came over, stayed and stayed and stayed. When they weren't dead quiet, they were shrieking.

I'd resigned myself to my fate.

Olivia visited. Actually did bring me a fish cupcake. We sat in my room the way we always had, facing each other cross-legged on my bed. The spaces we occupied, the roles we filled—those were the same, but the girls who filled them had changed and were now miscast. There was nothing, it seemed, left to do or say. Nothing substantial. Except for the first thing I asked: "Did you tell people?"

"Tell people what?"

"About the funeral. About Dad. Did you tell people what I said?"

"Oh. You mean your…theory?"

I sighed. "Yeah. That."

Olivia placed a hand gingerly on her chest. Recoiled. "*No.* Oh

God, no. No one except for Miles. I think. Actually, no, yeah, I was talking about it with a couple—"

"*Olivia.*" I tumbled on to my back, my skull narrowly avoiding the headboard. "Olivia," I said again, this time to the ceiling.

"What? What's wrong? People were asking how you were, and I, no offense, I was like *well, no, she's not so hot*, and obviously they asked *why*, so I said—"

I clicked my phone to life, pulled up the texts, showed her the screen. Said nothing.

When she was finished reading, she looked at me, blinked, and said, "That's creepy."

"I already feel like shit. I don't need anyone knowing about the finer details of it. Or contributing. Or, I don't know, even thinking about me at all. Okay?" I prepared myself for her well-meaning axioms, for her to say she'd done more research and it was common for people to—

"Like I said. People are worried about you." Oh. So I wouldn't even get the axioms.

"Yeah, I get it. I've lost it."

"No, that's not—" She exhaled through her nose. "Well, look. If you're that concerned, why don't you go to the police, or something? Isn't that how it works?"

I shook my head. "They said they looked into it."

"And?"

"And nothing."

"Well, then maybe you should listen to them."

This wasn't a normal conversation, but the words still came more easily than they had any right to. We were operating at a certain distance, I think. Any too-long thought about how we were discussing the implications of my dad's possible murder would have sent me spiraling, so I didn't consider it for too long. I thought about me and Olivia aged eight. The pair of us running circles in the cul-de-sac, digging for fossils, riding bikes. That all seemed so far away. Not just that: hostile.

"Or," she continued, "didn't your dad have literal files on everybody? Wouldn't one of them say if a patient had, like, murderous tendencies?"

Olivia was right. There was a cabinet in Dad's desk containing handwritten documentation of every patient he'd ever had. And I knew that because I'd stumbled across it unlocked one day, and even though at that time I probably wasn't even old enough to understand any of it, he'd made it known that was no place for me. "I can't open those," I said. "It's illegal, firstly. And he... I don't think he would have wanted that."

Olivia shrugged. "Then I don't know. I'm sorry someone's being creepy about it—and, hey, I'm sorry I said anything. I won't talk about it anymore. But, like, maybe it's not good to linger on that stuff."

Little Olivia and Sydney, running circles in the cul-de-sac. If I had been suddenly transported back there, confronted with a younger me, would I have told her what she had to look forward to? Maybe she could prepare herself. Maybe she'd be more grateful for what she had. Maybe she'd look harder, speak softer, hold tighter. "Yeah, maybe."

Tuesday. Tried to watch *The Wicker Man*. The original, obviously. The last scene had always been my favorite part, but now, it made me sort of sick. There was something too real about burning alive, looking on while the rest of the world danced.

Wednesday. Made some questionable Google searches. How to control a car remotely. How to cut brakes. Fast-acting poisons. How to fake a suicide.

It was those things that led me to videos of car crashes and the car crashes that led to the ToD.

The home page was enough to warn anyone that they were somewhere they'd probably rather not be. It was a relic of the early internet: no layout, only a flashing button in the center that scrolled like a theatre marquee that read: BY ENTERING, YOU VERIFY YOU'RE OVER EIGHTEEN.

I clicked. Hoped that no one would follow up on that verification.

ToD stood for Time of Death and was essentially a lawless, mortality-based equivalent of YouTube. Mortality of all kinds. Building jumps and armed robberies and accidents and war footage. Car crashes. Mostly footage from security cameras that was almost definitely obtained illegally, some of it recorded on the phones of people who happened to be in the wrong place at the wrong time; the only rule was that someone in the video had to die.

It was addictive, to say the least.

I avoided anything overtly gory, which wasn't difficult, since most of the videos only had about five pixels to work with. Couldn't really watch anything with the sound on either.

Listen. It was sick. I knew it was sick.

But I was thinking about every horror I'd ever watched, and how the monster was always scarier when you didn't know what it looked like. When you can't see it, it could be anything. And *anything* is always scarier than *something*. *Anything* is incomprehensible, an infinite amount of horrors—and you can't fight *anything*. But then the monster gets some gratuitous money shot, and it's either a person in makeup or a puppet or bad CGI, and it becomes a tangible thing. An assailable thing. Abstract is scarier than physical. Unknown is scarier than known—not because of what it is, but because of all the things it could be.

So that's what I was doing, I think. Making it known. Becoming acquainted with death. I pasted Dad's face onto theirs, his face from the hospital room when he was still kicking, hooked up to God-knows-what levels of machinery, all pumping and pushing and beeping, but he got worse and worse and worse until the nurse said softly, "Okay, I think he's going now," and Mom held his hand and whispered in his ear, because hearing is the last sense to go, and I left.

Didn't watch. Didn't want to watch. Didn't want to know how his face would contort or how his lungs would beg for more breath or how Mom would wail when he flatlined; hearing it muffled behind the door was enough for me, thanks.

So I had to see it now. I had to.

Saturday. Finally left my room, which was actually surprisingly clean. All my clothes, mostly consisting of Pleasant Hills–themed

25

sweatshirts and skinny jeans, hung neatly in my wardrobe, since I hadn't changed; the usual pile of empty plates from snacks that sat on my nightstand wasn't there, since I hadn't been eating; my bed was made, green checker-print duvet crisp and fluffy, since I hadn't been sleeping. Though there was a decidedly human-shaped imprint in the beanbag that sat against the far wall (the walls being an almost neon fuchsia—a non-decision made by younger, stupider me), facing my TV and, by extension, my PlayStation. Leaving felt like exiting a bomb shelter into nuclear fallout.

Someone else stared back at me from the mirror. A puffy-eyed beast, face swollen beyond recognition. I—and I mean this in the most affectionate, self-loving way—didn't think I had ever looked more disgusting than I did in that moment. Sadness isn't some clean, porcelain thing; it's raw, and ugly, but mainly, it smells. I hadn't brushed my teeth in a week, let alone bathed, and I was even paler than normal, so sickly you could see the blue veins running down my neck, branching off like centipede legs. My own face unsettled me. Wasn't me.

I splashed my eyes with icy water, ripped through the matted parts of my hair with a brush until my scalp burned, and shuffled downstairs.

Dad's office was off the kitchen, and the door was shut, the way he'd left it. I turned the knob until it clicked, and tiptoed inside.

The office wasn't even that old—it was built right after I was born—but due to his proclivity for buying things secondhand, it smelled old, like mothballs and dusty mahogany and well-loved books. It was small, but felt cozy instead of claustrophobic. The ceiling lights were warm and golden and the walls a deep red, covered in giant photographs of nature scenes. Mostly Yosemite. Dad also seemed to be fond of mirrors—he had more than a few positioned at seemingly random intervals—and I liked to imagine him asking a patient to look into one and tell him what they saw.

My earliest memories were grainy. Crouching in the den, stubby fingers clutching the windowsill, hoisting myself high enough to get a peek at whatever unfamiliar car had pulled into the driveway. A woman in a blazer putting on five coats of lipstick before coming in. A couple who'd pull up, argue, then never actually come inside. The man with the wrinkles and kind eyes who'd wave at me through the window—until Dad noticed, and then I never saw him again.

But most of them were unmemorable in the best way possible. Normal people. Normal people with normal clothes and faces and jobs. Just with some buried things too.

I collapsed on the patient couch in a heap, positioned the slouchy cushions until they were comfortable under my back, and moved my attention to his desk. Still spotless. Meticulously organized. On top of it sat his computer, some white roses that had gone brown and crispy, and a picture of him and me that Mom had taken at Niagara Falls on the ferry that travels underneath the spray of the waterfall. Both of us were wearing these ridiculous plastic ponchos. In it, his hair's not gray, and I'm so small that I barely reach his waist.

Underneath the roses and the picture, of course, were the patient files.

I could have opened the files right there, spilled the contents, turned the endless sheets into wallpaper so everyone could get a look. Maybe Dad had left some freaky cassette tapes behind for me so I could avenge him. Maybe me rifling through the patient files would have distressed Dad so completely, as he watched from the afterlife, that he might have actually been shocked back into existence.

Maybe June Copeland was there.

I wouldn't. I couldn't. Ransacking your dead dad's sock drawer is one thing, but his confidential documents seemed another thing entirely. He wouldn't have wanted me to. I couldn't do it.

So I sat there, let the room bring back a flood of memories, and dipped myself in.

The spring after I turned six, a robin had built its nest in the cluster of trees behind our house. Dad was completely elated, paternal, and guarded it vigilantly until the eggs arrived. He'd hoisted me on to his shoulders to get a look; four of them, speckled and cyan, looking impossibly fragile and wonderfully smooth. I'd fantasized about how satisfying they would have felt to hold.

We checked every day to see if they'd hatched, careful not to intrude on the mother, as per Dad's request. But there was a storm a couple of weeks later. And afterward, I was back under the canopy hunting for worms to roll between my fingers when I saw them: the eggs had fallen from the nest and sat in a heap, lodged between the tree's roots.

I looked around to make sure nobody was watching and picked up an egg, one hand on top of the other, the way I would eventually hold my first communion wafer. It was heavier than I imagined—I only had experience with the plastic, Easter variety of egg—but also smaller than it had looked before, its shape dwarfed by my palm. I turned it over to find a crack running along the length of the shell, wide enough in the center that you could just about see inside. And I don't know what possessed me, but suddenly, I wanted nothing more than to know what secrets it held.

I picked at the fracture. The shell chipped away easily, and the being underneath began to take shape: not quite embryo, not quite creature; wet fluff that would never grow, or feel the sun, clinging to sickly, pallid robin skin; a bruised, bloated eyelid; the fleshy beginnings of a beak. Nothing more than a blob of vaguely biological matter. It was horrible, and ugly, and I wanted to see more. But the chipping away meant the egg was no longer structurally sound, and it crumbled in my hand. The sharper fragments of shell sliced through the little blob like it was paper. Crimson blood crept from inside it onto me.

Dad had seen it all. He washed away the evidence. Let me cry in his office. There were no accusations; he didn't scold me. I wasn't crying because I was afraid of the repercussions, but because I knew I had held death, and it wouldn't come off by washing my hands.

Sunday. Mom entered my room without knocking and informed me I'd be going to school the next day.

"Seriously?" I asked.

"Mm-hmm." She perched on the corner of my bed. "Having a routine again will be good for you."

"Did one of your mom forums tell you that?" I regretted the taunting question the moment I asked. It was too much.

Mom set the bottle of water she'd been holding onto my night-stand, gentler than the protruding veins in her neck might have suggested she wanted to. I wasn't really looking, though. I was busy pressing my fingertips into my eyelids until the darkness flexed underneath. This was the tunnel, the one back to normal, and if I could let go, let it take me, then maybe, maybe...

"I understand it probably feels early. I do. But you can't afford to fall behind. Not this year." She put a hand on my head—it made me jump—and smoothed back my hair. "You still have a whole life to lead. We both do."

"I don't." Saying the words gave me goose bumps. I guess I'd been thinking it this whole time but hadn't actually said it; that I wouldn't do anything substantial for the rest of my life except feel this way. I had been buried too, and there was no point pretending otherwise.

Mom sighed, then did that mom thing where she kissed my head and inhaled at the same time. "Go take a shower."

3

OLIVIA AND I SAT IN the commons, waiting for the morning bell to ring, as we always did, and I swore people were staring at me.

They tiptoed around me as if I were a dandelion that had gone white-tipped and any misjudged breath could blow me to smithereens. They were scared of me, I assumed: a bad omen with legs, contagious bereavement. And the staring. God. I'd worked to cultivate the image I'd had since freshman year. All I wanted to be was a girl who kept her head down, but nothing I did would be enough to conceal the body chained to my ankle.

Maybe I was being paranoid, which meant I was also being

egotistical. Anyone who's paranoid has to be, a little bit, to think you matter enough for anyone to care about you, or gossip about you, or sneak looks at you. But even though I'd recently felt crushed by the weight of my own unimportance, I couldn't help but think that after two long weeks without me, the leeches of Pleasant Hills High couldn't get enough of my blood.

I leaned across the table to Olivia, speaking quietly but loud enough to be heard over the low roar of conversation. "You're noticing, right?"

A crumb of muffin tumbled from her lip to the ground. Something about it grossed me out. "Noticing what?"

"People keep looking at me." I spoke with my teeth squeezed together like a vise, the way a ventriloquist makes their dummy talk.

Olivia stiffened. "Are they?" She caught the gaze of a group of sophomores two tables away from us. They turned away so quickly, they probably got whiplash. "Oh, wow. Yeah. They're not even trying to hide that at all." She shrugged. "Maybe they're looking at someone behind you." I turned—there was a wall.

"They're saying my name."

"Maybe they're saying *chimney*. Or *kidney*. *Kidney vinegar*. Ew. Gross." Olivia spoke with the last bite of muffin still in her mouth, her words thick and gummy on the way out, and rolled the wrapper into a ball. "They're just surprised. I think people assumed you were never coming back." She tossed the wrapper to the trash can next to us, but it hit the rim before falling to the floor. "Drat."

I glanced around the commons as Olivia went to pick up her failed shot. The place had never inspired particularly warm or fuzzy feelings, but there was something almost sinister about it now, though nothing physical had changed. There were still the unsightly strips of warehouse light, yellow-tinted, turning all the students into a horde of jaundiced zombies; the purple-and-gold pennant on the far wall, proclaiming us the Pleasant Hills Panthers; a couple of browning potted plants peppering the speckled vinyl floor. All the same in shape, but now, someone or something was turning the saturation down a tick every time I blinked. Everything seemed inexplicably different, but really, I was the only thing that had changed.

I took inventory. Back, against chair. Feet, on floor. Head, somewhere else, desperately trying to reattach itself to body. For a split second, I could have sworn I was watching myself in the third person, like a movie, hovering, separate. And God, I didn't look good.

Olivia's chair legs screeched against the floor, and I was sucked back in. "If it makes you feel any better, I don't think they're being, like, malicious, or anything. I think they feel bad and want to help, but they aren't sure how, you know?"

"I guess," I said, even though I doubted their intentions were more benevolent than selfishness.

Miles joined us at the table. He was Olivia's most recent boyfriend, a guy who looked like he had too much outside and not enough inside, a PANTHERS WRESTLING shirt stretched across his wide chest, with sleeves that looked like they might have been cutting off the circulation to his biceps. I didn't know much about him, but from what I knew about studious, sports-averse Olivia, they seemed a bizarre pairing.

When his gaze caught mine, Miles stuck his lips out in a way that

I would have considered extremely patronizing coming from anyone else, but since it was Miles, I think he was trying to make sure he was expressing emotion properly. "Hi, Sydney," he said, running a hand over his crew cut. "Sorry."

Olivia elbowed him. "I told you, she doesn't want to talk about it," she said, which was almost definitely worse than her not saying anything at all.

They started to argue about the logistics of talking about something versus apologizing for it, and despite how little attention I was paying, it seemed like things were getting heated. No worries; if they broke up, Olivia would have a replacement before I could blink. She'd had ten—eleven?—different boyfriends since freshman year. If I sound bitter, I really wasn't. Maybe I envied how easy it was for her to let go.

And then there was June.

She was sitting across the commons at a table with Heath and a few others I recognized as members of the elite. Heath had just said something that really made her laugh, apparently. Flash of teeth. Eye crinkle.

I didn't know why I cared so much about a girl I barely knew. I wasn't even sure I liked her. The way she navigated the world struck me as disingenuous, a sort of blasé approach to life that seemed to me dishonest, or unnatural, or cultivated, or all three. She spoke to everyone with a sort of cool disconnect that they all interpreted as warmth. I wasn't sure she had ever felt pain in her life.

But if she had been seeing Dad, then there must have been something more.

I could've asked. We'd very clearly made eye contact at the

funeral, unless I truly had been hallucinating, but I doubted it. The moment had happened. It wouldn't be that strange for me to go up and say something, right? I quickly came up with a story—I needed her address because we were sending out thank-you cards. Did people do that? *Thanks for the mourning?*

I willed myself to rise from the table, my heart beating faster still. It wouldn't be a big deal. It would be—

The bell rang for first period.

Now it would be weird. Now I would be chasing after her, and it would be weird.

So Olivia and I said goodbye, and I peeled off alone to the east wing.

I shivered as I walked past the courtyard, which had to be one of architecture's most remarkable blunders; it was rumored that Pleasant Hills High accidentally got the plans for a school in Los Angeles, so the windows were flimsy and thin, capable of keeping nothing out and nothing in, and the place was perpetually cold and damp. It had been built in the early twentieth century, apparently, and you could tell. Its hallways were cramped, despite Pleasant Hills not being very populated, and its layout was counterintuitive, a labyrinth of dead ends and dimly lit corridors with chipped layers of decades-old paint and anything broken mended with duct tape. I'd felt a weird camaraderie with the building in the past—if the walls could talk, and all that—but now, it felt as if it were out to get me.

Stares kept coming. But if I couldn't see them, they maybe weren't there, so I walked with my head down until the tiles beneath me were no longer tiles, but trampled grass and mulch and branches.

I'm hiking with Dad. At the River Styx.

It's summer. I can't see him, but I know he's close, because I feel incomparably safe. A swampy gust of air rushes from ahead—it's either just rained, or it's about to—and I breathe the tendrils in through my nose and out through my mouth. Something above us chirps. Dad calls from behind me, "I used to be as quick as you, you know."

"Oh yeah?" I ask. "What happened?"

"I learned to slow down. Start taking it all in. It's called mindfulness.*"*

"How close is mindfulness to arthritis?" And when I turn to smile at him, there's a crunch beneath me. Maybe it's a twig snapping, or a beetle's back breaking, but once I feel the pop...

I looked up, and Dad was never there at all.

It took until the moment I reached my locker to discover that I had forgotten my combination. I heard the universe laugh. One tragedy doesn't disqualify you, it said. There's still a lifetime of mild irritation to look forward to.

I entered every sequence of numbers that felt at all familiar to me. Two or twelve? Definitely twelve. Or twenty-one? My hands shook. Lockers were being shut, and each slam sent another jolt through my system. And then it was quiet, but I was still there, sweating on the lock until the first-period bell rang. I gave the metal a solid kick to its jaw.

I could go home, I thought. What difference would it make? I had a tragic backstory and everything, so I practically had an excuse to drop out and become a hermit, if I wanted. What kind of monster would tell the girl with a dead dad no?

But I didn't feel like turning on the waterworks today, so I trudged to homeroom.

I put a hand on the doorknob, twisted, pushed…but it didn't budge, which ruined my plans of entering stealthily. I made out Mr. Carlisle through the sliver of a window, scowling, but when his eyes met mine, they softened. The door opened with a click.

"Sorry I'm late," I said, to rub it in a little more.

Mr. Carlisle shook his head like he'd seen some particularly disturbing roadkill. He might as well have; I didn't feel too far removed from a flattened raccoon, brain splattered onto the blacktop. "Don't you worry. Come on in."

I did, and twenty heads all swiveled in unison to see the perpetrator. *Hello, everyone*, I wanted to say. *Welcome to the freak show.* I contemplated charging a dollar to anyone who wanted to get a good, uninterrupted look at me. *Come and meet the unfortunate soul experiencing real, gen-u-ine grief!*

But Bea, as always, was not looking.

Since freshman year, Bea and I had been playing this hilarious game where she pretended she couldn't physically see me, and I pretended I didn't feel like offing myself every time I saw her, and then we'd go back and forth like that for a bit until I considered peeling off my own flesh. But today must have been different; she was so *obviously* avoiding me. Eyes fixed ahead, jaw clenched—I swore I heard her teeth grind when I walked past to take my seat.

The second half of a movie flashed from a projector onto the wall of the darkened room. I had already seen it, so during class, instead of reading the Wikipedia page for "rigor mortis" like I'd planned, I kept my gaze firmly locked on Bea. She didn't look too dissimilar from when I'd known her—band tee, sad eyes with sharp liner—but her hair was shorter now and pink at the bottom. Olive skin still clinging to some leftover summer tan.

When the bell rang, I waited around to see what she would do, let her walk ahead of me—and on the way out, she dropped a folder. I shot to pick it up.

"Here," I said.

She didn't even look at me, just took my offering as if it had levitated to her hand, and left.

I wasn't going to mention it—certainly not to Olivia—but she'd noticed something similar.

"Hey, did you see Bea today?" she asked at lunch over the low chatter, peals of laughter, and clattering of plastic trays. Miles seemed to be struggling to peel open his container of yogurt. "She was being so weird today in chem. She's in my lab, and I was like, *hey, Bea, can you grab me a flask?* And, you know, she did, but she wouldn't even look me in the eye. Like I was freaking Medusa or something. And, you know, it's not like she'd ever been all that nice to me anyway, but it's always been more indifference than active avoidance, you know?"

"Yeah. She looked—I don't know. Worried about something, almost."

"Have you even talked to her since—you know?"

I shook my head, picked at the crusts of my peanut butter sandwich, and rolled the scraps between my fingers.

"Livvycanyouopenmyyogurt?" Miles said quietly, as if I wouldn't hear, as if this yogurt lid was a tangible barrier between his internal self and the expression of his masculinity.

Olivia nodded, then continued her diatribe. "Well, I'll tell you what: if she's feeling guilty all of a sudden, or whatever, she's about three years too late." Olivia waited until the last word to rip off the yogurt lid for emphasis. It wasn't particularly effective. "Yeesh. Imagine being her. I don't know how someone can live like that, you know, be able to go to sleep at night, knowing they haven't even apologized."

"Who are we talking about?" Miles offered. It was perhaps the first time he'd willingly involved himself in one of our conversations instead of sitting there, ripening.

"Bea Fuller?" Olivia said. Miles still looked bewildered, so she elaborated in a shout dressed up to look like a whisper: "The girl who outed Sydney."

That's what Olivia liked to say, because it made me look better, but it wasn't entirely true.

It was the summer before freshman year, and Dad had convinced me to try out for the soccer team. Practice was held in this enormous field, surrounded on all sides by thick woods. Bea and I liked to stay after practice sometimes to hunt for interesting-looking leaves, do handstands, climb trees.

I thought she wanted to kiss me back. It seemed implied. Because of the idyllic setting, or her hand on my knee, or the way her lips looked like they were searching for something every time I shifted my weight against the dewy late-July grass. She had told me she liked boys and girls, and that she liked my freckles and the way my voice trailed off sometimes, so I leaned all the way in, in, in, until there was no more room to lean. Her lips parted, and so did mine, but she knew what the whoops and hollers coming from the tree line meant before

I did, so she pushed me off. Shouted. Made a real good show of it. That was the first time I was ever called a dyke, because it was the first time anyone had enough information about me to conclude I was one.

It was too late for me. They had already seen. Bea had managed to deflect part of the blow away from herself with her initial hostility, so they weren't quite as relentless with her as they were with me. I had this fantasy after the fact, that she and I could have faced it together— but that's not what happened, of course. She hated me. Freshman year, I was the only girl out in Pleasant Hills. People smacked books from my hands. Looked at me and laughed. Thankfully, they seemed to get bored of me by winter break, with help from the demeanor I'd adopted to make myself as invisible as possible.

It'd continued for a while, but now I worried that all the work I'd put in had been for nothing.

When you lived in a fishbowl, everything seemed bigger, magnified, and no one was safe. People said that in Pleasant Hills, everyone got their scandal. Fifteen minutes of infamy.

This was mine.

Do not go gentle into that good night. It was Dylan Thomas's most famous poem, a villanelle, which has something to do with the number of lines—nineteen of them, I think—and the rhyme scheme. Normally, I wouldn't have remembered that, but everything that happened in class that day was branded onto my brain.

English was the last class of the day. It was also the one class I shared with Olivia, so I thought I was safe. How naïve of me. She had warned me at lunch that we were starting our poetry unit—she couldn't stand poetry, but I didn't mind, really; the idea of losing any sense of self between the lines of something abstract seemed comforting.

Mrs. Farr introduced the poem as easy and relevant, which should have been my first clue. She had Jamie Uren, an unfortunate name for the girl who we all remembered had pissed herself during the fourth-grade spelling bee, read it aloud.

"Do not go gentle into that good night," Jamie began, hesitant. Mrs. Farr was known to eject people from the classroom if they didn't put the pauses in the right places. "Old age should burn and rave at close of day."

And as she continued, I was imagining. Daydreaming. Day-nightmaring.

Though wise men at their end know dark is right...

The silhouette of a man. Slumped against a giant redwood so tall that its peak disappears in the milky clouds, branches melting into indigo. Only crickets.

...because their words had forked no lightning they...

I can't see his face, but I will soon; moonlight is flowing in from behind me, as agile and quick as a fire, and when it dances up and onto his face, I recognize him.

...do not go gentle into that good night.

Dad's eyes are closed, limp, and I reach for him, but something's pulling him down, into the tree roots. Hands yanking and tearing, and I can't get to him in time, and he's dragged deeper, deeper, deeper…

"And you, my father, there on the sad height," Jamie read.

I swallowed.

"Curse, bless me now with your fierce tears, I pray." The spit caught in my throat.

"Do not go gentle into that good night. Rage, rage against the dying of the light."

Mrs. Farr let the words settle, and then turned to me. "Sydney," she said. She was going to ask what my interpretation was. Seemed slightly cruel to call on me, but whatever. I could feel Olivia's eyes on me. I think she knew something was wrong before I did.

I chewed my lip. It was obvious. Not only obvious, but something I could actually get behind: not succumbing to death. Telling the grim reaper to fuck off. Don't go without a fight. Rave and burn. Rage. But Mrs. Farr didn't ask for my interpretation. "I don't think there's a better poem for you right now," she said. "I thought you might want to use this time to talk about your dad."

And then I left. I just left.

I couldn't believe I was doing it while I did it. My feet started moving before my brain told them to. Or maybe my brain told my feet to move before telling *me* what exactly was going on. Either way, I was leaving, apparently.

Mrs. Farr called after me, but I kept going. Slammed the door and everything. A scream gurgled inside me.

Rage, rage.

I made it to the front of the building before anyone tried to stop me. "Excuse me!" the woman in the office called. I kept going.

I straddled my bike and shot out of the parking lot.

Rage, rage.

Right on Main Street. Left on College. Past the baseball fields, down the hill.

Twelve along, four down.

I counted right. I knew I counted right. So it was definitely Dad's grave. It had to be. But I had no idea what June Copeland was doing there.

4

THERE WAS SOMETHING PICTURESQUE ABOUT the scene, the fiery maples and the headstones planted in meticulous rows, and the girl in the middle of it all, sitting cross-legged at the grave that wasn't hers to mind.

When it came to fight or flight, it seemed I had opted for a useless middle ground, one where you stand there, mouth agape, and do absolutely nothing at all. A part of me wanted to watch June from afar, with the buzz at the back of my skull reminding me she could turn around at any moment. Some sort of sick endorphin rush. But she wasn't supposed to be here. This was *mine*. This was meant to be a haven, a safe place, and this girl whose life was exponentially easier than mine was taking away the one thing I had that she didn't. I hated her. I *hated* her.

I was trying to figure out what to say, or if I should say anything at all, when the decision was made for me. I shifted my weight, and my bike creaked impossibly loudly, and June, despite being a good thirty yards away, heard. Her head snapped around, hair flowing behind her like the tail of a comet.

We locked eyes. A long second passed. "Sydney?"

I barely recognized my own name. Wasn't sure why the fact that she knew it made me shiver.

I flipped down my kickstand. Fine. This was happening now.

June stood and dusted off her jeans, which were dark blue and tight all the way down to her ankles. She wore these mud-splotched Doc Marten boots, which were kind of cool, but whatever. She shouldn't have been here. Not here, not at the funeral, not in my head.

I traipsed forward, navigating around the headstones as if they were mousetraps. "What are you doing here?" My words were barbed, but I didn't care.

Apparently, it didn't take much to make her sink. She curled in on herself, linked her fingers together at her hips. "I'm so sorry," she said. "You're right. I shouldn't be here. I should go. I'm going."

But the way out was past me, so she had to move closer, her gaze trained firmly downward. And I don't know why—maybe because the situation was hopelessly awkward, or because I felt I'd been too harsh, or because of the way her face caved in, but before she could leave I said, "It's okay. You...you don't have to."

June stopped, still maybe ten paces in front of me, and looked up.

"Seriously," I said, aware that what I said next would likely make her uncomfortable. "He's essentially public property now. He might as well be, like, a bench."

June stared. Blinked. *Yes, surprise, I'm a weirdo. Firmly drawing a line in the dirt between your world and mine.* This was not how normal people spoke about dead loved ones. But the unexpected happened: she laughed. Hesitant at first, probably to gauge my reaction, but then it bounded from her, deep and musical. I wasn't immediately convinced, but I found myself smiling in return, not because what I'd said was especially funny but because it was funny that I'd run out of school to find the homecoming queen at my dead dad's grave.

"Are you sure?" she said. "Really. I can totally go."

This was my chance. *Take it back, Sydney. Tell her to beat it.* But I didn't think I wanted that—my curiosity won. "It's fine," I said. "Honestly, it's…it's nice to have…company." What was I doing?

June nodded, seeming to understand something I didn't. "Okay."

She sat back down at the plot, and I sat opposite her, Dad wedged between us. We both knew the question that was coming—*What the hell is going on?*—and it was a matter of which of us would be the one to ask it.

It started raining. Not enough for me to care about it—*a gentle misting*, Dad would have called it. Light rain was *a gentle misting* and heavy rain was *a deluge*. He'd say stuff like that with some not-quite-English accent that he thought was the funniest thing ever. (I wake up early on a wet Saturday, come downstairs and he says, shit-eating grin plastered on his face, book in his lap, "Were you *awoken* by the *deluge?*")

June spoke first. She pulled her olive-green jacket tighter around her waist, hugged her knees to her chest, and laughed despite herself. "I should probably explain, right? You…you must think I'm stalking you or something."

At first I thought it best to feign indifference, but little flames of anger still flickered in my belly. No, I wasn't indifferent. I cared a lot. "You probably should explain." But that was too mean.

June was quiet, then she exhaled. "I'm so sorry, I—"

"You were at the funeral."

She nodded.

"Not for very long," I added.

She shook her head.

I felt in control of the conversation. Not because I'd taken it; she was letting me have it. "Did my, uh, speech scare you off?"

June didn't laugh at this. "No, that wasn't—"

"It's okay," I said. Right. Jokes about murder accusations during moments of bereavement paranoia were off-limits. Maybe because the paranoia had actually scared her off. "Why'd…why'd you leave? So quick?"

I found myself wanting to hear her speak again. Her voice was low, raspy, but in a nice way, like she'd spent the night talking over loud music. "I was there alone," she said. "And, man, I didn't want to be weird. And it felt weird. To hover. After you saw me I felt like I wasn't supposed to be there. Didn't want to draw any attention."

Ha. *She* was worried about being weird. I went to address the elephant in the room. "Sorry, why were you even—"

She'd known the question was coming and interrupted: "I was seeing your dad."

There it was. With my suspicions now proved correct, a pang of jealousy arrived. She had memories of Dad that I didn't. I tried to imagine them sitting in his office together, June sprawled over the couch, Dad listening intently, but I couldn't get the image to materialize. He was something to June that he never was to me. She didn't just remind me of it all—she was a part of it all. "Yeah. I'd been seeing him. Wanted to pay my respects, I guess."

But how could she have been? Why did June Copeland need Dad?

She could tell I was taking too long to respond. I apologized. "You're not his regular clientele, I guess." I didn't know shit about his regular clientele.

June smirked. "No?"

"They were usually, uh, older," I said, because I suspected it to be true; as far as I knew, he didn't see many kids from the high school.

"Mm," she said, slightly deflated. But she had this knowing look—the kind of knowing I guess you only saw if you looked straight into her eyes.

"So, what," I said, nodding toward the headstone, "you couldn't get enough of him, or…?"

That brought her back to life. "Like, basically that." We laughed. "So, he was really great. I'm sure you know that already, but he… yeah. He was so helpful when stuff was shitty, and, yeah, stuff has been shitty, so I thought I'd…stop by. God. Sorry. That feels stupid to say to you." I got the impression she was really considering her words. I wasn't sure if I was grateful for that or not.

"Don't worry about it."

"Okay, wait, let me get this out of the way. I want to say sorry, but that seems super-patronizing, but I also don't want to say nothing because that seems really inconsiderate"—a nervous laugh—"so I don't really know what to…do right now."

I reached for the phrase: *It's okay. I don't want to talk about it.* But that didn't feel right here. It didn't feel true. "I'm sort of working under the assumption that everyone is sorry by default. You know? No one's like, *Fuck you and your dead dad.*"

That made her laugh. "Maybe that's what I should have done. Kept you on your toes."

I smoothed my face over with the heel of my hand, like I was massaging something out of it. "But, yeah. It, uh, sucks, pretty bad, it turns out. Surprise, right? I'm kind of exhausted." Why the hell was I telling her all this? "I haven't slept for, like, a week."

"I get that too," June said. "Insomnia. Not fun."

I wanted to ask why. What kept her awake? There could have been all sorts of reasons; though I didn't imagine that sleep felt too much like death to her. Then I remembered: I'd gotten up early the day after the funeral. The flowers. "There were flowers on his grave last week. That we didn't leave. Were you—"

"Yeah, that was me. Mysterious flower-bringer. God, you probably think I'm so weird."

"No, it's okay," I said. An invitation for her to explain.

"I wanted to… So, you know, I got spooked at the funeral, but I still wanted to give him something, so I dropped them off after everyone left. Your dad did…a lot for me. And something, like, happened.

49

It's complicated. Whatever. So I wanted to give him something. Anything. I'm saying a lot of things right now, but I'm not really sure if any of them mean anything. Words."

Something *happened*? What did that mean? But she seemed anxious about it, so I didn't prod. "Words," I said back. Wait. I was still supposed to be in class. Which meant she was too. "Don't you, uh… Aren't you supposed to be in school?"

"I have early release." She nudged a rock toward me with her foot. Smirked. "Aren't *you* supposed to be in school?"

I took one sharp breath, now so deeply rooted in this absurd situation that the previous absurd situation didn't seem so bad anymore. "It's complicated." June smiled again, and I figured that was her way of telling me to keep going. "I ran away."

"Um. Care to elaborate?"

I kicked the rock back toward her. "I was having a temper tantrum."

She laughed again. "Oh my God. So you just walked out?"

I nodded.

"That's—that's *exemplary*. You have personally done what I've dreamed of doing every day for the entirety of my high-school career. They let you leave?"

Fine. I saw why people liked her; she was warm and spoke like you were the only thing in the world that required her attention. But she wasn't how I expected. I felt embarrassed—that I'd built up this whole character for her in my head, and had formed opinions on that character, without ever hearing the actual girl speak. I liked her, I decided. I liked June Copeland.

"Bereavement perks," I said. I looked toward Dad's headstone in an attempt to inject some sort of reality into this largely unbelievable situation. How long did it take for a human body to decompose?

"What are you thinking?" she asked.

"Uh, nothing," I said, then reconsidered; brutal honesty had worked thus far. "I guess I was wondering if he's turned into…I don't know. Worm food."

"Dude. Is that seriously your sense of humor?"

A hot confidence rushed through me. I wasn't sure why, but I suddenly felt like it was very important to impress her. "Oh, that's just the beginning. Bit the big one. Gave up the ghost." She snickered. Maybe it was just very important to make her laugh. "Pine overcoat."

"Shuffled off this mortal coil?" she said, and I laughed, recognizing the line as Shakespeare. "Are you in AP Language this year?" I nodded. "You read *Hamlet* next year. It'll be right up your alley."

"Why?"

"I mean, people have their opinions about it, whatever, but it's mainly a whiny baby, lamenting about death—"

"Am *I* the whiny baby lamenting about death?" I asked, tongue lodged firmly in my cheek.

She laughed. "No! It's like, I don't mean you're whiny, I mean, you'd probably think it's funny. I… This feels inappropriate. This feels like a weird way to have this conversation right now."

I rested my chin in my hands and eyed the headstone again. "If I can't laugh at it, or anything, then, I don't know. I'm gonna…" I stopped. Why was I telling her this? All the red lights in my brain flashed, and the sirens went off: *abort, abort, Sydney's sharing intimate information with a total stranger, get her out of there!*

But I didn't go. I stayed. We stayed. Talked for a while, laughed so loud, I hoped it'd be enough to wake the dead, *all* the dead, and I'd get to walk off with Dad, and maybe some kids would get to speak to Grandma's skeletal remains—but instead of from below, the rumbling came from above. The rain picked up. Heavy, fat beads of it.

June looked up and squinted, the spray from the gentle splashes against her cheekbones clinging to her eyelashes. "Uh-oh. You came on your bike."

I knew rain like this; the sky was about to open. "It's okay. Luckily I'm water-resistant, so."

June ignored the bad joke. "Let me give you a ride."

"Uh," I said, eloquent. She was looking at me so expectantly, with this glint in her eyes, that all possible answers seemed to be expelled from my head. But I couldn't. I hadn't been in a car since… And I had no intention of changing that. "It's fine. Really."

"It's the least I can do. And, hey," she said, smiling, "it's not like I don't know where you live."

What was my excuse? I actually enjoyed riding a bike in the pouring rain? I decided to opt for aggressively declining instead of explaining. "I don't—really. I'm okay. Thanks, though."

June looked taken aback and seemed to search my eyes for something. "Well, either way, I'm getting out of here. You coming?"

She jumped up, I followed, and we ran between the grave plots, icy wetness inching itself underneath the collar of my sweater. I pretended we were being chased, that we were running from something, but we were fine and happy because we knew it wouldn't catch us, and ahead of me, June moved like her body had a whole world in it.

See ya later, Dad.

I hopped on my bike without bothering to wipe off the seat, and June stopped outside her car for a second too long, like she wanted to say something. "Hey!" she said, needing to shout to be heard over the rain. I turned to her. "I'll see you around, okay?"

"Yeah, see you around!"

She smiled, I waved, and she drove out of the parking lot.

I stayed there for a bit. Let the rain clouds swallow me up.

After I'd made it home, peeled off my wet clothes, and wrung out my hair, Olivia texted me.

Olivia: THAT WAS AWESOME

It took me a second to remember what she was talking about. Oh, yeah. Farr-gate. This, of course, had been eclipsed by June-gate.

Me: Yeah, thanks. Best thing I've ever done, probably

Olivia: lol. it was wild. are you ok? want me to come over??

Me: Don't worry. I have a fucking tome's worth of worksheets I need to start on

Olivia: ok. nice word!!! godspeed my rebellious friend!!!

It wasn't *really* a lie. I did have a fucking tome's worth of worksheets I needed to start on. But mainly I was planning to sit in bed and stare at the wall and think about whatever the hell had just happened to me.

That was weird, right? That was weird.

June was nothing at all like I'd thought she'd be. Who would have thought she would be the one to laugh at my "dead dad" jokes? I figured maybe she'd felt bad for me and that was the only reason she'd given me the time of day. A charity case. Maybe I was being delusional. But there might have been some truth to it, considering my first assumption was correct.

It wasn't inherently strange that she was a patient of Dad's, but the way she'd spoken about him *was*. She'd said something had happened. What did that even mean? What kind of drama do you have with your therapist? Either way, she had shared *something* with him, something located on the side of Dad's double life that I knew nothing about; in a Venn diagram of Dad and me, this girl lived in the intersection. There was something meaningful about that. Something important.

And I wanted to know what it was.

I did eventually end up trying to do schoolwork as per Mom's request, but worksheets that normally would have taken me five minutes were taking forever. They made no sense. They might as well have been in a different language, and all I could think about was June and this awful heaviness battling a searing lightness somewhere in my stomach. It made me want to puke.

So I flipped open my laptop and searched her name.

Hardly anything came up. No Facebook. No Twitter. Nothing personal at all, actually—only stuff from the Pleasant Hills School District website that I already knew about her: all the academic awards she'd won, the clubs she headed. A few pictures from when she'd been a cheerleader, backlit by the floodlights and beaming out on to the stadium, Panthers uniform and purple pompoms and all.

But Heath's online footprint was much larger.

He instantly appeared on Facebook. He was irritatingly

good-looking, charming, even when two-dimensional. His most recent post was about homecoming, a picture of him and June going to the dance freshman year next to a picture of them being crowned king and queen—a corny "look how far we've come" thing, with more than two hundred likes. There was an album of them on vacation in Hilton Head, June sprawled out in a bikini and doing cartwheels in the waves. The posts went back years. There was something uncomfortable about watching a relationship unfold from only one side, but from what I could see, they seemed kind of infatuated with each other.

Thinking of infatuation, naturally, made me think of Bea. Why had she been so weird? What was her problem? Summer. The July before freshman year. Around then, I'd imagined someday being old and shriveled and having someone ask me about my first love—and it would have been her, all braided pigtails and gapped teeth and the most ridiculous snorty laugh I'd ever heard.

Oh. That's what this feeling was.

Absolutely not, my own fucking brain. God. What was happening?

The momentary lightness was suppressed by a tidal wave of grief.

Dad. Dad sitting at the foot of my bed with his hand on my ankle, which I can feel, but barely; my nerves have gone haywire and are now firing at random intervals. How can a body fine-tuned to keep you alive so gleefully tear you apart?

It's freshman year. My parents have found out. I'm too far gone to ask how, but I know they have, based on the way Dad lumbers into my bedroom like he's on his way to his own funeral. I've spent the previous few days at school being harassed. Pushed. Pointed at. In class, a teacher mentioned Lesbos and everyone snickered. It will go on relentlessly for weeks, weeks, until after Christmas break, when it'll calm down, become a weekly occurrence instead of daily, and then they'll all forget, because Sydney Whitaker is quiet, uninteresting, doesn't even flinch anymore; it's not fun to terrorize an indifferent mouse.

All I can say to Dad is that I didn't want it to happen like this. I didn't want it to happen at all, but especially not like this.

Dad says my strength is incomparable, but I don't feel particularly strong; I feel rotten, used, embarrassed. I'm sure that I'll never feel worse than I do in this moment.

Oh. Just you wait.

I waited until Mom had gone to sleep because I didn't want her to ask questions about what I planned to do.

I wasn't going to *open* it, you know. I was just going to *see*.

I tugged on the handle of the filing cabinet, but the door didn't budge, so I rummaged through the other drawers and compartments until I found a key that looked small enough to fit.

The files were organized alphabetically by last name. There might have been a hundred patients there. I kind of squinted my left eye so as not to see the first names, then found the end of the B's. Byers. Conley. Copeland.

Opened my eye all the way: June.

I positioned the manila tab between my forefinger and my thumb and traced over Dad's handwriting, the nearly illegible half print, half cursive. I would never open the file. How could I? As I crouched there, Dad was probably slamming his ghost hands on my shoulders and wailing, "*Paaatient confidentiaaality*, Syd!" Merely touching the folder made me nervous. But here she was.

I shut the cabinet, locked it again, put the key back where I had found it.

And when I collapsed back into bed, my phone buzzed.

Anonymous. The restricted number.

Your dad deserved it.

Buzz.

And so will you.

Buzz.

Dyke.

IT WASN'T REALLY THE *DYKE* that bothered me. Entirely uninspired. Try again.

It wasn't even the *Your dad deserved it*. That sounded almost childish, like some valued contributor to the human race was sitting around and twiddling their thumbs, thinking: *What's the worst thing I could say to this bereaved individual?*

It was the *so will you*.

Not so *did* you. As in, you deserved his death and the repercussions of it. But so *will* you. As in something that hadn't even happened yet.

I thought about messaging back. Asking, *Um, yes, excuse me, are you sure you meant to threaten me?* But it wasn't the fear of the confrontation that held me back; it was the fear they'd say more I didn't want to hear.

God. Who hated me enough to send this? Did I even have enemies?

Bea?

But she wouldn't. Right? God. Maybe she'd been kind of a shitty person, but she wasn't evil. Was she? And even if she was, why now? Why get back at me *now*?

I sucked on my sandpaper tongue. Screenshotted the conversation without replying and sent it to Olivia, who texted back almost immediately.

Olivia: uh, what the HECK

Olivia: wth do they mean "and so will you"???

Olivia: typo???

Me: I don't know. I don't think so

Olivia: soooooo creepy

Olivia: wanna come over and watch 'flix later??

Her changing the subject so nonchalantly made my blood boil. Maybe she was trying to be helpful. Maybe she was doing what I'd asked—pretending everything was the same. Regular programming. But nothing was the same; the decay was creeping into everything, and I was pretty sure I was the only person in the world who could see it.

October became November, and two Dad-less weeks became two Dad-less months. My encounter with June became a memory. Everything became death.

Time passed relentlessly, and because I rarely slept, days seemingly didn't end or begin, just rolled into one another. This illusion was facilitated by the fact that it was always dark and freezing cold. Bone-shatteringly cold. The chill had arrived in full force, dripped into me and clotted along the underside of my flesh. Snow covered everything like a second layer of skin; it clung to branches and gathered in clumps that looked like giant, gray tumors. Most days, I shoveled the driveway at Mom's request. I switched to the bike with the winter wheels. I liked to watch the blizzards from my bedroom window, or Dad's office, remembering that thing in *How the Grinch Stole Christmas* where he implies that each snowflake contains its own tiny universe. I liked to watch them smack against the ground, melt against the salt on the sidewalk. *Splat, splat, splat.*

Any gossip about me at school, imagined or otherwise, had seemingly stopped. I guess they'd all got their fill of my despair. Misery, when finite, is a fevered game of limit-pushing, running your finger quickly through a lighter flame or jabbing a knife in between your outstretched fingers. Something to get the adrenaline pumping. But when it gets to be too much, you can shut it off, catch your breath, and nothing's lost. Turns out, it's a lot less fun when it's not on a switch.

They'd all moved on. I figured I was supposed to as well. Two hours was enough to kill Dad, I guess, so why wasn't two months enough to heal me? Two months, two lifetimes, two hundred Big Bangs.

And the texts. I'd waited to see if there was a follow-up, but there wasn't. Even my anonymous harasser had gotten bored of me. I'd kept an eye on Bea, just in case. She still refused to even acknowledge me, instead seeming *angry* when she accidentally caught my eye in film class. I wasn't sure if she was able to hold a grudge for two years, or why that grudge was seemingly being exacerbated by the death of the target's dad—but she was the only person I could think of who had enough history with me to have a motive. The *so will you* reared its head at unexpected moments; I was surprised how much the words had actually unsettled me.

And June. If I hadn't held her file in my own two hands, I might have been able to convince myself I'd made the whole thing up. I barely saw her at school. Didn't hear from her. Except for one time when I passed her in the hallway, and I swore she glanced over at me before she walked into my blind spot. Other than that, though, she was as distant as she'd been before I'd spoken a word to her.

The most prominent actor in my life, though, was Death. A former side character who had stolen all the leads. Since death had become the new lens I filtered everything through, how could I ever trust myself? I was obsessive. Death became my new neutral. And more terrifying than not being able to think straight was *knowing* I was not able to think straight; I could *feel* my mind slipping. I'd have much preferred some sort of ignorant melancholy, where I wasn't acutely aware of why I was thinking and feeling everything I did. God, I was aware.

I was terrified.

I didn't want to die. I didn't want to *die*. Whenever I thought about it, the inevitability of the thing, this dull, aching dread would swoop over me, settle into my pores, and the only thing I could do was let it pass. Nothing prevented it. Nothing ended it.

But Dad had done it. To so vehemently fear the thing he was forced to confront made me feel borderline pathetic. I wished more than anything that I could summon the courage to look into Death's face, to say I wasn't afraid, because fearing it gave it power over me, over *Dad*, and I knew that, but it didn't even matter because I was a coward.

I was afraid, afraid, afraid.

One night, I crept back into Dad's office and took out all the folders from the cabinet.

I wanted to face them. To feel them, to drag a finger along the outside and coax out the knowledge through touch.

I spread them all out on the floor like playing cards, like some magic trick where I'd scoop one up, flick it open: Is *this* your murderer?

I raged without any idea of where to aim it, nursed blame without any idea of how to allocate it. *I get it, Dad.* It was confidentiality. For my sake. For their sake. I understood. But if he had *told* me, maybe there would've been some hint, some clue, *something* to tell me that one particular person was at the end of their rope.

My eyes flicked to June's file.

Even her. There was something unsettling about Dad having seen someone who went to my school, about the fact that she'd been here, spilled her guts, and I never would have even known. Not only was Dad overseeing the collective world of Pleasant Hills, but *my* world too. He should have told me. I should have known. I should have known June had been here.

This was *his* fault, said my brain, for underestimating me. Did he think I couldn't handle it? Hiding all this darkness underneath his nonchalance, his secrecy, when maybe telling me could have saved his life. If he had told me, this might not have even happened at all.

No one even looked into it. No one even cared.

That doesn't happen in Pleasant Hills, they said. Of course it didn't. Nothing happened in Pleasant Hills. Everything was great in Pleasant Hills.

I couldn't open the files. I couldn't.

I knew if I began, I wouldn't stop. Dad would have disowned me. He wouldn't have wanted it.

And I also knew that even if I did open them, I couldn't be objective. Innocuous things would look like intent. You can't see clearly when everything is death.

I couldn't stop thinking about Dad, the folders, the swerve, smash, gone, and barely anything helped except for the baths. I'd run them so hot, I could barely stand it, then lower my head until my ears were fully submerged, and stay there like that. Just me and the interminable lulling of the water. Then I'd dip again, except now it was all of me, and I'd shut my eyes and hold my breath until I felt moments away from passing out, thought maybe that must be what dying feels like, and I'd do that over and over again until I felt sufficiently nauseous and stupid.

Or I'd go to the ToD. It practically became a staple of my daily routine. Mainly, I was struck by the sheer quantity of videos. I figured the probability of actually catching someone's death on video was pretty low, which meant the amount of death that had to be occurring to account for all the footage was incomprehensible. God, it was so easy. Humans were fragile. Soft and fleshy. A single slip was enough to kill one. *Oh, it's a little icy out today, better walk slow, whoops, smack, dead. I'm late, better hurry without looking both ways, whoops, smash, dead.* All the hopes and dreams and loving and longing snuffed out in a flash like it had never meant anything at all.

I knew it wasn't ethical. These people I was watching die had families. Kids. People who wouldn't watch these videos themselves, let alone be at peace with the knowledge that thousands of death voyeurs were doing it. Not only watching them—leaving comments. Trying to be funny, to outdo one another, like it was all fake, like these people were actors, like they were never really human.

Barox90, on a video of a guy getting hit by a bus: he got busted :(

Warrenwelder, on a particularly shaky video of a car crash: Goddamn, just keep the fucking camera on the subject. It's NOT hard.

GetMeRich, on a video of war combat: ACHIEVEMENT UNLOCKED: Headshot Honcho.

Want to know what's worse? I laughed at some of them. A lot of them.

Because if I didn't, I wouldn't have been able to handle it.

But what if, somehow, someone had a video of Dad? Camera positioned on the ceiling of the hospital room, looking down at him with his limbs outstretched like a mounted beetle, gasping for his last breath?

Comment from Bender989: If you turn up the volume at 38 seconds you can hear him gurgle.

Well, I wouldn't like that at all, I decided.

So I didn't think about it anymore.

It was the first week of November, and I was sitting in Dad's office.

I had worked through most of the ToD's backlog and now had to sort the posts by most recent—a digital vulture, circling and licking my lips at the thought of any scrap of rot. Starved and brave, I settled on one that the comments promised was particularly disturbing—a freak accident, a couple driving along when some cargo from the truck up ahead comes loose and crashes through the windshield. Weirdly, the screaming made me feel barely anything at all.

And with my headphones on and my back to the door, I had no way of knowing that Mom had come into the office.

I instinctively slammed my laptop shut when I finally felt her there, but it was too late. She saw. And her eyes glazed over, wide and unnatural as a recently stuffed bit of taxidermy; she said nothing as she moved toward Dad's desk.

Mom and Dad both had the emotional recklessness of a napkin, which had its pros and cons. Dad was sometimes so rational that he came across as unfeeling, and Mom figured that everything left unacknowledged might just go away. I'd never been shouted at or grounded in a fit of anger. I almost wanted them to do it. *Come on. Give me something to work with. A little melodrama for once, drenched in feeling and passion and rage. Rage!*

But Mom never did. Especially after Bea. I was sure that had something to do with it too; that part of my life was another helping of things we found it impossible to talk about, for whatever reason. We wore spacesuits and floated aimlessly through the ether, our radios dead and a soundless vacuum between us. Before, Dad had been the cord that at least tethered us together; now, there was nothing keeping us from drifting to opposite ends of the void.

I tried to make contact. "What?" I asked. It was unnecessary. I already knew *what*. Only now did I notice the black trash bag in her hand. "What do you want me to do?" I wasn't sure if I meant in this exact moment or indefinitely. "I'm grieving. This is me grieving."

Mom didn't say anything. She riffled through the top drawer on Dad's desk, and emerged with a key.

The key to the patient files.

"What are you doing?" I asked. My words were barbed with a new indignation, and I didn't even bother to hide it.

"Clearing out the desk. I was gonna throw some of the furniture on Craigslist."

"You're selling Dad's stuff?"

"Not *everything*. But what are we gonna do with all this, honey?"

"Oh, yeah, I don't know. Might as well smash it. Burn it." Mom glared at me, and I understood why. I was being unreasonable. But, God, I couldn't help but think that Dad would still need it. If it stayed where it stood, if he came back, everything could return to normal—emptying the room was an acknowledgment that no one needed it anymore. The desk was staying. "I want the desk."

"Sydney—"

"Seriously. I'll use it."

Mom sighed. "No. No. I don't think—I don't think it's healthy to hold on to stuff like that." She unlocked the filing cabinet and went to toss its contents.

No! I shot from the couch. "You can't throw those away."

"I can't?"

"Like, legally. They either need to be sent away, or shredded, or something." I was talking directly out of my ass. But I needed them. Just in case.

"Oh, I don't have time for that. I won't tell if you won't, hmm?"

"I'll do it. I'll *do it*. Please? I think it would've been important to Dad."

That won. "Okay," she said once, then again. "Your way. That's fine." I sat back down, content with my narrow victory—but Mom wouldn't quit. She took this big, exaggerated breath, sat too close to me, and said, "Why are you watching that stuff?"

I didn't know what to tell her, really, so I shook my head, swallowed what felt like a rock. Examined her face. Her freckles were exactly like mine, and I wondered, if you mapped them all out on the both of us, where they'd overlap.

"You doing that, and saying those things, I just... I don't know, baby. I don't know how to help you."

Unable to meet her gaze, I spoke to the ground beside her. "I can't act like it didn't happen."

Mom pretended I hadn't said anything. "I was talking to Alyssa Smith's mom. Do you know her? I think she's in the grade above you."

I nodded.

"She sent Alyssa to this support group after they got divorced.

Alyssa, I guess she really loved it. It helped her a lot. Talking to kids her age who were going through the same thing, you know?"

I didn't like where this was heading.

"Well, I looked, and the same place has one for teenagers who have lost somebody. Starts in December, around the holidays. Hm? I booked us in for a consultation with the counselor in a couple of weeks."

"I don't need to go to a support group," said the girl who'd watched a video of a man being squashed by a train ten times in a row that morning.

Mom winced—at what, I wasn't sure—and tucked a loose strand of hair behind my ear. "It'll be good for you."

"Mom, I don't want to go. Please."

She looked at me, and for a horrible second, we were frozen there, but then she rose, plodded away, and shut the office door softly behind her.

Everything was wrong.

I wasn't going to a fucking support group.

If there was anything I was certain wasn't going to help me, it was singing "Kumbayah" with a bunch of strangers in some sad therapy office, drawing pictures or doing breathing exercises or talking about *feelings*. How patronizing.

It occurred to me that I was surrounded by a therapist's entire collection of books—at least one of them had to be on grief, and, if I read it through, I realized I'd probably be able to convince Mom I'd been miraculously cured or something.

I dragged a finger along the bookshelf and stopped at a book called *Grief Counseling and Grief Therapy: Fourth Edition*. Bingo. No secret passageway opened when I plucked it out, disappointingly. I took the book to the couch and opened it to the table of contents; a section titled "Chronic Grief Reactions" caught my eye.

It is not unusual for patients to only seek help two to five years later, saying that the death still feels unresolved and that they haven't returned to their normal lives.

My stomach dropped.
I was going to feel like this for another two to five years?

Anniversary reactions are common for ten years or longer.

I wanted to rip out my hair.
I got the hell out of that chapter and flicked idly through the rest of the book until I got caught on a dog-eared page with a passage highlighted in yellow.

The functioning level of the surviving parent was the most powerful predictor of a child's adjustment to the death of a parent.

The rest of the section was about how parents should best behave to ensure their kids don't fall off the deep end, basically. It was all highlighted; at first, I thought by Dad, but as I read, I realized they were all things Mom had been attempting to do.
I tried to swallow the guilt, but it wouldn't budge.
And then came the knocks. Three of them, on the window.
I turned to look. June Copeland grinned through the glass.

SHE WAVED, BEAMING, LIKE SHE wasn't trespassing.

For a moment I thought I might be dreaming. Not because what was happening was especially nice, but because it was so intensely unbelievable that it couldn't have actually been happening, like all your teeth snapping out of your mouth or inexplicably forgetting that one must wear clothes to school.

My stomach rolled. I clicked my phone to life to check the time— it was just past midnight.

June knocked again and gestured toward the patient entrance, the door that led outside, or, conversely, *inside*, like this whole time

I'd simply been confused as to what to do next. Yes. The door. How novel. But in her defense, I *was* just sort of staring at her, unblinking, probably drooling, not because I wasn't sure what the logical course of action was, but because opening the door would make this real, and I wasn't sure if I even wanted to participate in whatever sort of late-night shenanigan this was. Maybe if I pretended this wasn't happening, then it would go away.

But then I realized how hypocritical that was and got up to let her the hell in.

The cold hit me straightaway; a frigid gust of wind whipped June's hair across her face. "Evening," she said, casual, over the buffeting air.

"Hi, uh, what's—"

She shouldered her way past me, which I thought was to get out of the cold, but then she collapsed into the shallow indent in the patient couch like she owned the place, and stretched her arms so high above her head that a sliver of taut stomach emerged from underneath her jacket.

Not that I noticed.

I shut the door, and with the howling muffled, the main sounds were fabric rustling on fabric and the perpetual chaotic screeching in my brain. "Uh," I muttered, "yeah, get comfortable, I guess."

Meanwhile, June's frown was almost childlike, as if she'd opened all her presents but was expecting more, and her forehead creased. She eyed me, then looked down beside her to where Dad's copy of *Grief Counseling and Grief Therapy* lay, then looked around all at once like she'd unexpectedly arrived by teleportation. She exhaled through her nose. "I'm sorry."

I wasn't totally sure what she was apologizing for. "It's okay, I guess, but—"

She popped the smaller knuckles on her left hand. "Apparently, I"—*click*—"get sort of hyper"—*click*—"or something"—*click*—"when I'm nervous." *Click.* The last one practically echoed, bouncing off the bookshelves and the picture of the ghosts at Niagara Falls and Dad's desk and my chest. I doubted every word and movement, worried that my sleepy frontal lobe had created them for me. "And I think that makes me seem rude. I'm really not rude, I don't think, but if I *seem* rude, then I guess that's the same thing as being rude. Shit. I'm so sorry. If I—"

"No, that's fine, I... Why are you here?" I lowered myself into Dad's leather chair, opposite June.

She shifted and threw her legs over the arm of the couch. I straightened my spine. "I was bored, I guess. Wanted someone to talk to."

"Really?" I asked. "Don't you have, like, friends?" It sounded meaner than intended, so I doubled back. "Heath?"

"Honestly, I thought you might like some company too. We hadn't talked in like, what, a month? I wanted to see how you were doing."

I shifted. Felt like I was being dissected.

"I didn't know if you'd even *be* here," she continued, "but I remembered that you mentioned not, like, sleeping, and I had a hunch."

It wasn't really the unexpected visit that cemented my belief that something was strange about June Copeland, it was this. Her replies. I wondered if she did it on purpose—a bunch of little mysteries, protecting her like armor.

72

"You couldn't have come up to me at school, or something? Like a normal person?" I said this next part under my breath, aware there wouldn't be much truth to it but driven by curiosity as to what she'd say. "I guess you wouldn't want to be seen with me."

June searched for words, then scoffed, seeming to struggle to find them. "I swear to God, I'm not, like, whatever Regina George piece of trash you think I am. I promise. Okay?" I hadn't seen *Mean Girls*, but I knew what she was implying. I folded in on myself, embarrassed I had even had the nerve to say that. Maybe that was what I'd thought before. Not now.

A new sound: the soft hiss of her breath, and I listened as she inhaled for five seconds, then exhaled for five more. I couldn't help it; I matched the rhythm once, then again, until the room itself seemed like it took a breath too. June's shoulders relaxed, and I watched her become the girl from the cemetery, sincere and light.

"Okay," she said, "I lied. I just lied to you."

"About what?"

"I wasn't bored. I'm having a really bad, shitty night. And sometimes when that happens, I like to go for walks. So, I was passing the cul-de-sac anyways, and I feel like—I enjoyed talking to you. Before. And I saw from the street that the light was on in here. So."

"Yeah, okay. Yeah. That's fine."

"Okay."

And then it was sort of painfully awkward, and neither of us knew what to do, so June got up and left. I'm not joking. She lifted herself off the couch, opened the side door, then shut it behind her.

A half a second later, though, there was a knock.

I smiled despite myself. Got up and answered.

"Hi," she said as if we hadn't already spoken, in some animated Valley-girl accent, and offered her hand to shake. "I hope this isn't, like, a bad time, but I was passing by and was wondering if I could come, like, hang out."

I took her hand in mine. It was warm despite the cold. "Oh, sure, come on in."

"Cool, my name's June Copeland and I am, evidently, a complete weirdo."

"Yeah, I'm Sydney Whitaker, I'm...a bitch."

She snorted with laughter, and I followed suit. "Okay," she said while we resumed our previous positions. "We're cool, right?"

"Yeah."

"So. Starting over. What have you been up to this fine evening?"

I decided it would be best to rewind to a point before *Grief Counseling and Grief Therapy*. And the ToD. "I was, uh, watching a movie."

"What movie?"

"*It Follows*."

June smiled. "Ooh. Are you some freaky horror buff?"

Heat rushed to my cheeks. Suddenly I felt very self-conscious: hair up in a greasy ponytail, sweatpants with years-old stains, bare feet with toenails I hadn't looked at in weeks, let alone clipped. And she was here, completely polished, like she'd done her makeup just to come and sit on the couch. "I take offense at 'freaky.'"

"*Why?*"

"Because it's a perfectly normal—"

"No, I mean, why do you like them? I can't stand being scared."

"I don't know. I sort of like to prove to myself that I can handle them. And I guess not much actually scares me anymore."

"Do you think you're desensitized or something?"

"I mean, sort of. I guess I am."

"*So* weird. You don't seem like the type."

"What do you mean?"

"I just picture, like, a *goth*."

"I *am* decidedly un-goth."

"What's your favorite?"

"Favorite horror movie?"

"Yeah."

"You can't—you can't pick a favorite."

"You totally can."

I smiled again. There was a lot of smiling. "I don't know, I like different stuff at different times, I guess. Okay, what stuff do you like? Let me judge you for that."

We laughed. "I'm not judging you!" she said. "Oh, man. Books! Yeah. Books. Music. And I actually like, um, robots."

"Robots?"

"Yeah. I kinda want to go to school for robotics engineering."

Christ. If I hadn't felt inadequate before. "Okay, what's your *favorite*?" I asked, imitating the way she'd said it.

"Touché... Wait," she said when I laughed. "I'll try to answer. All three?"

I nodded. "Ten seconds. Rapid fire."

"Okay, I guess I like *Their Eyes Were Watching God*, but I might be saying that because I just read it, my favorite robot is Sophia, the one who says she's gonna kill everyone, and, God, like…I can't pick a song. I like this album by Arcade Fire—*Funeral*?"

"So, you only *sort of* picked a favorite book, and then you had the audacity to pick an album called *Funeral*."

Her frown suggested she thought I was serious at first, but I broke, smiled, and then we both came apart in completely inappropriate laughter. Something about the way we spoke reminded me of dancing, one foot moving to match the other, a quiet swapping of dominance. I worried I would step on her toes.

"Sorry. But, er, speaking of which." She swung toward me, crossed her legs. "How…are you?" She didn't say it the way it's normally said, with a sort of indifference as to what the answer will be; this was heavier. She meant it.

"Yeah, I'm, uh, yeah, I don't know. Fine, I guess." June raised an eyebrow. I worried she could read my mind: *not fine, not fine*. "Mom, uh, my mom wants me to go to a support group." I said *support group* slow, like I was trying to pronounce words in another language.

"Oh yeah?" June replied. I nodded. "Were you studying up?" She glanced over at *Grief Counseling and Grief Therapy*, then tossed it to me over the coffee table.

"Yeah, sort of. I don't know. Honestly, I don't think I want to go." I didn't want to talk about me. Flicked through the pages again to have something to do. "But other than that, yeah. I guess I'm fine. How are you? You said…you were having a bad night."

"I'm okay. I can get kind of—stuck in my head."

"I'm sorry."

"It happens."

"Have you, uh, gotten a replacement therapist?"

She laughed. "Well, that's the problem. The position remains unfilled. But yeah, no, I haven't. I'm getting there, though. Yeah. Getting better."

I wondered what June would've said if I brought up the fact that I had a folder containing all of her deepest darkest secrets nestled directly to my right. Maybe she'd already realized. To be fair, none of her secrets necessarily had to be deep or dark. But if they were, they were in there.

"If we're being honest, I don't really wanna talk about me either," she said suddenly.

"Then what do we talk about?"

"Well, maybe we don't have to *talk* about anything. Like, jokes are all well and good, but have you actually heard *Funeral*?"

"What? Uh, no, I don't think so. I don't know. Maybe? There's songs that I like, but I don't really pay attention to albums or anything."

"Okay, wait." She put her phone down on the coffee table and tapped it until she seemed satisfied. "This is the first song on the album. It's my second favorite."

It started optimistic, with strings and a tinkling piano, but then it swelled and got heavier. June said it was called "Neighborhood #1."

Olivia was a song-skipper. The good part of a song wasn't even until the climax, right before the end, and she'd always get distracted before we even made it that far. But June was savoring every note, and at a couple of points she looked like she'd wanted to say something but stopped herself for fear of interrupting. When it ended, she looked at me and smiled. "Nice, right? But, okay, I guarantee you've heard this one. It's sort of a hipster anthem."

Weirdly enough, I had. I remembered it from an old *Where the Wild Things Are* trailer. I couldn't remember what it was called, but it had this really powerful guitar part and these crescendoing moments of pure sound, and when he sang, God, it was like you could *feel* it, all the moments where his voice wavered but then grew stronger; and it *was* beautiful, but maybe not quite as beautiful as I felt it to be, because before I knew it, I was crying.

It was thoroughly embarrassing. I didn't even know why I was crying. It wasn't just the song. I think it was everything, the moment, holed up in my dead dad's office with the wind swirling behind the window over the snow-blanketed, monochromatic dark; it sort of felt timeless, off the grid, as if we were in limbo, and honestly, the idea didn't sound all that bad.

It took me a second to realize June was crying too. I assumed she, like me, had her own reasons. Then the moment faded, like a film lifting from in front of my eyes, and she said something so completely understated that both of us laughed. "Pretty good, huh?"

"Yeah," I said, sniveling pathetically. "Good taste."

"It's called 'Wake Up.' I guess song meanings are sort of up to your interpretation—some people think it's about, like, renouncing religion. A million little gods. That kind of thing. I see it as...coming to terms with all that stuff. It's like a loss of innocence, but maybe in...a good way, if that makes sense."

It did make sense. Everything about her made sense.

That's when her phone buzzed.

She whipped it out like it had electrocuted her, processed whatever was on the screen, then went all dark from the inside out. It oozed through her eyes. "Ah, damn. Damn, damn, damn."

"What's wrong?"

"It's my mom. Turns out I'm, like, not actually supposed to be places in the middle of the night. Who knew?" She softened and looked at me. "I'm sorry. I gotta go. Really great five minutes, though."

I surprised myself with how upset that made me, like something I ought to take care of was slipping through my fingers. I didn't want her to leave. I figured it'd go back to the way it was after the cemetery—pretending like we'd never spoken. That sounded terrible. I liked her. "Oh. Okay, yeah."

"Hey, do you—do you want a ride tomorrow? To school?" My heart dropped.

"Why?"

"Huh?"

"Why are you offering?"

"I… Because you're funny? I like you? And I live close."

I had to ask. "June?" She looked at me. "Do you feel bad for me?"

"Why do you seem so surprised by the notion that someone could actually like talking to you?"

I'm not—I'm surprised that you *enjoy talking to me.*

But I didn't say that. It came out as: "I don't know."

"At the cemetery—when you didn't want me to drive you home— was that because you were afraid? Like, to be in a car?"

I nodded, reveling in the simplicity of not having to explain to somebody why I was doing something or why I felt the way I did.

"Well, don't worry. I—don't want you to do anything you're not comfortable with. Seriously."

"No. That'd be nice."

"Really?"

"Yeah."

"Okay. I'll…see you tomorrow."

I remembered the time. "Today."

She smiled. "I'll see you today. Pick you up at seven?"

"Sounds good."

Later, at the end of the school year, after everything had happened, I hated myself for never questioning the small things. But when she said it was her mom on the phone that night, I had no reason to believe she was lying.

7

WHY DID I SAY YES?

I woke up after a sumptuous two-and-a-half hours of sleep, pulsing with the knowledge that June would be there soon—alongside the recognition that I had made a terrible mistake.

I was rarely so easily swayed. Maybe it was the nighttime or the exhaustion or the intrigue, but something about her had forced me to make a decision I wouldn't normally have made, and even though it was only mere hours later, I wanted nothing less than to sit beside the helm of a metal deathtrap, no matter how compelling the captain.

June. None of it had seemed real. None of it had made sense. I wasn't the sort of person girls like her visited in the middle of the night; that sort of thing didn't happen to me.

But I'd said that when Dad died too. Clearly these things *did* happen to me, over and over and over. I decided I'd have to reevaluate my self-image.

What had she even been doing outside?

I found her account unconvincing. Not because I didn't believe her, necessarily; she really might have been having a bad night. Fine. But why did she think I could help? What made her think she could trust me?

I should have been happy about this. There shouldn't have been anything upsetting about a pretty girl, who liked books and hipster music and *robots*, driving me to school in the morning. But it *was* upsetting, because it wasn't right, and the trades the universe required for us to even have arrived there were unfair. This wouldn't have been happening had there not been a cemetery containing the putrefying corpse of my dad for us to meet at, or had there not been something the matter with her in the first place, bad enough that she had to seek out Dad, and then me. Our relationship was born from misfortune. Not the best start.

We both had our issues, clearly. But I stood on top of mine like a parade float, and hers—I imagined she kept them somewhere else. In a safe. Underground.

And then there was the more immediate issue that she would soon be on her way in a car that could kill me. Strike that. A car that could travel fast enough for a sudden stop to kill me.

But it'd be fine. It'd have to be fine. Anything could kill me.

Get in the damn car, Whitaker. Let her handle the rest. The idea of relinquishing any sense of control over the situation was comforting, maybe, somehow. *She'll be in the driver's seat. If something happens, then it happens, and I won't have anything at all to do with it.* But I wasn't sure I even had the capacity to relinquish control of anything; you can't relinquish something you didn't have in the first place.

I still had an hour until June was supposed to show up, so I decided to do my makeup, something I'd hardly even thought about since the end of the world. Tinted moisturizer. Mascara. I tried to fill in my eyebrows, but my hands were shaking and heavy, and the pencil swipes ended up too thick and uneven, so I scrubbed them off. This wasn't helping; mascara made the bags under my eyes darker, blush accentuated the ghoulish boniness of my cheeks, and lipstick settled in the downturned corners of my mouth. I didn't feel pretty. I felt tired. I felt like death. This was an unproductive exercise, like putting glasses on a corpse, and anyway, none of this would even matter—*it doesn't matter if you're pretty when you swerve, smash—*

Ugh.

Stop.

I thought of Mom. Hated that she'd been in the office, maybe late at night or while I was at school, thumbing through Dad's books for something, anything, that could help, that could help *me*. Highlighting. Dog-earing. Committing to memory.

I'd been too harsh.

And even worse—when I went downstairs that morning, there were sheets of trifolded paper strewn all about the kitchen island, and I couldn't help but peek: bills. Crawford Funeral Homes. The hospital.

Holy shit. How the hell did it cost so much to *die*?

I overcooked some blueberry pancakes as a peace offering, then covered them in plastic wrap so they wouldn't get cold and popped a green tea bag into a mug. Left a note.

I'm sorry. Love you.

It struck me like a meteor to my chest that I wouldn't have to specify who the note was for.

June was punctual, and I was a mess.

I'd been waiting in the driveway since 6:45, hoping the cold would rouse some sort of strength within me, or at least freeze the panic, but I hadn't had much luck either way. I was focused mostly on breathing, the air sharp and slicing the back of my throat, when June crunched up the driveway. At least, I assumed it was her. The headlights were so bright against the pitch-darkness that I couldn't see anything except for the silhouette of the car and snowflakes drifting lazily in the glow. With the spotlight fixed on me, I felt a bit like I was being beamed up.

I took an unsatisfying breath and moved forward.

Somehow the sweat on my palms hadn't frozen, I realized, as I tugged on the door of the passenger side.

"Morning, girly," June said, all singsong, after I'd collapsed into the seat.

"Hi," was all I managed to squeak out.

June or the car. I couldn't settle on which scared me more. Of course, it wasn't the car that scared me, it was the sudden stop, and it wasn't June that scared me, it was myself in front of her.

I couldn't swallow. God, I hadn't thought it was going to be this bad. But I had to do it. Exposure therapy. I couldn't go my entire life without ever being in a car again. But when I looked out over the dashboard, all I could think about was whether Dad had enough time to think about anything before the windshield carved up his torso, if unconscious really meant unconscious, how half a second of blinding, earth-shattering pain probably feels longer than a whole entire life…

"We don't have to do this," June said. I turned to her. She'd noticed my unease, evidently, and her eyes slanted in a sympathetic grimace. "Like, listen, I know it isn't what this is about, but I'm a good driver, and I'll—I can go slow, warn you at turns. Whatever helps."

I studied her face, all big eyes and full cheeks and warm skin. *She* didn't look tired. And if she was thinking about how pathetic I was, she certainly wasn't showing it.

"So, drive?"

I chewed my lip, which wasn't enough of a response. Nodded. "Yeah. Thanks."

We started down the street.

The silence was unbearable. Just tires crushing thin snow and June's nails clicking against the steering wheel. The world spun past with a strange sense of unreality; the light from the lampposts was too bright, but everything else seemed somehow too dark, and even the way the falling snow trembled felt menacing. I got an overwhelming sense that I wasn't really here, that *we* weren't really here, like we were actually sitting stationary on top of one of those rolling street screens they used in old movies. The experience should have been accompanied by a shrill violin crescendo.

But nothing leaped from the shadows. Nothing jolted to a stop.

Each passing headlight threatened to ram into us, my heart skipping beats in response to each imagined collision. But nothing hit. Nothing broke. Nothing died.

It was fine.

June kept looking at me; for any feedback, I assumed, which was kind but also made me very aware of my own face. "How can I help?" she finally asked, maybe five minutes in, when I'd taken to jamming my middle fingers into my temples.

Say something. Anything. I tried to hide my embarrassment by speaking quickly. "Can you just talk?" Any stimulus. Anything besides doom.

We pulled up to the intersection of Main and College—we'd be at school in five minutes. I looked to her; she smirked, the blaze of the stoplight casting a deep red glow on to her face. "Oh, man. Yeah, I can do that. About what? Anything?"

"Yeah. Anything would be good." Green. Forward. I paid close attention to the glove compartment, tried to will the heat into me to keep my teeth from chattering.

"Oof. Okay. That's a lot of responsibility, Whitaker."

Whitaker. That was nice.

"Okay. We're going to do a stream of consciousness thing here and hope for the best. I like that it's snowing today. I think it's pretty. I...had some yogurt for breakfast. With blueberries. I love blueberries. God, is this all I have to talk about? Am I really that boring?"

I let her voice wrap me up, tuck me in, rub my back.

"I actually sort of like driving to school in the morning because it's kind of that weird time where it's dark out but people are awake and have the lights on in their houses and stuff, and I like to look inside sometimes and see what the people are doing. Is that weird?"

"A little."

"It's like—what are they called—liminal spaces? Places that are just for moving through instead of staying in. That's what the drive feels like. Normally I'll listen to music or something. I have a whole Spotify playlist specifically for mornings. Lotta chill vibes. We don't have to do that right now. Some other time. Um, okay, what else… I was actually kind of bummed this morning because I found out one of my ferns has mites, so when I get home, I have to sort that out."

"Ferns?"

"Oh yeah. I'm a plant mom."

Due to the strangeness of the night before, I couldn't decipher the tone of the ride. The cup holder between us felt bulky, and I couldn't stop my legs from fidgeting.

"Also…I'm sorry I dragged you into this, dude. I'm not sure the environmental benefits of carpooling are worth whatever, like, mental deterioration I've forced upon you."

I scoffed. "Is that what this is really about? The environmental benefits?"

"Oh, for sure. I took one look at you and thought, 'Shit, that girl looks like she has a significant ecological footprint.'"

I smiled.

"No. I told you, I live on the way, anyway, and, you know. Whatever helps."

"Whatever helps," I repeated.

"Fine. If you're so set on this being a quid pro quo arrangement, then I'm not doing this to be nice; I'm expecting compensation within three to five business days."

"That's not true."

"For real. Three to five, Whitaker. Also, we're here." She was right. We'd made it. In one piece.

The morning hustle and bustle was in full force, the parking lot brimming with activity, school buses pulling up one after the other and releasing kids in swarms. June looked at me. "Not so bad, right?"

"No."

June pulled into her parking spot—all the seniors had designated spaces—and someone honked at us, which made me jump, embarrassingly. Heath was in the car opposite, with someone else in the passenger seat: Greg Wilson. He was on the varsity swim team with Heath, as well as one of the privileged few always sort of flitting around Heath and June in hallways and sitting with them at tables. Heath smiled and waved, and June smiled and waved back, and I felt myself melting away.

"Morning," June called once she'd left the car. I found myself feeling disappointed that our time had been cut short. Reality flooded back in; the lights were no longer blurry.

"Hey!" Heath and I made eye contact for what I realized was probably the first time ever. He had these big features that commanded attention, and perpetually smiling Gap-model coy boyishness that made him even more handsome; the sort of eyes that suggested he was in on a joke that you weren't, but he'd probably tell you if you asked. Shoulders back. Jaw set. When he looked at you, it was like he was looking through you, into your guts and out the other side.

I had decided preemptively, and for little reason, that I should dislike him.

Greg followed behind. He was shorter than Heath, had stark blond hair that almost glowed in the low light.

June gestured to me while gathering her books from the back seat. "You guys know Sydney, right?"

This felt like a job interview. I flashed my best closed-mouth smile in the hope of offsetting my insecurity. "Hi."

Greg looked at me for what seemed like half a second too long and gave a shy, noncommittal wave, then said his own name as a suave sort of introduction. Heath leaned coolly against the door of his Audi and introduced himself too, even though I obviously already knew who he was. I appreciated the humility of it. "So *you're* the stowaway," he said.

"Aye," I said, before realizing that was a really bad opener, and when Heath's smile grew wider, I kicked myself internally and said, "uh, stowaway made me think of pirates."

"Well," Heath said, "yo-ho."

June didn't speak. Just eyed the three of us.

Heath still gave me his full attention. Another bus had arrived, and I was glad for it; the thought of being seen with this group of people excited me in a way I couldn't explain. "You know, I didn't believe June when she said you were a junior."

"Why?" I asked.

He had a hand flat against his shoulder. "You need to be at least this tall."

Greg made a sort of *oooh* noise while June looked to Heath, an intensity in her eyes that I couldn't place. "Don't."

"It's friendly banter!"

I needed some material. Quick. "I thought you were a senior"—I nodded down to his pretty terrible leather brogues—"not a senior citizen."

I cringed so hard, I thought my eyeballs might squish out of my skull, but Greg did another *oooh* with more fervor, now, suggesting he was on my side. Heath grinned, lighting up his whole face. Looked at June. "See? Banter!"

"Those are pretty bad," Greg said.

"They're *Tom Ford*, dude."

June rolled her eyes. "Okay, comedians. I'm going to homeroom, but I hope you all have, like, a wonderful day at clown college or whatever."

"We're coming, honey." Heath looked at me with his eyebrows raised, while Greg also just sort of looked at me, generally. "Man. I didn't know she was like this with you too," Heath said teasingly. My belly skipped rope. We had a *joke*. There was something effortless about it all, and I felt a sudden sinking—was this what I'd been missing? Why didn't talking to Olivia feel like this anymore? I'd shut myself out for so long that I had forgotten how wonderful it felt to be included, to be seen, to be heard.

I didn't want to like Heath. But I already did.

I hadn't even opened my paper bag to start not-eating before Olivia was chewing me out at lunch, like we were fucking married, or something. "Where were you this morning?" she asked. "Miles was late"—she shot him a look—"so I had to sit there alone like a, like a quarantine patient."

"I *told* you I'd be late," Miles said.

Olivia shrugged. "I'm not placing blame," she said, despite placing blame. She looked back to me and raised her eyebrows. "So? Where were you? Your bike wasn't in the rack either."

I'd known this moment was coming. "Uh, someone gave me a ride."

"You can't just say that like it's a normal thing that happens. Who?"

"June Copeland."

Olivia froze, mid-peel of her packet of fruit snacks. "Okay, you're gonna have to explain that one."

"Explain what?" I said. I knew full well what I had to explain.

"You know June? That's cool," Miles said, which was maybe the first time he had contributed anything to a discussion voluntarily since the beginning of the school year. Either way, I was kind of pleased with myself. Yeah, I *did* know June, and it *was* cool.

"Is it, Miles?" Olivia said. "Why's that?"

"I don't know. She seems nice."

"She seems *hot*."

"I didn't say that!"

Olivia turned to me. "Miles thinks she's hot."

"Liv!"

"Go ahead, Sydney. The counsel is waiting for an answer."

I probably should have thought this through. "I, uh, met her at the cemetery."

"*What?*"

"She was a patient," I said. "And was visiting. And we, I don't know. Got to talking."

Miles nodded solemnly. "That makes sense. You can't be hot, smart, *and* mentally stable. Gotta pick two."

Olivia looked at him incredulously. "There are so many things wrong with what you just said. Which two am *I*, then?"

Miles blabbered something in defense, but I was already annoyed; he couldn't talk about June like that. He didn't know anything about her. "No. It's not like that. She's not like that."

"Oh my God," Olivia said.

"What?"

"Do you *like her*?" she asked, with all the tact of a fucking nail gun.

I froze. "Are we eleven?"

"Oh my God!" Olivia leaned backward, letting this realization settle into her, like it was *important*, for some reason, when it really wasn't at all. "You do." She clicked her tongue. "This is a dangerous road to tread, little Sydney. A dangerous road."

"Okay, but you're not exactly an expert, are you?"

She stopped, looked at Miles, and then back to me. "What's that supposed to mean?"

"I'm just saying. You don't know what's best for me."

"Right."

"That's all I was saying," I snapped. It really wasn't any of her business. I spent the rest of lunch silently watching the clock, thinking about where June might've been, then wondering if I could be there too.

The November of my junior year became permanently etched into my mind as the first month of June.

She drove me to and from school every day without fail. Ten minutes there. Ten minutes back.

During those twenty minutes, I seemed to exist on another plane entirely. Even if I had spent the night freaking out or half the day picking at toilet-cubicle graffiti, once I sat in the passenger seat, it'd all evaporate. The driving became less frightening each time until I hardly thought about it at all. June was light, all yellows and oranges, and we quickly became something like friends.

Friends. Despite not seeing each other outside of those intervals, the relationship grew into something the two of us could slip in and out of without too much hassle. A skin I grew and shed each day.

This may have been because I was too emotionally porous for some sense of closeness *not* to grow. Everything felt hugely impactful and important, and June, at the time, seemed to be no exception. June convinced me we were all open books if only we found the right person to read us.

She was touchy-feely from the beginning. Little things, like grabbing my bicep when she laughed, or pushing me gently when I teased her, or picking loose hairs off my clothes as if we were monkeys grooming each other. If I hadn't known any better, some days, it seemed like she was looking for excuses to touch me—but I did know better, of course. She was like this with everyone. This was why everyone liked her, and I was as gullible as the rest of them. I was not special.

I fell for it anyway.

"Girl, you have toothpaste on your face," she said, then licked her thumb and jammed it into the corner of my mouth.

I half-heartedly batted her away. "I put it there on purpose."

"And you missed a huge chunk of hair in your braid."

I felt the back of my head. I had.

So we sat idling in my driveway while she undid my hair and wrapped it again, goose bumps flaring on my arms when she gathered the wispy bits at the nape of my neck. "You're a mess," she said. She ended up doing perfect Dutch braids in barely a minute.

From then on, I contemplated doing my hair badly every morning.

"Whitaker," June said, "I have a question for you."

"Okay. Hit me."

"What's your favorite thing about yourself?"

God. I didn't even know. I guessed I was smart, but June was smarter, and I guessed I was funny, but June was funnier. Then, finally, I said, "My sense of self-preservation is pretty, uh, honed."

She scoffed. "Yeah, all right. Not totally what I was looking for, but that works."

"Why do you ask?"

"I'm just wondering."

"What about you?"

She thought for a moment. "My empathy," she said. "Well, I don't know. That used to be my favorite thing, but now I'm not so sure."

"Really? Why?"

"I think sometimes you can become, like, so focused on making sure everyone else is okay that you forget to make sure you're okay," she said. "Like you're spending time mowing someone else's lawn when your house is on fire."

Yikes. Was I the lawn? I made a mental note to be less needy. But where—*what*—was the fire?

"Describe how you're feeling right now in five words."

"Like, five words maximum?"

"No, exactly five."

"Okay." I held up my fingers to count. "I feel—"

"I suggest not wasting your first two words on repeating the question."

Put the two fingers back down. "Normally scared, but currently happy."

"Five words and your main one is *happy*? Boring."

"Delighted. I'm delighted. Fine. You go."

"Inside, looking out a window."

The trees had gone completely bare by the time Dad's voice wasn't there anymore.

I kept trying to summon up the sound, but it wouldn't come. I could visualize him with his mouth moving, but nothing would come out besides a weird news-anchor voice that didn't sound like his at all.

How could I forget? How could I *forget*?

I hated my brain for doing this to me. To him. How could it do this? How dare it?

But I was my brain, and my brain was me, so *I* had forgotten. But maybe it wasn't really something you actively *forgot*, and more something that went away. A candle doesn't forget its flame; eventually, it just doesn't burn anymore.

Despite all of June's talk about fires and windows, I told her all this on that Wednesday morning, an abject sense of betrayal hammering away at my insides.

She was quiet for a long time, which I was grateful for at first. I knew if I'd told Olivia the same thing, she would have given me three separate pieces of unhelpful and slightly patronizing advice by now. But eventually the silence became so long that I'd worried I'd at last crashed through her outer limits and had irreparably freaked her out. Finally, at the red light on the corner of Main and Summit, June turned to me and said, "Did you know I can read palms?"

I looked at her, expecting her to crack, but she didn't. "Seriously?"

"Yeah, give me your hand."

"Palm-reading isn't…real."

"Silence, naysayer. Hurry."

I gave in because I wanted her to touch me. I offered up my left hand because it was less sweaty than my right, and June took it, examined the lines, or whatever, and hummed quietly to herself while I tried to keep from shivering. After a moment, her face fell. "Oh no."

She was dead serious. I didn't think I'd ever seen her so serious. "What?"

"It says…" A pause. "You're a *dork*." We looked at each other for a second, my hand in her hand, neither of us saying anything. And then she cracked into this goofy surprised expression, her mouth wide open and her eyes huge. "Oh *no*! What will we do?" A honk came from behind us; the light on her face had gone green. "All right, all right," she said, switching her attention to the road.

"That was nasty," I said, trying to suppress what I knew would be a dumb, toothy grin. My skin tingled where her fingers had been. "Nasty trick."

This was when I realized *why*, exactly, I got along with June, and why it was so easy to trust her—she didn't treat grief like a problem to be solved, but a constant to be endured. She created all the little moments of clarity that became the iceberg tips in an existence spent primarily dragging myself across the ocean floor.

Having a dead dad was part of my identity now. I knew that. No amount of self-care changes what you are, or what you can have, or the hand you've been dealt. June knew that too, I think, so she was helping me learn how to ride the unbroken wave.

Pleasant Hills received another real dumping of snow two weeks later. Everyone had been hoping for a snow day, but given our diligent fleet of salting trucks, the roads were clear by five that morning. I knew that because I watched it happen from my window. I didn't mind class not being canceled, really; it meant I got to see her.

On the ride to school, I mentioned to June how much I hated the snow.

"You *hate* it?"

"Whoa. I was not expecting that much opposition. I thought that was a normal opinion to have."

"Oh, is it? No. I think it's amazing. It might be the novelty of it. Like, you don't really get this in So Cal. Don't you at least think it's pretty?"

"Not really. I don't know. It's just...monochrome. I guess it's kind of pretty when it first falls, but by the next day the roads are all covered in dirty gray sludge and everything's...wet. I don't know. And there's nothing to do in the winter."

"There's this, like, famed sporting event held every four years that begs to differ."

"Right, yeah, sorry I don't know how to freaking *luge*."

June laughed at *luge*.

"I don't know. I just don't like anything about it."

"There's Christmas."

I scoffed. "Yeah, really looking forward to that. I don't know. Everything's..." I blew a raspberry. "Dead." June didn't speak, so I kept talking. "Dad, uh, and me, every year as soon as it got warm, we'd start going to the River Styx every weekend. To go hiking. We did pretty much the same trail every time, and, I don't know, it never got boring, for some reason. That was our absolute favorite thing to do." The past tense strangled me. "And it's so depressing to think of it all frozen over now. I'd hate to…I don't know. Honestly I'm not sure I'll ever even go there again."

"You should go back, Whitaker. It might be good for you. If you were to, like, actually see it again—I'd bet it's prettier than you think. Anyways. Maybe it wouldn't hurt to make some new memories there either. Reclaim the place. You know?"

I looked at her, traced the soft outline of her face with my eyes: the curve of her nose, her chin, her Cupid's-bow mouth. "I'll take your word for it."

It was becoming increasingly apparent that I did, in fact, like June Copeland in a way that was more than platonic.

I'd smile whenever I saw her, the action as reflexive as kicking when my knee was tapped. It was more embarrassing than anything; we wouldn't even be talking about anything funny, and I'd have to try to keep a straight face.

In pre-calc, I started dashing a short line through the middle of my sevens, the way I'd seen she'd done it in some worksheets she left in the back seat.

I was thrilled and surprised in equal measure at the ease with which I could say things to her, strange or otherwise. I told her every-thing. Well, most things. I told her how I was feeling on my bad days. I left out the parts where I thought maybe Dad was murdered, where I spent most of my free time watching people die.

Of course, I couldn't act on my feelings toward her. Of *course* I couldn't. If she realized it on her own (because I liked to act as if it *wasn't* obvious), my life could have been made even worse than it already was. I'd have to move schools, maybe. Change my name. *Local girl's dad croaks—but girl is still horny for June Copeland.* Despite the likeli-hood of her being straight. Despite her being taken. So I kept it quiet, kept it selfish, and absentmindedly basked in her presence, bathed in it, lived in it. I was happy just being with her, living on the same planet, breathing the same air. But there was always an element of uncertainty. The understanding that there had to be something else to all this.

Dad. June never mentioned whatever had happened while she was seeing him. She never even brought it up again. And everything else about her: she'd barely ever talk about Heath or her parents either. Of course, I never really asked. What would I say? "So, tell me a little bit about your *home life*." I didn't necessarily think it weird that the subject never came up naturally in conversation, because I didn't exactly expect it to, but considering our relationship was based entirely on my late father, I thought maybe there'd be something. Anything.

Her reluctance to share fed a particularly ugly fear that maybe she could hardly even tolerate me. That this was all only happening because she felt some strange sense of obligation to my dad after *what happened*. The *what* of that sentence was as elusive as she was. On days where I could say *Dad*, I tried to ask.

"So, uh, how long did you see him for?"

"Oh, man." June thought, drumming her fingers against the steering wheel. "Six months, I think."

"So, I guess…how was he?"

"In what way?"

"I mean, did you like him? Or, I guess…what was he like?" I knew what he was like, of course. But I wanted to know what he was like with her.

"He was great. He was patient and understanding and had this, essence, I guess. Really warm. Funny. I get why you loved him so much. Of course I do. I know that's part of the job, but he never made it feel like that." She paused. Swallowed once. "And he gave me incredibly discounted sessions."

"Really?"

"Yeah. Like, almost free. My parents were—they're weird, about that stuff, so, yeah."

"What do you mean weird?"

"Like…" She let out something between a sigh and a grunt. "It's hard to explain. Sorry, I don't want to dump this on you or anything, but my parents are divorced, and I'm not close at all to my dad, and my mom—eh. She's one of those people who thinks mental illness can be cured with, like, a positive attitude and multivitamins. And she would *not* have agreed with me going."

"So, she didn't even know?"

She shook her head. "She doesn't really know anything about me at all."

"Yeah. I get it."

We were quiet for a moment. Longing for all the things we lacked filled the empty space.

"So," she continued, "I guess I was kind of on my own, trying to figure stuff out. Yeah. He was a good dude. Or maybe I was such a head case that he thought it was his civic duty to sort me out."

"Did he?"

"Eh. Almost."

Something about the conversation made it feel like Dad had been sitting in the back seat this whole time, but I'd never turned to look.

Of all the issues with my less-than-innocent fondness for June, the most apparent problem was Heath.

I caught myself looking out for him at school, paranoid he'd be able to tell how I felt by seeing my face when I looked at her. But truthfully, I didn't *really* want anything bad to happen between them, because as much as everything in me fought against it, I liked the guy. I couldn't help it.

In December, while I was waiting for June after school, I was on the ToD, watching this particularly incriminating video of a building jumper, and Heath had come up beside me without me noticing.

He ran a hand through his hair, exhaled, and puffed out his cheeks. Yeah. He saw. "I'm sorry. I didn't mean to—"

"No, it's not your fault. I shouldn't be doing this here anyway. Uh. Yikes. That's embarrassing."

He got in close to me and I needed to tilt my neck upward

to look at him. "Listen. This might be weird of me, but I…" He pinched the bridge of his nose. Even now, I was worried this was some sort of confrontation. "So, I actually lost my mom too. A few years ago."

I shuffled my feet, unsure how to react. Unsure how he wanted me to react. Why hadn't I already known? That seemed like the sort of information that would've done the rounds. Why hadn't June mentioned it? "Oh, um, man. Why didn't you tell me before?"

"I worry with these things there's a fine line between sharing and seeming like you're trying to one-up the other person, or take away from their experience. We may have gone through a similar thing, but nobody's grief is the same."

"Yeah. I mean…yeah. For sure."

"Either way, just know I've been there, even if I haven't been exactly *there*. And maybe that's marginally better than being surrounded by people who haven't. Who…can't even point it out on a map." He chuckled at his own metaphor in a way I found endearing.

"No, yeah. Definitely."

Ugh. He had as many pity points as me. I didn't even have that going for me anymore. And a part of me felt like he really had made that information known to make me feel guilty. That was the cynicism, but it couldn't stay for long; he was too damn nice, and charismatic, and every encounter we'd had—though they were mostly brief—was pleasant.

But my affection for June, left unkindled, wasn't really hurting anybody. Was it?

Maybe nobody except myself.

One long night, I came up with a special and horrible game. My mind felt like it was balancing on a tightrope, and any misstep or slight breeze could send me tumbling into the void. The tightrope was always there; here, there was no *Don't look down*. Every direction was *down*. But the game was foolproof. Entirely effective. Any time I found myself wavering—thinking about death or dying or ends or Dad or the ToD—I'd force myself to think about June instead.

This was creating troubling links in my head. I knew it was.

But it worked too well to stop. *Think about June. Flip my mind overtop of itself, push everything else out until she's all that's left.* June laughing at a joke I'd made, or June speaking, or June existing. This didn't serve, exactly, to balance me on the tightrope; it *disintegrated* the tightrope. It made it so the tightrope had never existed at all. There was no gravity. I could float there, comfortable, and never worry about the fall ever again.

Whatever helped.

What's the point of living if—

June.

We're all going to die and the universe is indifferent and—

June. Her hands on me and her face close to mine but what does it matter if she, if Dad—

June. June smiling in the driver's seat. Dad decomposing in the driver's seat—

June. Heaven is June in the driver's seat. Hell is June in the driver's seat. There is only June in the driver's seat.

And at night, my consciousness would slip away, repeating that smooth, delicious mantra in my head.

There is only June in the driver's seat.

THE NEXT TEXT CAME DURING a phone call with June two weeks from Christmas break. Calls had become a regular occurrence; they'd begun when I'd left a notebook in her car and she'd called to tell me, and then just kept talking. I could neither confirm nor deny I'd left the notebook there on purpose.

I had her on speaker while I played *Bloodborne* on PlayStation and she narrated an episode of *Robot Wars* to me; apparently, it was a good one.

"Dude, Whitaker, you need to turn off *Birthblood* and get an eye of this absolute walloping."

That was when my phone buzzed.

Your dad would be so disappointed in you.

Seriously?

Did this have to happen *now*?

"Uh, June?" I said, making sure I didn't stammer. "I gotta go."

June didn't say anything at first; I thought I heard someone else talking just out of earshot. "Oh, that's okay. I have to go too."

"Okay. Talk to you later."

I hung up and tried to swipe the text away, but realized I should wait to see if there'd be anything else, any follow-up, or if this was all they had for me—and when it seemed like it was, I resolved to tell Mom.

This was no coincidence, now. She'd have to understand.

Mom was sitting at the kitchen table, the skin under her eyes bruised and thin, her hair clipped away from her face in a heap; in the three months since he died, she'd gotten three different haircuts and still never wore it down.

I caught a glimpse of the papers she'd been reading. They had the same familiar headers: bank, hospital, insurance...

"I wanna show you something," I said. "Well, I, I need to tell you something, but I need you not to freak out."

She abandoned the papers and moved toward me, slowly, as if I were a sleeping animal who'd attack if wakened. "What is it?"

I handed her my phone. Explained the texts. That I'd been getting them since the funeral. Whenever they mentioned Dad, she recoiled, but subtly enough that maybe she thought I wouldn't notice. "I think maybe this might have to do with Dad, okay, and I think we should go to the police and tell them about what's been happening and then maybe they can do something—"

"Sweetie." She set my phone on the kitchen island, put her hands gently on my biceps, then moved one to my face. "We're not doing that. You know we're not doing that."

"What do you mean? It's all here, Mom. They have to do something."

"They don't." She moved away, obviously thin, even in her baggy sweatpants, and lowered herself back to the table; she'd already checked out. "They don't, because there's nothing *to* do."

"Mom, read them again. Read the texts. This person sounds like...they *sound* like they could have done someone harm."

"I'll call your school to tell them, but that's all."

"No, don't. I'd rather you not do anything than call the school. The school won't know anything because it doesn't have to do with the school, Mom."

"Sweetie, it's just... People have been picking on you for years."

That stung, but I wouldn't show her. "Not like this. You know it. Not like this."

"I think you're seeing things that aren't there."

"I want to go to the police."

"I said no, Sydney. There's been enough buzz around this house recently, and I—I don't have the time. I absolutely do not have time."

I scoffed. "You don't have time? How can you say that?"

The paper she held creased beneath her grip.

"How can you even say that, Mom? People are saying these things to me, and you don't have *time*? Someone is...is stalking me, and you don't have time? Someone might have killed Dad, and you don't have—"

"*No*." She said it so loudly, I swore it echoed.

I stopped.

"No." She scooted out from the table again and looked me dead in my eyes; she looked somewhere far away. "You cannot keep saying that. Stop it. Sometimes these things happen, and there's nothing we can do, and there's not always somebody to blame. Thinking there is... It's making it impossible for both of us to heal. Do you understand? Nobody—nobody did anything to Daddy."

"Mom."

"*Nobody*. You *stop it*." She gathered the papers, straightened them against the table with a sharp *thwack*, and went to leave. "The support group meets next week. It might be a little short notice, but I'm going to make sure I get you in."

I felt like I was talking to a brick wall. No, not exactly that—a brick wall that hated me. "Mom—"

"I'm making this decision. You don't have a say now. And your father would have wanted you to go as well. This is the right thing," she said, maybe more to convince herself than me.

"Really? Do you know that?"

"I do."

And that was how I found myself at Constellations Healing.

The office was located three towns over, in a square that vaguely resembled Pleasant Hills', quiet and colonial with wreaths hanging from front doors and ribbons draped on lampposts. It was five days before Christmas; apparently they'd wanted to squeeze the first session in now to give us some holiday-themed coping tips or something. And although I absolutely was not looking forward to any of this, I sort of found myself thankful for the distraction.

Mom and I climbed, the stairs groaning beneath our weight—some sort of omen, I decided—until we reached the fourth floor and stopped at a door with a glass panel that read CONSTELLATIONS HEALING, surrounded by some peeling and discolored sticker decals of shooting stars.

Ah, yes. This was the place.

A bell rang softly above us as we entered the windowless waiting room, which was cramped and gray and smelled like stale lavender. Mom went to the reception desk while I made myself comfortable in a couch across the room.

That was when I noticed the other kid.

He sat in the plush armchair opposite me, sunken in deep enough to suggest he'd been fossilizing there for a while, flicking through a battered copy of *The Time Machine* by H. G. Wells too quickly to actually be reading it. He was my age, I guessed, with dark brown skin entirely free of pimples. He tugged at his red beanie, which concealed what looked like a head full of short dreadlocks. Fiddled with the clear-framed glasses that dominated his face. Was he here for the support group? I could ask. This was my chance to start anew. The ease with which I'd become close to June had instilled in me a newfound confidence, and I thought maybe I'd been needlessly dismissive this whole time, that people *were* good and honest, that we *were* open books. I resolved that I was surely going to become best friends with this kid I'd been staring at for five seconds.

"Hey, are you here for"—I referenced my pamphlet so as not to seem too eager—"teen bereavement? The support group?"

He looked at me incredulously. Oh God. Maybe he was mute. Maybe that's why he needed therapy, because he was fucking mute, and I'd just tried to initiate a conversation with a mute kid. "No," he said finally, bored and drawn-out and sarcastic, one step removed from a sigh, in a voice lower than I'd anticipated. "I'm here for the ambience." And then he returned to flipping through *The Time Machine* at an inhuman pace.

Nope, I was right. People were the worst.

If pretentious, baby-faced, sad kid didn't want to make friends, then I didn't either. "Okay. Sorry." I slumped back into my chair.

Mom returned and kissed me on the head. "All right, baby, you're good to go. Play nice. Back in an hour."

I winced in embarrassment as Mom left, the door chiming behind her.

Baby Face glanced at me, then returned his attention to the book. "Play nice," he deadpanned.

"You first."

A woman emerged from the door that led from the waiting room toward whatever other horrors awaited us. She had a worn, kind face, and looked like she'd gotten dressed under the impression that it was 1974—paisley maxi skirt, long blond hair draped around a cotton shirt. "Leo? And you must be Sydney, right? Hello, chickadees, why don't you come on through?"

Ha. So he had a name.

We trailed behind her like ducklings. "You're a little early, but I figured you could come in the office, familiarize yourself with the various sights and smells and auras."

I rolled my eyes internally.

The office was hardly big enough for the seven chairs it held, all positioned in a circle. This was it? I'd envisioned this being like AA, or something, with twenty people and ample legroom, but this was not like that. Leo followed behind me like we were about to be executed via a swift gunshot to the back of the head. He plopped himself down across the circle from me, much more heavily than necessary, and I lowered my head. I suspected this boy might have been a human bomb, and I wasn't interested in positioning myself inside his blast radius.

The woman told us to make ourselves at home, but I *couldn't* because the room was too small and poorly lit and it felt like someone was watching me. Probably *Leo*. I comforted myself with the thought that Mom was most likely right—Dad would have wanted this.

The next entrants came in a pair, their matching heads of thick, dark hair and wide-set eyes suggesting they were siblings. The boy was older and walked ahead of the younger girl, who was just a wisp, petite and birdlike; she couldn't have been older than thirteen. She walked with her eyes fixed on her phone, the way she swiped the screen at occasional intervals suggesting she was playing a game. The boy gave me an uncertain, closed-mouth smile, but said nothing.

They were followed by a chubby girl with big eyes and these electric-blue box braids that I wanted to compliment, but it would've been awkward, so I didn't.

112

"Hurrah! That's everyone." The woman from before sat, a notebook in hand, and took a breath, eyeing the lot of us. We all focused on her so as not to have to pretend anymore that we weren't trying to sneak glimpses of each other. Leo appeared to only be interested in the ceiling tiles. "Thank you all for being here, firstly. I met with all of you individually—except you, Sydney—but to refresh your memory, I'm Gerry."

Leo wouldn't stop jiggling his leg up and down.

"So, this first session is focused mainly on breaking the ice. Don't worry, we're not gonna do anything too in-depth. My philosophy is that, you know, no one is going to get anything out of this experience unless we feel comfortable with each other and free to share. I know, I know, at first glance, this stuff might seem boring, but personally, I cannot think of anything more exciting than meeting fellow members of the human race." Gerry spoke with her hands, these smooth, fluid movements that were maybe too over the top in normal conversation, but here, they were almost hypnotic. She had us introduce ourselves—name, age, who croaked and how, and something she called *availability*, on a scale of one to ten. How *here* we were. How willing we were to participate.

The siblings started. Their older brother had overdosed. Jacob confidently rated himself a ten in here-ness; Nora, seemingly unsure what to do with herself, refused to speak at all. Jacob mumbled an apology and draped an arm around her shoulder. "She's a little nervous," he said.

The girl with the box braids, Jasmine, laughed nervously when she gave herself an eight; her grandma had died because she was old.

Then it was me. "I'm, uh, Sydney. I'm seventeen. My dad died in a car accident last September." It occurred to me that I was the only one who'd said the month, then felt like a freak. I sensed Leo glancing at me, but I didn't want to give him the satisfaction of looking back, because I was pretty sure I hated him, and I was pretty sure I wasn't really here at all. I was in the car, I was swerving, smashing, stopping, but I lied to remove the attention from myself. "And...seven, I guess." *Negative seven*, I thought.

"Leo. Seventeen. Rather not say about the rest." Gerry said that was fine, but then asked him how here he was, and he said, "I'm far, far away."

Wow. That's really cool, man.

Come on, I wanted to say. *We're all trying our best. Just say who crossed the fucking rainbow bridge.*

We spent most of the hour playing a game creatively titled Move, where Gerry would give a statement, and if it was true for us, we'd have to get up and go to an empty chair.

Having been told by people since Dad died that they knew how I felt, it was weird to be in a room of other kids who actually *did* know. Well, at least partly. I wasn't convinced anyone felt the exact same way I did. That was the rub about being human. You had all these tools to express yourself, art and music and poetry and stuff, but no one would ever truly know how you felt unless you somehow managed to create a projection of your brain and played it on the wall. Even then, it might not be as vivid. Even then, it might not be as close.

But here we all were, popcorning in and out of our seats, some desperate dance to convince ourselves that yes, there were others, and yes, they understood. Even if they didn't.

114

The game started with statements like, *I prefer hamburgers over hot dogs*, but the statements slowly got more and more real, and—no lie—Leo and I moved on the exact same ones. Every single time. To the point where I thought maybe he was doing it to get a rise out of me, but I looked at him, and I could tell by the furrow in his brow that he was thinking the same thing. Everyone who played video games. Everyone who liked horror movies. Obviously, none of the things were particularly uncommon. Then it became: Everyone who struggled to talk about feelings. Everyone who felt it was difficult to talk to their parents. Everyone who thought life was unfair.

By the end of it, I couldn't help but laugh. I looked at him from the opposite end of the circle, really looked at him, and his lower eyelids twitched the slightest bit—enough to let me know he thought the same. We'd made peace.

And that was it, pretty much. Painless, if slightly infantilizing. *Only seven more to go*, I thought as Gerry gave us all a handout titled *Physical Effects of Grief*.

"Sometimes our bodies can react to our emotional state in ways we're not expecting," she explained. She went down the list. All your standard fare. Loss of pleasure. Decreased energy, motivation, initiative. Weight loss. Hypersexuality.

I shifted in my seat. It felt like everyone was looking at me, even though none of them actually were.

Gerry gave us two more handouts, but then it was eight o'clock, and she said it was time to go, and to my complete and utter surprise, something about the energy in the room shifted, crackled, and on the way out, Leo spoke.

"I like your shirt," he said after five excruciatingly long seconds of me pretending I didn't notice he was staring.

Not entirely sure what I was wearing, I glanced down. It was my SUMMERISLE TOURISM BOARD shirt, subtle enough to mean nothing if you didn't know what it was referencing. "Thanks," I said. "You've seen *The Wicker Man?*"

"Yeah. One of my favorites. The original, obviously."

"Obviously." I decided to test his limits. "Are you being nice now because I like the same niche shit as you?"

He smiled faintly. "I'm sorry for being a...grump. This is the second group I've been to, and I'm...I'm kinda burnt out, man. You know? I was pissed off that I even had to be here again."

"Yikes. Your second?"

He nodded solemnly. "My mom is convinced—I don't know. That if I spend the rest of my life doing support groups, maybe I'll get better. Picture, if you will, some eighty-year-old man in a teen bereavement group. *Yes, I'm spiritually here,*" he said in a croaky voice.

I laughed. Fine. Leo had grown on me, and I wanted to talk to him more, but Mom was in the lobby, and I didn't want her to think I'd made any friends. I gave him a half smile. "See you in two weeks, I guess." Then I turned on my heel and left.

I looked him up afterward.

It might seem a bit excessive. Whatever. Not like I had anything better to do.

After we found out I'd been accepted into the group, Mom had forwarded me the email from Gerry, which had been sent to all the other parents too—and luckily, Gerry's counseling training seemed to have excluded how to bcc an email, which meant I had a list of neat and tidy parent email addresses, complete with last names. One of those last names had to belong to Leo. A quick search on Facebook, and bam. I'd find him.

There was a Leo Townsend, but he lived in California, and a few Leo Smiths. But Leo's last name was Anderson, and I almost missed him, because his first name wasn't actually Leo.

I'd be pissed off all the time too if my fucking name was Galileo.

Flipping through his profile pictures, I found it hard to believe this was the same grumpy bastard I'd met. But the most recent picture was from two years ago, anyway. It showed him smiling with another guy, and they were pressed against each other in a way that suggested it wasn't platonic. I pieced it together—ha! Another gay! In the wild! His listed relationship status confirmed this.

But the picture after that was him and a different guy, who looked a lot like him, weirdly.

And the commenters were saying things like *I'm so sorry* and *He loved you so much* and *It isn't your fault.*

The picture was tagged as *Alexander Anderson*. I clicked on the resulting link, which took me to his profile. His profile had become an *In Memoriam* page.

Twins. They were twins.

All right, Galileo. I get it.

Christmas sucked—but not really for the reasons I'd expected.

Uncharacteristically, I had been dreading the break; break meant no school, and no school meant no June, which meant no tethers, no soft, cushiony landing, no reason *not* to spend entire days staring at the wall or scrolling through the ToD. Foolishly, on the drive back from the last day of classes for the year, I had thought maybe she'd invite me over or give me something or insist she found the thought of two weeks without me as criminal as I thought of two weeks without her. But I didn't get any of that. Just a promise to text and an awkwardly diagonal hug over cup holders.

I was afraid of myself when left to my own devices. I didn't like that person much in the fleeting moments I encountered her, and I certainly wasn't interested in being handcuffed to her.

Christmas. The grief book in Dad's office had warned that today would be bad. I woke up feeling mostly empty. Tired, but that wasn't anything new. I still wasn't sleeping much, because I couldn't sit in the dark for any considerable amount of time without a variety of awful thoughts intruding, spinning around on my brain stem, pole dancing, mocking me. Instead, I opted for playing video games or watching movies until I passed out, then I'd wake up in the middle of the night with the title music humming faintly. But this morning, I couldn't even bring myself to open my eyes. Christmas. Dad loved it. The minute after midnight on Thanksgiving, he'd feed me a steady diet of those Claymation Christmas specials, which were all sort of creepy but in an endearing way. I liked the uncanny-valley-ness of them, all the jerking unnatural motions sort of reminiscent of how I felt I navigated through the world. Especially today. Especially today, because today I was due to have an *anniversary reaction*, a reaction I'd have for at *least* ten years and probably for the rest of my life—every Christmas and every birthday forever there'd be a Dad-shaped hole, where I'd remember in vivid Technicolor that he should be there, he should see me graduate and get married and grow old, and for fuck's sake, he should at least be there on Christmas so we could—

Breathe.

June.

June. I wondered what she was doing. If she was still in bed. What her family did on Christmas—her not-close dad, her not-understanding mom. Had she even thought of me since the beginning of break? I would have done just about anything to see an itemized list of everything she thought about on any given day. Oh God. I would have given *anything*.

Mom knocked on my door at ten that morning. I pretended it had woken me up; I wasn't sure why. "Santa came," she said.

I propped myself up on one elbow. "No, he didn't." I think I was trying to make a joke, but it came out like some defiant proclamation from an eight-year-old.

She smiled, the rest of her face straining in protest, then leaned against the door frame with her arms crossed. "We're gonna have a little day in. Okay? There's no pressure. No pressure to feel...feel anything at all. Deal?"

I wiped the non-sleep from my eyes and smacked my cheeks. "Deal," I said, not convinced.

Mom had gotten me an excessive number of presents. I worried that I'd been placed on some give-a-sad-kid-the-best-Christmas-ever list, but the meticulousness and uniformity with which everything was wrapped suggested it had all come from Mom. New sweatshirts, and gift cards to restaurants, and a drone. With each new thing I unwrapped, she'd watch, then take a sip of her coffee before saying that we could take it back if I didn't want it—it was so damn quiet in the house, just crinkling and tearing and plastic scraping plastic, and Mom slurping and saying we could take that movie back or that gift card back, and it was honestly the most uncomfortable thing in the world. God, of course I appreciated it, of course I did, but I also couldn't stand it. And I thought of Mom at the kitchen table with her stacks of folded papers, kneading her forehead and sighing—how could she have done this? How could we afford this?

When the pile had been exhausted, she looked at me for a long time, then finally said, "You're not happy," in the weirdest way I'd ever heard. She didn't say it as though she expected the presents to make me happy, like she was disappointed that they didn't, but as though it was a statement of fact, almost robotic, like she'd assessed and come to a conclusion. "You're not happy." *No. No, I'm not.*

But it wasn't because I was unsatisfied; it was because I was sad for *her*, and I was sad for *us*, and I was sad that the world had ended and there was nothing we'd ever be able to do to get it back, but I couldn't say any of that, so I went with: "You said I didn't have to feel anything."

Mom thought for a moment, then got up and left. I worried I'd driven her away or something, but she came back from the front room with another present: small, rectangular, and wrapped in glossy red paper. "This was in the mailbox," she said, and handed it to me. It wasn't particularly heavy, and it had my name printed across the back in what looked like impossibly neat handwriting. "I figured it was from one of your friends."

Weird. Olivia? Definitely not. She wasn't one to shove a present in the mailbox; she'd want to give it to me in person. Seeing as the list of people I could consider "friends" was practically microscopic, there was only one name left.

Breathe.

I tore at the paper with a new hunger, suddenly feeling very validated, like this had all been worth it—June *had* been thinking of me, enough to come all the way over, to give me something. *I should have gotten something for her*, I thought.

It was a book. A pale green cover with a drawing of a distinctly sad-looking guy on the front, and above it, the title. It took me a second to read, even after the paper had been cleared away. I must have been reading it incorrectly. No, no. There it was.

Healing Homosexuality.

I instinctively grabbed for paper to conceal the cover, as if I could rewrap it somehow, and if I did, then maybe the moment wouldn't have happened—I never would have opened it at all—but it did. It had happened. Someone had put a fucking copy of *Healing Homosexuality* in my mailbox.

Thank God, Mom hadn't watched me open it. She had her back to me, refilling her coffee, which gave me enough time to sneak behind her toward the stairs with the book pressed to the side of my thigh, turned cover-side in. "Thanks for everything, Mom," I said. "I'm sorry. I love you."

This was suddenly very real. I could handle texts; my skin had grown so thick that I was practically one big callus.

But this was real world. They'd been to my *house*.

They'd driven to the cul-de-sac, come to my house, put their grubby fingers on my mailbox.

With each encounter with whomever this was, I could feel myself being dragged away from the shore, forced further into a situation I didn't ask to be a part of. I was reeling and needed someone to tow me back to solid ground. Someone else needed to know. But who? I couldn't tell Mom—not after how it had gone the first time. She'd freak out, and in the pit of my stomach, I still wanted to believe her that this was some elaborate bullying scheme, that the death of my dad had amplified me into more than a blip on everyone's radar, and like last time, they'd get bored of me, and this would all go away eventually.

Bea? Could this have been her? I didn't know. I didn't think she had the guts to do something like this—but the truth was, I knew nothing about her anymore. A lot can change in two years.

I couldn't tell June. Not now, when everything was going so well. I'd scare her off.

I texted Olivia.

Me: Are you home?

Olivia: nah. with miles's fam. his grandma just called me oriental. excuse me, miss, do i look like a rug

Me: Yikes. Do better, Miles and company.

Me: Do you know when you'll be back

Olivia: uhhh dunno. we still need to have dinner n stuuuuff

Olivia: why? are u ok?

Me: I'm mostly fine. Just lemme know when you're back

Olivia: affirmative!!

While I waited, Mom and I spent the day watching various festive media in silence until, at one point, she tried to mask a sob with a cough, and when it became painfully apparent that it was, indeed, a sob, she disappeared upstairs. I felt a pull to ask her to please stay, that we could talk about it, but I couldn't manage to get the words out. I listened to her plod up the stairs, followed by the soft click of her bedroom door.

Later in the day, my phone buzzed again when I wasn't expecting it. Thanks to what must have been some Pavlovian conditioning, the sound nearly made me jump out of my skin. I checked the name: June.

June: Merry X-mas Whitaker! From me and Heath. xo

And then a selfie of the both of them smiling, June in a cream turtleneck and Heath in a Santa hat, a stack of cherry-red wrapped presents piled up behind them.

She had thought of me.

Me: You guys too!!

I considered taking a picture to send back but thought better of it. (*Yeah, here I am, alone, in my empty house. Festive.*) I willed her to say something else, *anything* else, but she was only giving me well wishes and everything had run its natural course.

Moments later, Olivia texted me. She was almost back. I wasn't totally sure why, but I didn't really want to see her in the house right now, so I made myself some microwave hot chocolate and found a little spot for myself in the backyard, dusted some spiderwebs off a linen chair from the garage, and lit a fire.

I'd made sure to bring the copy of *Healing Homosexuality*.

The silence of the cul-de-sac was even more pronounced than usual, and the long shadows cast by the fire and the trees were entirely unsettling, so much so that Olivia made me jump when she arrived.

"Ho ho ho!" she said, her words muffled by the comically large scarf wrapped around most of her face. "Good holiday tidings."

I sipped my not-quite-lukewarm hot chocolate to have something to do with my hands. "Hey. Do you want a chair?"

"Nah, I'm good. I've been sitting *all day*. One big Christmas sit. Miles's family is huge—like, he has all these little cousins and, my God, it was cute at first, but we actually watched them open presents for two hours and thirteen minutes, and I know that because I timed it. Oh, look." Olivia thrust her wrist into my face, revealing some sort of generally pleasant bracelet.

"That's...nice."

"Miles got it for me. It's Pandora. It's the ugliest thing I've ever seen. I love it. Did you get anything exciting?"

"Actually..." I handed her the book.

It seemed to take a second for her eyes to adjust to read the title, because she was quiet for a moment, then said, "Oh my God. I knew she was kind of awkward about it, but oh my *God*."

"No, it's not...it's not from Mom. It was in my mailbox this morning. Wrapped, with my name on it."

"You're kidding me."

124

I stared into the fire and the fire waved back. "I am very much not kidding you."

She flipped it open. Gasped. "Have you looked *inside?*"

My gut twisted. "No, what?"

Olivia handed me the open book. I couldn't quite make out what it was in the dark, but it looked sort of like a newspaper clipping. I leaned in closer while the firelight ricocheted off it, and it clicked— *Benjamin J. Whitaker, age 46, passed away Monday, September 14th*—it was Dad's obituary.

I didn't say anything. I couldn't think of anything to say. I was pretty sure Olivia was blabbering—there was a shrill buzzing assaulting my left ear—but the anger bubbled and bubbled and made my hands shake and my nose run.

Then Olivia plucked the book from my hands and threw it into the fire.

I reached for it uselessly, watched the flames dance and lick and destroy, the man on the cover warping and convulsing until he was gone. I glared at Olivia. "Why did you do that?"

"Why wouldn't I? You don't need to read that, Sydney. You really don't even need to look at it anymore."

"But what if it was..."

"What?"

"Evidence?"

Olivia tilted her head. "Evidence of what?"

"That...I don't know, that..."

"Seriously. You don't need to look at it. And there. It's symbolic. Literally burning, because it doesn't matter at all. Okay?"

I wanted to fight with her, insist that it did matter. That every-thing mattered, all of this mattered, and still no one else noticed.

I thought about this for a while.

"Hey," Olivia said finally, something charged in her voice. "Let's play Ghosts."

Ghosts? It was potentially the weirdest thing she could have said at that moment. Ghosts in the Graveyard was a game we'd played when we were little, scurrying through the wooded labyrinth behind my house. Actually, it wasn't much of a labyrinth. But it was big enough to be disorienting at night, and that was all you needed for Ghosts. That and preferably more than two people. Dad would play, sometimes. Ghost would hide. Gravedigger would look. And if the ghost caught the gravedigger first, the gravedigger would become the ghost. "Seriously?" I said. "Right now?"

"Yeah. Come on. I'm trying to—I don't know. You used to love to play. Scared the bejesus out of me. Maybe it'd get your mind off things. You know? Do some dumb kid stuff." She headed for the tree line, started to shuffle through. "I'm Ghost."

"Fine. Thirty seconds," I told her while she crept farther in. The crunch of twigs grew more distant, and her black coat disappeared between the trees, and then it was me, counting up to thirty, saying *time's up*, and stalking in after her.

My footsteps were slow. When I was little, the woods gave me the creeps at night, and even now a sharp pang of fear sat at the bottom of my belly, waiting to strike, but it wouldn't. Not anymore. I had seen every scary thing in the world. I *was* every scary thing in the world.

I came to the dried-up scar in the earth where there used to be a creek, and flicked on my phone's flashlight so I wouldn't fall off the makeshift bridge Olivia and I had built over it with plywood we found in her garage. In the summer, there would sometimes be enough fireflies to light the way. By mid-June there'd normally be so many that it was hard to tell where the star-littered sky ended and where the forest began. They'd light up on the ground, even, so if you blurred your eyes the right way, it felt as if you were walking through space.

And then I saw...someone.

Still distant, maybe twenty steps or so away, trying to hide behind a tree trunk that was too small to conceal them completely, and something in my gut ballooned and popped and told me that I knew them, and that actually, there was something *sinister* about them, and that I needed to *run*—

"Ghost," I muttered under my breath.

I had to get out. I had to get *out*.

I turned and ran, hoping it was in the direction of my backyard—I couldn't remember. But I ran, and ran, until a loose log skidded under my foot, and I flew forward. I smacked against the thick-rooted base of a tree and stuck there.

Coppery blood worked itself between my teeth, and I sucked it down, the taste of it jolting some welcome life into me. Black soaked the corners of the world, and I tried to blink it away, to silence the ringing, and then there was Olivia, who crouched down to me and asked what happened, what did I see?

This was when I learned you could outrun the ghost.

GRIEF AND GUILT CAME HAND in hand. Guilt that followed smiling or laughing or getting any kind of mild enjoyment out of anything. Indulging in earthly pleasures seemed grossly hedonistic, somehow, after having experienced a Great Loss, so I learned to compartmentalize. The grief was always there, if not center stage, then lurking in the wings, or hanging from the rafters, or pulsing beneath the floorboards. But it didn't always need my attention. I could ignore it—for a little while, at least. I was always grieving, but sometimes I was grieving with an *and*.

So that morning, I lay stiffly beneath my sheets, hand edging along the elastic of my pajama pants, and thought about June.

June, who pulls the car over in the morning, who shows up in the middle
of the night, who pulls me into the bathroom at school, who yanks me close
and kisses me fast, like she's been meaning to and has just remembered, who
guides me in and kisses me slow, like this is the only thing we have to do for
the rest of time, who's all lips and hands and eyes while I'm all shakes and
shakes and shakes—

But then I thought about death. Death. Dad? No. June. Dead Dad. June. Dad...

Nope. That was enough of that. I felt stupid for even trying.

June, who I hadn't heard from. June, who'd promised to text.

It was New Year's Eve, and I wasn't up to much. I'd spent the past eleven New Years with Olivia, watching Ryan Seacrest host the countdown, and tonight, I assumed, wouldn't be much different.

Olivia: what do you feeeeel like for tonight? pizza??

Me: Yeah sounds good. Pepperoni pls.

Olivia: always OH and i think miles is gonna come if that's ok!!!!

Me: Will he bring a personality

Me: ;)

Olivia: har de har har

I was almost looking forward to the festivities; our ritual, if nothing else, was something familiar. Something that bridged the gap between the old world and the new one. Ryan Seacrest still looked pretty much the same, and Olivia's house still looked pretty much the same, and with everything else being equal, I could pretend Dad was inside.

Then June called.

It was unusual. Feeling extremely creepy—wondering if I had

some sort of masturbatory wish-granting powers—I transferred my phone to my left hand in case she was able to sense what I'd be doing with my right, and answered on the fourth ring. "Hey, June," I sang to the tune of "Hey, Jude." I was cooler over the phone.

"Oh yes, serenade me."

I laughed; hearing her voice calmed something in me that I hadn't realized was uneasy.

"So, question for you: What are you up to this evening?"

"Oh, uh, nothing." *Liar.* "Not really. Me and Olivia were just gonna, uh, hang around. Why? What's up?"

"Well, I don't wanna steal you from her or anything."

"No, it's fine." *More than fine. Steal me. Take me away.*

"I was *going* to ask if you wanted to go to a party and grab a coffee. Not, like, in that order."

My voice, evidently, had decided its services were no longer required.

"My fault. Context," June replied to my silence. "Heath throws this big New Year's party every year, and so I was wondering if you wanted to come. Oh, and since I was gonna pick you up, I thought we could grab a coffee before. I guess? Do people get late-afternoon coffee? We can. I do. Anyways. Offer's on the table."

"I mean, yeah," I said, worried my inexperience was oozing through the receiver. "Yeah. Sounds fun."

I sensed June raising an eyebrow. "You don't sound convinced."

"What? No. No, I'd love to come. It's just, I haven't really been to many *party* parties."

"That's okay. I can show you the ropes."

"Okay. Sure. When? Now?"

"Whoa! Eager! I appreciate your enthusiasm. I can pick you up around five? Stuff at Heath's won't start until later, but, you know."

"Okay. Yeah, cool. Nice."

"Do you have any other words of affirmation you'd like to share with the audience?"

My cheeks went red hot. "Positively."

June laughed, and all of me lit up. "Oh, Whitaker. You goon. See you in a bit."

"'Kay. Bye."

I hung up, tossed my phone on the floor, and flopped onto my bed.

This was a wonderful turn of events.

There was only one problem: Olivia. June probably wouldn't have minded her tagging along. But there was one thought sort of fizzing around near the back of my skull, in the place reserved for worst and most wicked of the lot: maybe I didn't want her to come after all.

I didn't think of myself as that much of an ass, so I called her.

"Hell*ooo*," Olivia said with the cadence of a slide whistle.

"What's up?"

"Hey, so, June just called me."

She gasped in a way that was so fucking annoying, I wanted to scream. "Interesting. Do tell."

"Heath has this party tonight, I guess—"

"I've heard about that! Do you remember when Alice Hannigan got pregnant? Pretty sure that's where the baby was conceived."

"Oh, fantastic. Listen—June asked me if I wanted to come."

"Oh."

"Yeah."

"Does that mean you're…you're going? To the thing? That's what you're saying. Right?"

"Well, yeah. I wanted to. But you could come with me if you want."

"Eh. I don't think so. Miles is coming, and I don't really think that's our kind of thing."

"I mean, if you wanted, I don't have to stay all the way until midnight. You know? I could still come to yours. Just later."

Olivia was quiet for a moment. "Before midnight, though?"

"Yeah. Yeah, for sure. Is that okay?"

"Yeah. I'll see you then. Ugh," she said, "my little girl is growing up."

June pulled into the driveway one minute early. Everything was as if she were picking me up for school, but today, I figured, was different. Today, anything could happen, and something about that made my brain stem sizzle.

"Happy New Year!" June seemed hyper. She hummed along to the Bombay Bicycle Club song that played over the speakers. Something about her sparkled; she wore dark red lipstick and thin eyeliner and a beanie that made her hair look even bigger than normal because of how it protruded from underneath.

"You're in a good mood."

"What? I was excited to see you."

My skin tingled.

She kept eye contact while putting the car in reverse, a mischievous sort of smirk on her face, then broke it to check her blind spot. "That's the part where you're supposed to say that you were excited to see me too."

"Is it?" I had made the joke unintentionally; it really wasn't a witty retort, but I was too nervous to say anything besides that.

June laughed and replaced the lyrics to the song she was singing with "You're an asshole."

"How are you?" she asked. "How's break been?"

"Yeah, uh, it's been okay. Boring." Besides the book in the mailbox. And my busted lip. And the fact that I had a literal hallucination. And Leo from support group. And Dad. And your folder in the office. And *you*. "How's yours been?"

June thought for a moment, like I hadn't asked her a canned question with a canned response; she was actually trying to answer as accurately as possible. "Illuminating."

"Illuminating?"

"Mm."

"Has anything, uh, in particular been illuminating, or generally?"

"Generally, I'd say."

"Okay. Uh—congratulations on that."

I got the sense the whole time we were catching up, she was thinking about something else, until eventually she finally blurted, "I have a surprise for you." By that time we were already at the Dunkin' Donuts drive-thru, and she had no more time to explain. "What d'you want?"

"I…don't actually like coffee."

"The girl lets me take her out for coffee, and she doesn't even like coffee," she muttered playfully under her breath.

A voice that sounded oddly familiar greeted us through the receiver. June ordered a vanilla latte for herself. "And a—" She looked at me; I shrugged. "A hot chocolate."

Once we pulled up, I realized why the voice sounded familiar. Bea, clad in full Dunkin' attire, stood behind the window. God. I'd forgotten she worked here. Of course she did. I couldn't throw a fucking stone in Pleasant Hills without hitting someone equally recognizable and unpleasant.

She greeted June excitedly—Bea was dating a guy called Will who hung around with June and Heath, so they already knew each other, which was terrible. I sensed June glance at me quickly, like an apology; an apology made uselessly, because *sorry* wouldn't do anything to quell the sudden hammering in my chest.

Maybe because of the angle, Bea only saw June. "Oh my God! Hey!"

"Hey, worker Bea," June said.

Bea smiled. "That's cute. Did you just come up with that? Oh, wait, your drinks, duh." She came back with two cups and handed them over. "I get off in fifteen—I'm going home to scrub donut off me, and then I'm heading straight to yours."

And that's when Bea realized I was there.

I didn't know if she looked at me or what, but I felt the weird, sudden silence fall on the three of us like a cartoon anvil, while I stared pointedly at the glove compartment.

June was the only one with enough sense to get us out of there. "Hey, thanks, gal—I'll see you tonight!"

"Yeah," Bea said. She raised her hand to wave, and at the last second, as we pulled away, I glanced back, and by complete accident, our eyes locked. She looked...odd. Sad.

Everything about the interaction made me angry. Angry that Bea was being weird, that June was friends with her, that Dad was dead and I was here, and all I could think about was Bea's clawed hands jamming a copy of *Healing Homosexuality* into my mailbox. June looked distressed, and since I hadn't told her about the messages and my suspicions, it wasn't because of that; it was because of my history with Bea, so even though the thought of explaining everything exhausted me, I needed to clear the air and get it out of the way. "What you think happened didn't happen."

June shook her head as we drove from the parking lot. "What do I *think* happened?"

"Seriously, I feel like I need to address this or else—I don't know. What Bea told everyone wasn't what happened. We liked each other—I mean, at least I thought we did, and I don't know, I'm sick of being pegged as some, I don't know, *aggressive lesbian*, when that's not what happened at all. Okay? That's not what it was."

The world rolled past. We watched as it went. "I believe you," June said, and I looked at her. "Like. No. God. Of course I do."

I wasn't even trying to hide my discomfort at this point, but her saying that made me ease up a little. "Do you?"

"I always figured that was the case. Bea seems, like, nice enough, but I totally believe she'd lie about something like that. I don't actually know her that well. Not at all. No, I know you better, and I—I don't think you'd do something like that."

I kept my eyes planted firmly on the dashboard. Tires *whooshed*. Windshield wipers squeaked. Girls sipped. "Okay. Thank you."

She shrugged. "Please don't think that changes my...perception of you, or anything."

I wasn't sure what she meant: what happened with Bea, or me liking girls in the first place. I assumed the latter. "I don't."

"No, because I mean, like, even I..." She grunted. "Never mind. We don't have to do this now."

We'd been silently driving for a few minutes when June spoke under her breath, as if she didn't care whether or not I heard. "That put a slight damper on my surprise."

We turned on to River Styx Road.

River Styx. I'd driven down this road hundreds of times. *We'd* driven down this road hundreds of times. Dad and me.

And I knew, based on that, that River Styx Road was a dead end.

"Is...this where Heath lives?" I asked.

June didn't answer.

We seemed to float down the road until we followed a left turn marked with a sign that read River Styx, down a steep slope then into the empty parking lot.

I was back.

June parked the car, the sudden stop jolting both of us backward. I felt her eyes on me while I sat there, doing nothing. It seemed like I was doing a lot of that these days.

I was back, and nothing was the same.

"I'm sorry," June finally said. "This was a stupid idea. I should have asked you first. I'm sorry. You hate it. I just thought, maybe if you came here again, if you saw it, then we could—I don't know. I don't actually know what I was thinking. This was stupid. I'm so, so sorry. Let's go to Heath's."

"No," I said too quickly, like every time she threatened to leave and I said no, no, no. Maybe it had been stupid of her. I hadn't decided yet. But I didn't care. "I want to see it. Let's go."

"Are you sure? I'm so sorry, I—"

"Yeah. Uh, yeah. Come on. It's okay." I was taken aback by the sheer force of her apology; I turned to examine her. "Are you okay?"

I swore I saw her blink back tears. "Yeah."

Car doors slammed.

I eyed the entrance, two flimsy-looking fence gates, and worried that I'd see his ghost. That maybe we'd crossed planes and were glaring down the entrance to the actual river to hell instead of an admittedly unimpressive excuse for a river with a melodramatic name.

"We don't have to, like, stay for long," June said. "It's chilly, anyways. And the sun's gonna set."

"Yeah, no, we probably shouldn't stay after dark. There's this, uh, path that goes in a circle. Over the river. It would only take a half hour or so. I don't know. Maybe more with the snow, but we don't have to do the whole thing."

"Yeah, okay. Let's do that."

She was doing it again. Injecting herself into places that weren't hers. She stood in the spots where Dad stood, slipped herself into his silhouettes and made them dance again. The faded wooden map. The unassuming path. These were mine and his. And now June was here. And I guess I wasn't upset about it, somehow. Maybe because the path was almost unrecognizable in the snow, without the trill of evening cicadas or the sizzle of the July sun.

We walked slowly, me in the lead, keeping guard, almost, as if something was going to leap out, as if this was actually a dream and the world was green, not white, and Dad was a few steps ahead. *You fell asleep*, I imagined him saying. *It was all a bad dream.*

We quickly realized that walking along a snow-covered trail without boots would prove difficult; the cold leaked through my shoes and numbed my feet. "Sorry," June said. "I guess I didn't really consider the, like, logistics of it."

I didn't mind. I sort of liked the feeling. "You don't have to keep saying sorry."

June looked at me, eyes wide, as if she hadn't even realized. Softened. "I apologize," she joked.

The Styx was a river in its own right, but only really a tributary that flowed into the larger Ohio River to the east. At its thinnest, it was hardly a creek here; at its widest, it was maybe ten long paces across, and deep. I guess it was named because the area was a bit depressing; a lot of the land on either side of the river was swamp. Mud. Quicksand.

We crept along the trail, which was hardly defined, the snow blurring the landscape into one uninterrupted sheet of white. Thick-trunked sycamores loomed over us, their placement messy. The trail had been carved to weave through the grove, so as not to disturb it. This was their home.

I had trouble reconciling my surroundings with the knowledge that this was *my* River Styx. Ours. It still was, just in different clothes. I wondered whether I was touching spots on the ground where Dad's footsteps had been, or if the trees remembered us, had heard our conversations, and maybe if they were cut down, all the ghosts of what we were could fly out, out, out. Not that I loved the thought of Dad being trapped somewhere, but there were worse places than in the trees.

He sort of *was* trapped. There was a divergence in the path; the left, I remembered, twisted toward the swamp, and the right went toward the river. But an aspen sat directly at the fork where the two trails converged. I knew this one. I cleared the snow around its roots, the cold pinching the skin between my fingers. He was there.

Aspens were easy to carve. The bark was soft and malleable, the sort that an eight-year-old might be able to slice away at with a particularly sharp branch.

I had seen people whittling their initials into trees on TV, apparently. At the time, I hadn't realized the gesture was pretty much exclusively romantic. I'd inscribed *S+D* into the tree—Sydney and Dad—sloppily enough that they barely registered as letters and almost looked like natural grooves in the bark; someone had to know where to look to even see them at all.

Is this all there is?

I traced the letters with the tips of my fingers, aware that June was behind me, but not really registering that she was watching. "Oh, Sydney," she said, understanding.

You're okay.

"He got *so* mad at me," I said. I wasn't sure if I was speaking to June or the trees. "He was kind of a nature purist. I think it was one of those, uh, parenting moments. I was trying to show him...I don't know." June said nothing. I stood. Wiped my face. "The river's, it's, uh, down here."

June followed me. Ahead of us, past more awnings and meandering pathways, the trail sloped downward, but before it got too steep, it turned into a bridge that led over the bubbling water. Styx wasn't the sort of river that *rushed*. It plodded. As if it knew it would get there eventually, so there wasn't any hurry.

Once we'd made it to the bridge, I lingered near the barrier and rested my elbows on the railing to watch the Styx bubble past. "Can we sit?" I asked.

"Yeah, dude. Go for it."

We cleared a spot by the end of the bridge, snow and ice tumbling down and dissolving away into nothing, and then sat, the silence situating itself on top of our eyelashes, in the creases of our clothes. There were no birds.

Is this it?

Panic swooped down, grabbed me by my shoulders, and fed me to its chicks.

"I hadn't even seen snow before I moved here," June said, breaking the silence. She kicked her legs back and forth above the drop. "It's pretty much what you'd expect."

"What was moving like?"

"It was rough, for sure. Definitely. At least at first. I worried about a lot. It was right at the beginning of high school, and I didn't know anyone here, and—I don't know, maybe it's stupid—but being mixed, I was like, oh my God, this is gonna be horrible, everyone's gonna be *racist*, whatever. And no. It wasn't stupid. Because there was some of that."

"I'm sorry."

"Hey, it happens. But, you know, there was this, like, overwhelming fear, because stuff would never be the same. I was leaving everything I'd ever known behind. And I don't have family there anymore, so, like, the whole of California might as well have burned to the ground, you know? There was no, like, *reason* for me to ever go back. Ever. And that was scary. Sad. I have this dumb memory of, like, driving away for the last time, and sitting in the back seat but facing behind us, you know, so I was always looking back at where we came from, because…I guess maybe I thought it'd, like, fall apart or something if I wasn't there to look at it.

"But looking back now, I'm like, that's *so* stupid, because of course I was gonna leave eventually. Right? I think—I think a lot of, like, fear, and sadness, and stuff comes from thinking things that won't last forever are gonna last forever. Good things and bad things."

She was so quiet that I worried I'd imagined her ever being there.

"That's not dumb," I said.

June shrugged. "Maybe less dumb and more selfish."

"Why?"

"Because things don't exist so we can be there to look at them while they do. You know…just because you love something doesn't mean it can't go on without you."

"Yeah," I said, "I guess."

"And then, once I'd actually gotten here, I sort of met Heath right away, and, you know. The rest is history."

"Did you ever see the redwoods?" I asked.

"What?"

"In California. The…the redwoods. Did you ever see them?"

She nodded. "I was in the Scouts when I was younger, and we went camping. Up north."

"Did they make you feel small?"

"Like a flea. They didn't even seem real. Like aliens had put them there or something. I was little at the time, and I bet ten of me couldn't even wrap all the way around the bottom."

"Did you…like that?"

"I don't know. I guess I didn't really like or dislike it. It just sort of *was*."

I don't know what possessed me to ask. But suddenly it seemed my thoughts and my words were one and the same—I was empty of everything besides what I was saying, now. There wasn't anything else. I might as well have been talking to myself. "Where do you think we go when we die?"

June scoffed. "I don't actually know. I don't think anyone actually knows."

"Because I don't think we go anywhere."

She shrugged. "Maybe. Maybe it's something more than that, though. Not clichéd, like, you know, heaven, or anything. I think maybe we float through the ether forever."

It was so scary, I almost started to cry. "That sounds horrible."

"No, I don't think so. Like, I don't think it'd be, like, Earth Sydney or Earth June. I think it's a version of ourselves, but…different. The kind that's happy to float." A gust of wind sent snow tumbling from the bridge, and I shivered.

I felt the urge to tell her, so strongly that I almost couldn't imagine *not* telling her. Not thinking of the fact that Heath might have already told her, or the obvious contradiction in trying to combat death with more death: "I've been doing something kind of fucked up."

"All right. What kind of fucked up?"

"I've been watching videos of people dying," I said.

To my surprise, she wasn't horrified. She actually smirked a little. "Where'd you find those?"

"Oh. You know. The internet."

"Do you think that's healthy?" she asked.

Oh, I adored her. She didn't ask why I did it, because she already knew. That you need to see it to understand, need to really *see* it—but no. No. Of course it wasn't healthy, but I wasn't sure I could admit it. "I don't know."

She didn't say anything else, so I kept talking.

"I'm so scared," I said, "that all of this, that this is it, this is all there is, and I'm worried all of this isn't even that good in the first place."

"Well, like, listen. The way I see it…I think we're lucky to even be here at all. To be, like, conscious? I think it's actually unbelievable. And the only reason you're bummed out about dying is because you're conscious in the first place. And a certain level of consciousness. Birds don't fly around worried they're gonna die one day."

"So maybe I wish I weren't able to think of that at all. Maybe this is stupid. Right? Like, maybe I don't even want to have lived."

"Whitaker. That's the most universally contested viewpoint of all time. Better to have loved and lost, and all that. Well. Better to have lived and lost. Like, look how beautiful this is." She said it with conviction, but her face sort of folded in on itself. "Look how lucky you are to be here at all." I couldn't shake the feeling that she was saying that to herself more than she was saying it to me.

I was looking. I told her so. I was looking, and all I could see were the cracks, Dad's blood rolling and clotting in the water, everything I'd ever seen and everything I'd never get to see coalescing into something ugly and awful, and I hated it. I hated it, it was horrible, it was dying, it was rusting and falling apart—the branches broke, shattered like glass, dropped into the river, everything collapsed, everything, everything, everything, everything dead, everything dead, goodbye, Earth! The sun would crash into Pleasant Hills and we'd all burn. Goodbye, me! "I don't want it."

"No. *Look*."

"I *am*."

"*Look.*"

So I did. I looked at her. Square in the face. And there was something else.

Past all the rot, something glittered, bounced off in fractals of light; the river shimmered.

It was her, all lights, all glowing in the bitter cold, her cheeks and nose rouged and her chapped lips and the dark spots on her jeans where the snow had soaked through.

It occurred to me—I was using her. I knew I was. "Why are *you* sad?" I asked her.

144

June took a breath and spoke, totally devoid of emotion, like she was reading off a grocery list. "I don't like myself very much."

How? I said that out loud too. "How?" It wasn't patronizing, but it wasn't really meant to be encouraging either; it didn't compute. How could a girl like that not like herself? And then after, without thinking, I told her. "You're everything."

June pretended not to have heard. "I just don't."

We sat there for a while, as the sun set. I made some joke about throwing ourselves into the water. The mood lightened after that. She ruffled my hair. We ended up finishing the trail and wrapping back around past the frozen expanses of quicksand. We ran, jumped, and dumped snowballs down the backs of the other's collars. I think we needed to let off some steam. Things were different. They had to be.

On the way back, we passed the aspen I'd carved. I didn't look at it again.

And back in the car, I clicked my phone to life.

Partying tonight, are we? Doesn't sound like you're all that upset.

They would not ruin this.

June asked if everything was okay. I said yes.

10

HEATH LIVED ON THE GOOD side of town. Realistically, the sprawling developments of middle-class houses meant all of Pleasant Hills was the "good side," but toward the north the driveways grew longer and lawns grew wider and houses were concealed behind veils of intentionally positioned trees.

"I'm glad you came," June said as we turned on to Longbrook: Heath's street. "I was really worried you'd say no. You don't strike me as someone who likes this sort of thing."

I scoffed. "Why did you invite me, then?"

June thought for a second. "I wanted to see you," she decided, even though her hesitancy suggested she had wanted to say something different. Regardless, my neck tingled. I couldn't help it. Even though I was kind of still recovering from the heaviness of our earlier conversation, any insistence that she wanted to be near me was enough to set my veins on fire.

The line of cars parked up against the curb implied the party had already started.

"Shit," June breathed.

"What? What's wrong?"

"I didn't realize it was so late already."

"That's fine, right? We're—I don't know. Fashionably late." I didn't want to let on how much I loved the idea of it: emerging into an already-crowded room with June next to me.

She crushed her knuckles against the steering wheel until they cracked. "Yeah," she said, then parked. "Okay. After you."

We started down the precisely shoveled path, and only after the first line of trees did I get a proper eyeful of the house. Until now, I hadn't realized there was such a thing as too much brick. It was completely overpowering, domineering, all browns and reds, and warm light spilled from the upstairs windows onto the front lawn. The place looked like it belonged on a postcard, or like it could be the setting of a murder mystery where ten people are invited to dinner but only one gets to leave.

"Whoa," I said.

"It's a lot, right?"

"Yeah. Beautiful."

"You think? I think it's super gaudy."

My cheeks went hot. "Yeah, same."

She smirked at me, then nudged me with her shoulder. "You fucking nerd. I mean, if anything, I can appreciate the...spectacle of it. But, nah. Not for me."

"What does Heath's dad do?" I asked, careful not to say *parents*.

"He's the city attorney." I looked at her, confused. "Yeah, I didn't know Pleasant Hills had a city attorney either. Apparently we do. And apparently, he's well paid. You know the Alderman Auditorium at the middle school? That's not a coincidence. He funded it. Gave them hundreds of thousands for it, I guess."

"Man. Why?"

June waved her arms in a theatrical swoop. "A love of the arts? No, I don't know. I don't know much about the interior worlds of the supremely wealthy."

"What's he like? Is he, I don't know, nice?"

"Heath's dad? I couldn't tell you."

"What do you mean?"

"I've only met him, like, three times."

"You've only seen your boyfriend's dad three times in three years?"

She shrugged. "He's always away. Doing...things. Not sure what. But, eh. Between you and me—I don't think he likes me very much."

She laughed, but I felt awkward, so I didn't say anything else.

Low, distorted music drifted from the house as we drew closer, then tripled in sound as we stepped through the front door.

The entryway was impressive; the ceiling soared above a black-and-white tile floor and a dual set of curved staircases that swirled up to meet a balcony on the floor above. People were dotted around here, but the real commotion seemed to be coming from farther inside the house.

"June?" someone called from the side room. Heath.

"Hey, babe," she said, unironically.

"Thanks for leaving me to set up by myself."

June stiffened. "I-I was—"

He appeared round the corner, grinning wide and cradling a stack of plastic cups. "I'm kidding. It's fine." They kissed. I felt awkward about it—and slightly taken aback that June had stuttered. "Hey! I didn't know you were bringing the freshman."

I made a big show of widening my eyes, pressing a finger to my chest and looking behind me—who, me? They laughed and I swelled.

June shifted. "Um, what are you doing? Do you need any help with anything?"

"Nah, everything's already finished, so. Why don't you get Sydney a drink?"

Not that I had thought Heath and June were rule-followers or anything, but the openness and the recklessness of it all wasn't something I had anticipated. The cops wouldn't come, would they? Oh God. This was the peer pressure everyone had told me about. This was the moment those alcohol-celibacy contracts I signed in elementary school had foretold.

Fuck it, I decided.

"Yeah. That'd be good."

We moved through the gargantuan kitchen, all dark wood and stainless steel, to a set of stairs going down into the basement: the epicenter of the roar.

We passed Bea.

She'd ditched the Dunkin' uniform, wore this tight black dress with long sleeves, and I swore when we walked past, she glared at me, like some creepy painting that follows you with its eyes as you walk. I struggled to hide my discontentment as we passed, so I resolved to not look at her at all. Could it have actually been her? Looking at her now, I wasn't convinced. But the person who sent the message knew I'd be at the party. It would make sense.

She would not ruin this.

I followed June down the basement stairs. The place was immaculate, but not really in a nice way; deep red walls and plush, gray carpet, with the sort of ostentatious, disconnected, glossy-magazine finish that suggested nobody who actually cared about the place had been involved in its design. An old *Pac-Man* arcade machine sat in the far corner beside a pool table, which I assumed was some attempt to make the place seem like human beings with interests besides gaining affluence lived here. It didn't really work, but with the amount of life that was crammed into the place, it didn't really have to.

June turned to me, now needing to raise her voice to be heard over the music. "I didn't know you drank!"

I thought about lying to make myself seem cooler. "I don't. Not really."

"What? This is your first time?"

I nodded, deciding now was not the time to explain that Dad had once let me have a sip of beer at our Fourth of July block party, which I'd promptly spat out.

"Oh God! Look at you, player. I honestly wouldn't have known.

You were so cool about it. *Yeah, that'd be good,*" she said, affecting my voice. "We're practically stealing your innocence." My belly swirled at the thought of June thinking of me as a little kid. Not in a good way. Also I knew she used *we* as a collective term to mean her and Heath, which didn't help. "You don't have to if you don't want to. A lot of people don't." The way her voice went up at the end of the sentence let me know she was lying.

But I *wanted* to get drunk. Stupid drunk. It wasn't that I had avoided drinking in the past; I had just never thought about it that much. But here it was. And I was willing to do anything to stop thinking.

The table at the back of the basement had the red cups I had seen people drinking from in movies; bottles whose contents ranged from clear to a sort of unhealthy piss-colored brown; Coke and Sprite and orange juice, which I guessed were mixers.

"What do you think you'd like?" June asked, eyeing the table and idly scratching the back of her head. "Well, no one really *likes* any of this. What do you think you can tolerate?"

"What do you, uh, put with the orange juice?" I felt like an idiot. Naive. But if June was thinking the same thing, she didn't let on.

"Vodka, normally. Want that?"

"Sure," I said. "I, uh, like orange juice." Oh, wow, that was cool. That was a cool thing to say.

June laughed. "Well, you won't like vodka." She filled a red cup nearly to the top with orange juice, then dashed some Smirnoff in like an afterthought, then handed the concoction to me.

"That's all?" I asked.

She smiled, her eyebrows furrowed. "Try it, then," she said, like a dare.

I did as she said, unhinged my jaw and practically downed the whole thing in one go. The orange juice was there, but underneath was this sort of empty burn that clung to the back of my throat and fizzed up to my nose and made my eyes water. I had to conceal a retch.

"Whoa! Easy, killer!" June said, snatching the cup I'd emptied. "The night is young. The night hasn't even been freaking conceived yet. Relax." Someone behind us called her name. "Oh, hey! Here, come on, let me introduce you…"

When she left, I pressed the mouth of the clear bottle to mine, and sipped.

I remember clinging to June like a leech at first. Being too nervous to be left alone.

I recognized all of them but knew no one. Most were seniors, and I'd been in classes with them or our lockers had been close together. Others I remembered from freshman year. From over-the-shoulder glances and stifled laughter. Maybe this was my chance to change things. Not that I cared about being liked by the people who thought it was okay to behave the way they had, anyway. But we all want to be liked. I imagined the crowd opening up to me like an outstretched hand and then closing around me, swallowing me, taking me.

I got drunk faster than I'd anticipated. I kept checking myself, checking my reality, like I didn't believe it would actually work. Right.

As if repeatedly emptying low-dosage poison into my body wouldn't do anything.

It wasn't necessarily an immediate happiness—like, I didn't really feel *happy*—but I felt like there was no reason not to be. Dad, firstly. But June, and the texts, Olivia, it all kind of melted away, dribbled down the front of my chest, out with the sweat. Gravity seemed to have gone on a break. My guts twirled. My mouth went numb, which was probably to blame for the alarming rate that my words were tumbling out of it. It was kind of a wonderful feeling, to think there was nothing more important in the world than my own words. Before, everyone in the room had been painted red, and now they were green, green, green.

I learned that I didn't like to share her.

In the car I had June all to myself—and even when she was with Heath, I'd sort of convinced myself that I wasn't allowed to be bitter. I was a growth, anyway; they were here first, and really, I trusted Heath. But here, to all these people I barely even knew, June was the belle of the ball.

They all loved her. She touched them, danced with them, and they all loved it, like she was some messiah who was gracing them with her presence, and at some point she took Kendall McIntyre aside and jokingly grinded on her, and I honestly thought I might be sick. At least in my mind, Heath was the one I would always need to give her up to. Ha. Give her up. As if she were ever mine. But seeing her flouncing around with everyone else, I couldn't help but feel alarmingly unprepared and painfully jealous.

The real reason it was painful, I suspected, was that there was nothing different about the way she touched them and the way she touched me.

But she didn't take any of them to the River Styx.

And while I was looking at June, Bea was looking at me.

I don't know if it was drink-induced paranoia, but God, every time I'd even glance toward her, I swore she was looking directly fucking at me.

And now the texts flashed in front of my eyes.

Doesn't sound like you're all that upset.

A switch flipped in my brain, a giant switch I'd been ignoring and that the alcohol had masked, but only for a bit, only for a *bit*.

Do you really think someone killed him?

I shouldered through the masses to make my way to her, and before I could stop myself, I had her cornered up against a wall. "What are you playing at?"

"What?" she said, recoiling.

"I'm so sick of—" I made some sort of primal noise, with my teeth clenched together. "I'm *so sick* of whatever it is you think you're doing. Just—why now? Why are you doing this now?"

"I—I don't know what you're talking about."

Dyke.

"Yeah, okay. *Healing Homosexuality?* Really? You know what? You—you can go *fuck* yourself. Can I know *why?* Like, why you've suddenly decided now's the time to get some weird revenge?"

"Sydney, stop. I have no idea what this is, I—"

"The texts."

"*What* texts?"

154

"Please don't lie."

I didn't mean to, but staring daggers at her made me see her as she was two years before, when I cared about her. I felt a pang of sympathy for the girl in front of me now. What was I doing?

"I'm not."

"Then why have you been acting so weird? Since my dad—"

"I'm so confused, Sydney."

"Why have you been acting weird?"

She sighed a big, full-bodied sigh. "I've felt so guilty."

"What?"

"I'm—I'm so sorry. For what happened. Seeing you the way you were, it—made me feel *awful*, so, so awful, and I didn't know how to apologize. It just, like, hit me, and I wanted to come to the funeral, but since I'd never made amends, I..."

"So, you've felt guilty? You've been acting like a freak because you felt guilty?"

"Yeah." We were quiet. "I'm so sorry for everything. I was gonna apologize, but it never seemed like the right time, and I wanted to talk to you here... But what were you talking about? Is someone harassing you? I—"

I turned on my heel and left.

My compromised brain had no idea how to process any of this.

So it acknowledged the information, felt very, very angry, and then promptly threw it away.

Later, June and I shared the corner of an L-shaped sofa. Normally I would have treated the gap between us like it might electrocute me if I touched it, but now, I collapsed into her, and she collapsed back and didn't push away, and our hips brushed against each other every time one of us shifted or laughed.

And in the moment, this was the most important thing.

I had forgotten about Bea completely.

I was aware of the conversation the way you're aware of your nose—I knew it was there, but I didn't care to focus on it. I mostly paid attention to my nerve endings, and the fact that June and I were so close to each other, the only motion required to kiss her would be to turn my head slightly to the right. I worried someone could read my mind, or that it was all too obvious. But no. They wouldn't know. This was a completely innocent, sleepover sort of contact.

My ears perked up when I heard my name.

"It's so weird to see Sydney drinking." The statement came from Greg, who spoke with this sleazy smirk I didn't like.

I smiled and said, "Sorry, who are you?"—half because I was drunk, and half because I honestly didn't know anything about him at all. It was funny enough to not be cutting, apparently, because the group laughed.

June asked on my behalf. "What does that mean?"

He proceeded to talk like I wasn't there. "Like, in school, I guess. She's kind of quiet."

June shifted. "You guys don't know her well enough. She's a fucking loudmouth."

I looked at her with faux outrage and elbowed her in the ribs,

156

which resulted in her shrieking and spilling her drink. She kind of half caught some of the liquid with a cupped hand. And I don't know what came over me, I seized her wrist and licked her palm like I'd been dared to stick my tongue on a frozen flagpole, and June giggled a ton, the sting from the alcohol and her laugh and the sheer publicness of it all blending into a moment that was almost euphoric. I watched as Greg leaned over to Heath and said loudly enough that we could hear but quiet enough that he could claim he didn't mean us to: "Threesome just waiting to happen."

We both stiffened, I think, but probably not for the same reasons. "Hey, man," Heath said, serious.

Greg smiled again. "Come on. You can't blame me."

Heath stood, towering over Greg. "What the fuck do you think you're doing?"

"Dude, come on, I—"

That was when June left and stormed up the basement stairs, polished wood creaking beneath her feet.

I followed her. I don't know what else happened with Heath and Greg because I followed her.

Up one set of stairs, then another.

June slinked into a room off the main hallway, and I shouldered myself in to find her sprawled out on what I assumed was Heath's bed, going by the Yale pennant that hung above it.

June tensed up, then relaxed when her eyes met mine. "God," she said, "you scared me."

"I'm sorry!" I said, too loud, too quick. "I followed you up here." I held on to the doorknob to make sure the force of my words didn't

157

knock me over. "Do you want me to leave you alone?" The roles had been reversed, I realized. Now it was me, interrupting June in the middle of the night.

June sniffed. Scooted over on the bed. "No. Come on."

I sat beside her slowly; any quicker and I think I might have toppled onto her. A wave of nausea rolled through me. "Are you okay?"

"Yeah, don't worry. I was just feeling sick."

Ugh. Her saying the word *sick* made my stomach rumble in the worst way. I tried to play it cool.

"Oh. Okay." I promptly flopped over on to my back, and she lay down next to me, hair spilling around her face like oil.

I was too drunk to press her about anything. My mind urged me to move on to the next thing.

And then, "You're so great, Whitaker."

I twisted my neck to look her in the eye. Giggled. "You're just *saying* that."

"No, no, no. You're exceptional. I'm so happy to have you. You're honestly so great, and it makes me really, really sad that the whole thing with Bea happened because now you don't believe that anyone could really, actually, like you."

"Okay," I said, like a complete idiot who fantasizes day in and day out about affection like this but shuts down when actually receiving that affection and says fucking *okay*.

She snorted. "*See?* That's what I'm talking about. You have no idea what to even do right now."

I felt thoroughly called out. But the interaction was tinted with such a carefree deliriousness that I didn't even care, the sort of lightness that suggested nothing we'd say here would ever prove of any consequence.

She fell back on to the bed, the aftershock making me bounce. "*Whi-ta-ker*," June said, sounding it out like a chant. "Whi-ta-*ker* at the Ri-ver *Styx*."

"*June*," I cooed, like a baby's first word. "That's a month. Why are you named after a *month*?" I said, as though it was very clever.

June changed the subject. "Oh. *Dude*. Hey. Speaking of. I was watching you chewing out Bea." Ugh. This. I willed her telepathically to rewind the tape. I preferred the babbling. "That was kinda wild. What happened?"

I could have lied. But it wouldn't have been a good one; mine and Bea's conversation obviously had some kind of context, and honestly, I wanted to tell June about the messages. Maybe I'd been rendered brave by what happened at the River Styx—that I'd convinced myself tonight would be a night of sharing—but also, maybe I wanted her to know. Or maybe it was too exhausting to continue lying by omission.

So I told her. I told her about the first one after the funeral and each one after, and the "present" I'd been given, every relevant event, all with drunken flair, and she listened intently the whole time, wincing at the parts that were bad enough to merit a wince; though not a complete night of sharing because I decided to leave out the parts where I thought all of this was perhaps the work of a murderer who'd happened to kill my dad. "Olivia and I thought for sure that it had to have been Bea, but, I don't know. You tell me. Did she look guilty?"

"She looked fucking terrified, is what she looked like."

I laughed. "Well, yeah. So I don't know. Now I feel like there's something going the *fuck* on and it's *pissing* me off."

"Well—who else...do you think it could be?" Halfway through the question, something changed on her face; maybe it was because she was drunk, or maybe because she realized the magnitude of the situation, or maybe she could see the red lights flashing *murder* behind my eyes.

"That's the thing," I said. "I don't know."

That was when I became really nauseous.

It was mostly the alcohol. *Definitely* mostly the alcohol. "Uh, sorry, June," I managed to squeak through the rising vomit. "Is there a bathroom?"

"Yeah, out and left—do you want me to come with you?"

"No," I said, already halfway out the room. "Definitely not. Thanks."

I made it in time. And then I was sick. Completely, beautifully sick.

I carefully wiped the seat with toilet paper and washed my hands twice, already feeling the fog lifting from in front of my eyes. Ah, yes. This was what the world actually was. I leaned on the sink, held on for dear life. Wiped at the wetness underneath my eyes. My braids had gone all loose and wispy, and there was a stain from an unidentifiable source smack dab in the middle of my hoodie. But there was still something lighter about me. My shoulders or my stance, or *something*. I wasn't sure.

"Did you puke?" June asked when I reclaimed my spot beside her.

"Oh, *did I*," I said. It seemed there was still some alcohol in my system.

"God. Tomorrow we're both joining AA. And…going to church."

I laughed. "Repentance!" I squealed, and while we were laughing, I started thinking about Dad, about how he knew her and I knew her but never at the same time. She could have been a uniting force, but instead, she was only a last desperate fiber from which the old world hung. I wanted to introduce her to him as I knew her, not as he did. What did he think of her? I was sure he loved her as much as I did. I was sure he knew more about her than I did. I wanted more than anything to talk to him about her, everything, all this…

Tears prickled at the backs of my eyes, and June, ever the empath, noticed and wrapped an arm round me. "Hey, hey. What's up?" she asked. So embarrassing, crying in front of her. It never really got less embarrassing. But then she started crying too, just a little. "Are you—is it—out of my field of capabilities?"

I nodded, and she pulled me in.

"Oh, Whitaker. Look at us. What a pair!" She glanced toward the window. It was pitch-black outside now, and it occurred to me that I had no idea what time it was. "Come on," June said. "I think we both need some fresh air." With a grunt of exertion, she lifted the window and maneuvered a leg through.

"Whoa. What are you doing?"

"The roof. There's a spot out here to sit." Her other leg disappeared, and then all of her was gone, until she poked her head back in. "Bring the blanket. It's fucking nippy."

I wasn't really excited about the prospect of sitting unsecured one story above the ground, but I had to keep up with her, so I grabbed the blanket and squirmed through the open window like she had, on to the roof, slippery with frost. I sat, but it was precarious at best; the portion we were sitting on was at a fifteen-degree angle, maybe, so it was flat, but not flat enough to ensure an especially strong breeze wouldn't send me hurtling to my death. Pushing my reservations aside, I handed the blanket to June, and she draped it around both of our shoulders, which delighted me.

"These parties are only fun for a little bit," she said, looking out on to the tops of the trees ahead. "And then I want to lock myself in a closet and curl into a ball. It's like, I'm only having any fun when I'm too drunk to realize I shouldn't be. Sorry for dragging you along. It was kind of selfish. I mostly wanted someone I could tolerate to hang out with."

"Oh, glad I'm *tolerable*."

"Not what I meant. You're more than tolerable. You're exceptional!"

"No," I said. "I mean, I'm not a party animal, or anything, but, yeah, I don't know. It was okay."

June nudged me playfully, which I would have enjoyed more were I not one unstable moment away from becoming paralyzed from the neck down. "Was it okay when you were puking?"

"Actually, yeah," I said, and she laughed. "I feel a lot better. Are you, are you okay?"

"Yeah. Don't worry," she said. "Thanks for putting up with my misguided attempt at a surprise. I'm sorry again…"

That's when she rested her head on my shoulder, and a bit of frizz from her hair grazed across my lips and stayed there, and I didn't brush it away. I craned my neck over the edge of the roof. It wasn't *that* high up. Three stories was normally the upper limit of survivability, so I wouldn't *die*; if I fell the right way, I probably could have made it maybe with only a cracked rib. Knees tucked, forward roll. If I fell on my head, though, I was a goner.

And from somewhere behind and below us, the countdown began.

Disorganized chanting at first, because no one really cares about counting down from twenty, but then it was fifteen, ten, five, four, three, two, one.

Happy New Year! Everyone shouted.

"Shit." June looked back inside, debating, I was sure, how quickly she could scramble off the rooftop so as to start the new year with people who actually mattered. "Heath's gonna kill me. Shit." She patted down her pockets. "The time just went. I don't even have my phone."

"He's not gonna *kill* you. Were you guys—were you supposed to—"

"Smooch, yeah. It's okay." She sighed. "It's okay. It'll be fine."

I could feel my sobriety leaking back into my vision, and in ten seconds, maybe, the question would become completely unaskable, completely untouchable, so I had to ask it *now*, now, or else I might never get the chance to ask it ever again. Was I misreading the room? The words were right there. Something I simultaneously needed to know but didn't want to ask. *Don't ask, back of my throat, up, up, tongue, tip, lips:* "June, are you straight?"

But Heath arrived before the words could.

There was a knock on the bedroom door first, followed by the creak of said door opening and then a sharp intake of breath. "June!" he said, sticking his head through the open window to meet us. "It's not safe to sit up here. I told you."

"I know, I know. We're coming in," she said. I was the closest to the window, so she gestured with her eyes for me to go back in, which I did, like a newborn giraffe with no legs or brain. June followed close behind; I was conscious of my butt in her face.

"There's ice on there in the winter, June. You could slip. And you're *drunk*."

"We're fine. Look. In one piece."

"That's not the point." He looked us both up and down, and I hoped I wasn't blushing. "What were you guys even doing?" he asked. My mental capabilities weren't currently sharp enough to discern whether or not he was asking because he suspected something.

"I just wanted some air, babe." And June made a beeline to him like she forgot I was there, or maybe because I was there, and wrapped her arms round his shoulders. His hands slithered on to her hips. She kissed him, long and hard, not just one kiss, but that thing where you think the kiss is done, but then there's more contorting and squishing. That kind of kiss. I watched. "Sorry I missed you at midnight," June said when their faces lost suction.

And then I remembered: the countdown. It was past midnight. Olivia.

Shit.

I clicked my phone on for the first time since I'd arrived: five texts and three missed calls.

9:02: hey!! hope you're having fuuuuun. what time do you think you'll be here?

9:50: pizza here!!! avec lil peps as requested. you can heat it up when you come :-)

10:55: uh so, miles's curfew is 11 (i know. on friggin new years) uh, so, he's leaving...lol. lonelyyyy

11:31: idk man. a liiiiitle bit bummed

12:03: ok. Happy new year. Glad u r having a good time see u whenever

Oh.

A timely reminder that I didn't, in fact, live in a fantasy and was instead primarily an asshole who let down her one friend in the naive hope she'd gain the affections of some faraway girl who didn't like girls.

"I have to go," I said suddenly, looking up from my phone. I think I might have interrupted the two of them whispering sweet nothings to each other, but whatever.

Heath spoke first. "Is everything okay?"

"Yeah. Well, I mean, no. I'm...I'm a bad friend. I was supposed to, uh, meet Olivia before midnight, and I'm such an idiot, I totally forgot—"

"I'll take you," June said, already moving toward the door. "Let's go."

Heath grabbed her hard by the arm. "Are you out of your mind?"

"I'm not drunk, Heath."

"You're joking. So irresponsible. Oh, by the way." He pulled a phone out of his pocket and handed it to her. "I found this in the grass in the backyard. Sure, you're not drunk. I'm taking you, Sydney," he said, like they were debating who should escort their daughter to soccer practice.

I banished any thoughts of potential car awkwardness and agreed. "Okay. Yeah. Let's go."

11

HEATH PLAYED VIVALDI. I WASN'T entirely sure what sort of music I'd envisioned him liking. All things considered, this seemed to make sense. He drummed his fingers against the steering wheel absent-mindedly, hitting each note in "Summer." I only knew it was called that because the screen in his car said so.

I attempted futilely to get ahold of Olivia. The fog in my brain—thinner, thankfully, but still there—meant typing anything was a slow process—in fact an insurmountable task. I couldn't get the words out. Wasn't even sure what the words were.

So I gave up. Watched the world outside zoom past. We might

as well have been flying through space, each passing streetlight some faraway star; being at the River Styx with June felt like it might as well have been a million years ago. It was even colder, now, and the heated seats made the car smell faintly like burning.

He wasn't talking, so I attempted to make conversation. "I think this is giving me anxiety," I said, referring to Vivaldi. Good one, me.

Heath kept his eyes on the road. "It's supposed to. 'The shepherd weeps, because overhead hangs the fearsome storm, and his destiny.'"

"Oh."

"Vivaldi wrote a sonnet for each of the four seasons. Pretty groundbreaking stuff for a composer at the time. That's translated, of course. It sounds much better in the original Italian."

"Yeah. Of course." I don't know why I felt as if I had to impress him, but I did, like I was hoping for his approval. Anyway, there was something endearing about him listening to Vivaldi directly after leaving a rager.

"Hey, so, I actually wanted to thank you."

The steadiness of his voice implored me to turn off my phone. "For what?"

"For everything you've done for June."

I wasn't sure I'd heard him correctly. "I mean, yeah, you're welcome! Happy to be of assistance!" And then I saluted him, which I liked to think normally would have been caught by the filter that kept me from doing things that were untoward as fuck. "What do you mean, though?"

Heath shifted. A lock of his hair tumbled forward and stuck there like a Superman curl. Even with the film of sweat on his forehead and the slight pink tinge to the corner of his eyes, he was still annoyingly handsome. "She was having a really rough time this summer. Was in a really dark place, actually, and I don't know if you know, but she saw your dad for a bit."

I widened my eyes like this was completely new information. I don't know why.

"Yeah," he continued. "She really liked him. But she's been happy, lately—I imagine you might have filled that gap for her, in a way. Don't you think?"

"Yeah, I mean. Yeah. I guess."

Heath hummed, like I had confirmed something for him. But I didn't think too much of it. I was focused on my heartbeat, which, instead of *ba-dum*, took on four new syllables: *she's been happy, she's been happy, she's been happy*. And then the bit of drunken truth spilled from me: "She's helped me a lot too."

"Good."

"I'm glad you said that, actually. I was worried I was sucking the life out of her, or something. Like, I don't know. Like I was a bummer to be around?"

"Well, maybe you're sucking the life out of each other."

I laughed too hard; based on the stiffness of Heath's lip, I wasn't sure I should have laughed at all.

"How have *you* been, though?"

I stiffened. "Yeah, I mean, I'm, uh, I'm fine, all things considered, I guess."

"Still watching those videos?" he asked, the corners of his lips curling at the last word.

"Not as much, no."

"I actually wanted to talk to you about those...texts you've been getting."

Oh God. Had he heard me and June talking? Maybe he'd followed us upstairs. How much had he heard? "How did you know about that?"

"Oh, sorry. Olivia. She was talking about it in student council. She wanted to run some kind of bullying initiative, and mentioned... yeah."

I slumped in my seat and powered my phone off, now bemoaning the fact that I'd left the party at all. Damn it, Olivia. Was it too late to ask him to turn round? "Oh. What about them?"

"So...hm. So, sorry, you probably don't want to talk about this right now, but, when my mom died..." He seemed to choke on the word. Took a breath. "I felt so alone. It's the main thing I remember from the time. Just feeling completely, utterly alone. It felt like people were looking at me, but not really, you know? Like they were looking through me, almost. Past me. And I would have done anything to get them to really, really look. Anything. To the point where I had some really dark thoughts. As in, maybe I wanted them to look at me even if I wasn't around to know about it. Do you know what I mean?"

"I guess. Sorry, maybe I—what does that have to do with—"

He sighed, like it was painful to say whatever he was thinking out loud. "I understand if maybe the messages are...as in, maybe the attention..."

We were both quiet for a moment. Vivaldi's second movement flourished to an anxiety-inducing climax. "You think I'm making it up?"

"No! No. That's not it. It wasn't right for me to bring that up.

Attention was not the right word. Ah. I can't—I'm not articulating myself correctly. It wasn't right to do this now."

I sat quietly, juddering slightly whenever we hit a bump.

"Am I still going the right way?" Heath asked, awkward. "June mentioned you lived on the way to hers. I've been going that way."

I swallowed twice before answering. Crossed my legs. Recrossed them the other way. "Yeah, no, you're good. It's the next left."

"Oh. Really?"

"Yeah. Why?"

"She's the next right."

A couple of more minutes crept past. Eventually, he pulled on to the cul-de-sac, and I pointed toward the house with the green shutters. I went to leave. "Hey," he said. "I'm sorry. That's not what I meant. Truthfully. I'm still here if you ever need to talk." His eyes suggested he meant it. I was struck by a wave of acceptance, looking into this harmless-ass kid's eyes, really, for the first time, with his dead mom and beautiful girlfriend and big house, and I was so jealous of everything, everything. The emotions were so annoyingly conflicting. I wanted to hate him. But he gave me nothing to hate. Maybe he was purposely being careful around me. Who knew? But honestly, at least this boy was looking after her. If I couldn't have her, I was glad he could.

"No worries," I said finally. "Thanks for the ride."

"Happy New Year," he said.

"Thanks, man. You too."

I slammed the door, and the sound of it rang in my ears, muffling the beginning of *Autumn*'s first movement.

Olivia wouldn't pick up the phone. I knocked on her door in a last-ditch effort to get some closure, at least, but Mrs. Good answered. She said Olivia was asleep, despite her bedroom light being on.

I sat in bed, not feeling particularly awake but not particularly tired either. In a weird liminal state, it occurred to me I was completely sober again now and my mind ticked along clearly, running through the events of the night in no linear fashion. Snapshots.

I did feel bad about Olivia. But who the hell did she think she was, telling people about the texts? We used to spend every waking moment together, the days of summer sprawling in front of us seemingly with no end. Everything that happened to me became Olivia's concern. I told her everything. The thought of her exhausted me now, and I didn't know why, or what had changed. Dad had something to do with it, sure, but even before then, the niggling feeling had been crawling under the surface—the thought that we'd both been growing, but in two entirely different directions.

Bea. I wasn't sure how good a judge I was, but I did believe it wasn't her. Her emotion felt genuine, despite my impaired perceptions, and the person sending the texts would be the sort of sick fuck who would want me to know they were behind it all. I felt like they would have wanted me to know it was them. Or at least they didn't seem particularly bothered about getting in trouble for it. *Getting in trouble.* That phrase seemed too juvenile now, for whatever this was.

With Bea acquitted, it could have been anyone. But who else *was* there? There was no pool of suspects. It was me, and everyone else. Me against everyone else.

And then that familiar horror of a thought, returning in one heavy wallop: that this had to do with what happened to Dad.

No. It couldn't have been. But it could have been.

Maybe Dad was killed. Maybe Dad was killed and the person behind all this killed him. Cut the brakes. Slashed the tires. Maybe, maybe—

Breathe.

June.

June. June at the River Styx. June in a beanie. June on the roof.

June. She was impossible to place. She was a mess of extremes, and I was a monotonous hum. Why had she taken me there, of all places? I mean, I had understood her reasoning. That she thought it would help. But why did she even want to help? And why did it always feel like for every word she said, there were three others she wouldn't?

I could practically feel her folder pulsating all the way from Dad's office. I contemplated opening it, the allure of knowing almost too powerful to ignore. I also contemplated bricking it up into the wall, so it could slowly starve to death, and I'd never have to think of it ever again.

I went to pull up the texts to read them closely.

My phone buzzed before I could.

I wasn't sure who I expected it to be. Maybe Olivia asking what had happened. Better yet, June asking if I'd made it back okay.

Neither.

Happy New Year, dyke.

Come on. Now they weren't even trying.

Me: Is that seriously it?

Looks like you had a good time at the party.

And then a picture. Dark, blurry, taken from far away and from an odd angle, but the subject was apparent.

June and me. Huddled up together on Heath Alderman's roof.

That's when the glass shattered.

A faint, distorted clink from downstairs.

Maybe Mom was still awake. Maybe she had dropped something. A mug. Right?

I slowly rose from my bed and crept out of my room, each step measured and deliberate.

Mom's room was across the hall. I nudged open the door, and there she was, duvet rising and falling softly with her breath.

Okay. This was fine.

I crept downstairs, turning lights on as I went, my footsteps nearly noiseless yet somehow still pounding against my eardrums.

Kitchen. Living room. Nothing seemed out of place.

Save for the periodic banging behind Dad's office door.

Bang.

Two seconds.

Bang.

Three seconds.

Bang.

The door to the office grew a pair of eyes and stared.

I moved closer, the world absolutely silent save for the banging and my heartbeat echoing in my skull. The world had never been so quiet and so loud.

Bang.

Closer, and the air around me grew colder. Colder.

Bang. Colder still.

I twisted the knob and pushed, everything in me tensing, expecting...I wasn't even sure what.

Empty.

The office was empty. But the door that led outside was wide open, slamming against the wall with each successive gust of wind.

And on Dad's desk was the picture of me and him at Niagara Falls.

The glass had been shattered and strewn around the frame, the fractured shards like birds flying away.

Mom called the police, who responded more slowly than they otherwise would have in Pleasant Hills. (*New Year's, you know how it is.*) One police officer—a shorter-than-average mustachioed guy with a neck as wide as his head—had a look around, as did we; nothing was stolen, it looked like, and there were no signs of breaking and entering, no open windows or picked locks.

"I...must have forgotten to lock the door," I said when Mom looked at me in surprise. But I couldn't have. I swore I remembered locking it.

"Does anyone besides you folks have keys?"

I realized. "Just my friend Olivia. She lives across the street."

He grunted. "You might want to have a chat with your friend Olivia."

Ha. As if.

"Well, if the door was open, isn't there a chance it was—I don't know—the wind?" Mom asked. I shot her a look.

"Not sure the photo would've been smashed the way it is on account of the wind. If you want my opinion, I think more than likely it was some drunk kids messing around. Saw an open door, thought they'd be funny, split when they heard you coming. They're running amok tonight, I'll tell you that. We've already had an accident on Miller, no one hurt, thank God—"

"Here." I thrust my phone into his face. "I think it might have something to do with this."

He took it, squinted, moved the phone away from his face and back again to try to find a distance at which he could actually read it. I felt Mom look at me. The police officer read it for a moment, then narrowed his eyes at me. "You gettin' bullied?"

I sighed. That felt like the understatement of the century. *Stalked.* I nodded. "Yeah. But I think it might not just be bullies, or whatever. This feels premeditated, and I think it might have something to do with my—"

He sighed. "You at the high school?" I nodded again; he grunted again. "Tell ya what: I think this is a case of nasty kids getting a little too brave. Hm? Trying to scare ya, or something."

This was enough. He was wrong, everyone was wrong, and they all needed to listen to me now, needed to understand that this was something bigger. "No. Sir, I'm sorry—"

"I'll have a chat with the principal there. Maybe he can keep an eye out, have an assembly, something—"

"Sir, I think this might be something to do with my dad."

Everybody froze. The officer straightened his back and said awkwardly, "Oh, er—yes, we all heard, and I, I am sorry for your loss—"

"Thank you for coming by," Mom said, and laid a hand on his arm to escort him outside. "We appreciate it. I'll, ah, maybe look into some security systems. Are there any you'd recommend?" *Click.*

I stood there, unmoving and sort of embarrassed, until she emerged again.

"Sydney Frances, I—what are you doing?"

"Why are you mad at me? I—"

"Do you realize how that makes me look?"

"Yeah, sorry to embarrass you in front of that *one* police officer."

"*Sydney!*"

"What do you *mean?* Why won't you listen to me? It's all here. All of it. I can show you. I didn't tell you on Christmas because I didn't want to upset you, but that present in the mailbox"—I tapped furiously on my phone screen—"it was from them. Whoever did this. It was some book about how being gay is a sin, with Dad's obituary taped inside of it, Mom."

This, of all things, seemed to have gotten through to her. "Why didn't you tell me?"

I threw my hands up, exasperated. "Because I thought you would do *this!*"

"We're going to figure out something to do about whoever this is. I promise. Okay? But"—her eyes glazed over—"but no more of this, Sydney. Okay? No more about Daddy. I hate to see you like—"

And then I left, stomped up the stairs, and slammed my bedroom door behind me.

Later, I sat in bed thinking of a conversation I'd had with him a couple of years before. We were watching *Twilight Zone,* and I was thinking about how crap it would be to know some unbelievable truth but have nobody who will listen to you, and I said, "Promise me if some bonkers shit happens to me one day—like I get abducted by aliens or kidnapped by ghosts or something—and I tell you about it, then you gotta believe me."

He propped his feet up on the fold-out footrest of his usual chair in the living room (nobody has sat in that chair since September). "I don't think ghosts are normally the sort to kidnap people."

"You know what I mean."

"Mm. Can't promise that. Might be a psychotic break."

"But I feel like I'd be able to tell the difference."

"You would *feel* that way, yes."

"Okay. Well. If I tell you a Kanamit is after me and you don't do anything about it, you're gonna feel real bad when they eat me."

"I think I would be *inclined* to believe you. Mainly because you're my daughter and I trust you. Though the Kanamits would be innocent until proven guilty."

I tossed a cushion at his head.

The only person who would believe me about my dad's death was my dead dad.

Olivia came over in the morning as per my pleading request, hair scrunched into a bun and forehead straining against her severely raised eyebrows. "How was *Heath's?*" she said finally, after silently pushing past me at the door and collapsing on our living room couch.

"Hey. I'm sorry. Okay? I really am. I totally lost track of time."

"It's New Year's. How do you lose track of time on New Year's? The whole holiday is about the time."

"We—I was drinking." Olivia's mouth hung agape.

"I'm—we're seventeen, okay? Relax. I wasn't paying attention. I'm sorry. I left right after I realized. I was gonna come see you, but you wouldn't answer."

She sighed. "I accept your apology."

"But something happened last night. With the message person."

Olivia rolled her eyes. "You're unbelievable."

"What?"

"You're only apologizing because you want me to play detective with you."

"No. I'm not. I would have apologized anyway. This is serious. Nobody is taking this seriously. Why isn't anyone taking this seriously? They're practically, I don't know, *stalking* me. They came into the house, Liv. They smashed a picture of Dad and me."

Olivia shifted. Crossed her arms. "I still think it's Bea."

"Dude, I *talked* to Bea."

"Yeah, all right, *dude*. Cool, *dude*. Since when do you say *dude*?"

"None of this is her. She had no idea about any of it."

She scoffed. "Okay, so you're not even a good detective. You seriously believe her?"

"Yeah, I do. Liv, really, I honestly think this has something to do with my dad."

178

She considered this for a moment. "So, what am I supposed to do about it? Do some, I don't know, some *hacking*? Start a Pleasant Hills patrol?"

"I don't know. Maybe firstly be—emotionally supportive? Or something?"

"I would have loved some emotional support yesterday."

"You could have just come with me."

"And you could have just *stayed*."

I was finished. "Okay. You know what, I—you can go. You can leave."

"Thanks for your permission."

"That wasn't—that's not what I was saying."

So this was how it ended.

I watched her leave, her dark shock of hair waving behind her. Things would never, ever be the same between us, and the sooner we realized—she realized—the better.

Class didn't start back up again until Wednesday, and I would have preferred to spend my remaining freedom inside, sulking, thinking, but I had to go back to the support group on Monday.

I wasn't exactly looking forward to it. Actually, I was grumpy as hell about it. Didn't want to be there. I felt like I had a whole host of problems that, even if I were the only bastard there, we wouldn't have been able to solve. I was upset about the fight I'd had with Olivia; I was, as always, in a perpetual state of discomfort about my dependency on June; I was also, apparently, the target of someone who was human trash at best and a literal murderer at worst.

Where would I even start?

Leo gave me a half-hearted smile when I arrived, which I returned. This boy was no longer a threat, I decided, and I liked that I knew more about him now than he knew about me.

That session, Gerry had us talk about emotions. "I know, I know," she said, "emotions in therapy? Groundbreaking."

We talked about guilt and death. As in, thinking that there was something you could have done, when, really, there's nothing that could have been done. Arguments don't cause heart attacks. You didn't have to cry at the funeral if you didn't feel like it. Stuff like that. Even if I had told Dad not to go driving that day, nothing would have changed. And I thought, maybe when there's meant to be a death, that death will happen no matter what you do. The grim reaper taking his daily cut of human life, and he needs to fill the quota. Some *Final Destination* shit. If Dad hadn't died driving, he would have been hit by a rogue bullet or choked on dinner or fallen down the stairs, all of which are probably worse than a one-and-done car accident, so really, he was lucky.

Anger and death. I was angry at everything. People. Death. The universe. Whatever. "The stages of grief—I'm gonna be honest here—are *bull*," Gerry said. "Sometimes the anger lingers. Or the denial. Or the bargaining. Or the fear. Any of it can stay."

She had us divide a piece of paper into four parts, and label each with *I feel guilty when*, *I feel angry when*, *I feel scared when*, and *I feel better when*.

Guilty when I smile, laugh, breathe.

Scared when literally anything happens.

Better when...

Better when I'm with June.

Gerry had us go around and pick one of our squares to talk about to the group, and when it was my turn, my stomach lurched. I wasn't really ever scared of talking in front of people, but for some reason, this time, even the thought of speaking what I was thinking made the world's tiniest spiders take to crawling all over my skin. The words I wanted to say rang clear in my head, but got caught on my tongue. "I feel..." I considered leaving it there. An announcement that yes, I did indeed feel. But they were all looking at me, so I needed to round the sentence off. "I kind of feel guilty for being alive at all." They were already quiet, but after I said that, it seemed like they got even quieter, somehow, like in movies right after a bomb goes off. I didn't specify that I didn't want any replies, but no one gave me any regardless. I felt Leo looking at me.

Then Gerry had us participate in one of what she called her "hippie games"—she had us all cross our arms over each other and grab the hand of the person next to us, then squeeze, so the squeeze would travel round the circle, as some positive energy transference, or something. When Leo squeezed, it was too hard, for too long—but I appreciated it. I think we understood each other. And I couldn't help myself, I had to look at him, so I did, but his eyes weren't narrowed, they were open, pained, and then he squeezed my hand again and nodded like I had done something very important.

He sat next to me after group in the lobby while we both waited for our parents. "Hey. It's none of my business, but is everything okay?"

"Why do you ask?"

"Not sure." He pushed his glasses up his nose with his middle finger. "You seemed a bit…heavy, in there." *In there*, like we'd escaped mortal combat.

"Yeah, don't worry about it," I said. And I don't know what came over me, but I thought he was trustworthy, and with Olivia all but gone, I was sort of looking to get anyone on my side. There wasn't any harm in him knowing. I wanted him to know. "Actually, it's not, it's all really fucked up, but are you sure you want to deal with this right now? It is kinda heavy."

"Okay. Hit me."

I lowered my voice. "When my dad died… Okay, this is gonna sound wild, but I was, uh, worried—paranoid, I guess, that somebody had hurt him. That maybe someone was responsible for it. You know? It's a long story, but he was a therapist, and I thought maybe one of the patients…you know?"

He scoffed. "You realize *you're* a patient."

"Yeah, no kidding. I'm not saying everyone who saw him was out to get him; it was just that one person *was*, and the whole thing… was not some random accident. And then afterward, you know, what a coincidence—I'm pretty sure someone started stalking me."

"Er. What?"

"Yeah, just, just let that one settle over the room."

"Like, stalking *how?*"

"The usual way, I guess."

"You're gonna have to fill me in."

"They started as, uh, texts. Calling me...names. Being creepy. That sort of shit. But then they, like, stuck a copy of some homophobic trash into my mailbox, which was bad, and then—here, let me show you." I brought up the picture of me and June. Leaned across to hand it to him. "They sent me that. That's me. And then they broke into my house—at least, I think they did—and smashed a picture of me and my dad."

"And what? You think whoever's doing this had something to do with your dad?"

I braced myself. "I know. It's out there, but..."

Leo blinked. "No, I think that makes sense."

"Really?"

"I mean, this *is* fucked. Like, it's...calculated, you know? Have you talked to the police?"

"The police think I'm being *bullied*."

He rolled his eyes. "I'm sorry, man. That's such a shitty thing to have to deal with...alongside everything else, is all."

"Yeah. I mean, yeah, it is." I shifted.

"I'm, uh—" Leo cleared his throat almost comically loudly. "Sorry. Are you gay?"

"Yeah."

"Me too. I'm. Yeah. Gay. Also. Sorry. Still getting used to that."

"I know."

183

"Come on, man. Don't give me that 'I could tell' shit."

"No, I honestly wouldn't have known. But I—I looked you up. I mean. You could've been bi, or whatever, but—"

"You looked me up?"

"Yeah. Sorry. I was just curious." I bit my lip. "Galileo."

He couldn't believe it at first, mouth open, but then he broke into a smile, bit his lip. "Unbelievable. What is this? Are you blackmailing me?"

I shrugged. "You have it as your Facebook name."

"Because I haven't gone on Facebook since—man. Not for a while. My—ugh. My dad's a freaking physicist. And I don't go by that anymore."

"Why? It's cool. But, uh, shouldn't it be *Lay-O*?"

"I've reached my question limit. Sorry. No more answers today." But he was smirking. And he offered to swap numbers. "In case you miss a group and need a picture of a handout, or something."

When I left with Mom, I felt full up, ecstatic to have met someone who so easily mirrored my frequency.

12

Me and June had gotten to school early, and I didn't really feel like talking to Olivia, so I headed to Mr. Carlisle's room before the seven-thirty bell rang.

Bea found me there. "Hey. I figured I should talk to you in person, after...you know."

I wasn't in the mood to have this conversation. Bea was innocent, which was all well and good except that it meant more important things were at stake, and I'd taken the liberty of purging her from my waking thoughts completely. "Really. It's fine. I think we were both a little out of it."

"Well, I was then, but I'm not now. And I'm sorry. And I want you to know that I've done a lot of growing up. And I'm sorry if it seemed like I was angry at you. I was angry at myself. I should have spoken to you when it happened."

I knew by *it* she wasn't talking about the party; she was talking about freshman year, leaving me to be a target, ditching me completely while the world fell around me when it could have fallen around both of us. I hated to admit it, but somewhere in me there was still a softness for her. Little jagged pieces of myself floated away. "It's okay," I said, and for the first time, I maybe meant it. "That's all I wanted, really."

Leo texted me during first period.

Leo: hey. this is leo. can you send me that picture the freak took of you?

Me: Lol the freak. Yeah can do. Why?

Leo: metadata, etc. there might be some clues. facetime after school?

Me: Cool, Sherlock

The thought that this could be a lead kept me optimistic for most of the day. "You seem happy," June said on the way home.

"I, uh, sort of am. Long story but I met this guy at the support group, and—you know those messages I told you about? We're gonna try and figure out who's sending them."

"Oh."

"You don't seem all that excited."

June slammed on the brakes; she'd almost run a red light.

"Whoa," I said.

"Sorry. God. I'm so out of it today. Just...be careful. Please. That stuff seemed kind of...I don't know. Serious."

I FaceTimed Leo around five.

He said a sort of formal hello, lifting a hand to wave and puffing out his lips.

"Hey. Is now okay?"

"Now is perfect. So, I had a little look and I did find something, but don't get your hopes up because it's not that much."

My stomach dropped. Not really a huge drop. My stomach *stumbled*. My stomach didn't realize it had reached the bottom stair and tripped. "Lay it on me."

"*So*, the picture was taken on an iPhone. And sometimes with iPhones there'll be a name attached to it, like, 'Leo's iPhone' or whatever—no such luck, but looks like it was definitely taken on an iPhone 4, which I thought was notable for its...obsoletion. Is that a word? Obsolete-ness. Basically I don't think that many people have them. Does that mean anything to you?"

I thought for a second. I assumed the folders in Dad's office wouldn't specify patients' technological leanings. "Yeah. Okay." I tried to cycle through images of the party anyway, only it was impossible to actually get anything to materialize; all the memories were blurry and too fast. It wasn't unlikely someone had that phone. More than one person. Even June did.

"No bells ringing?"

"Not really. I'll...I'll keep an eye out, though. Let you know if I remember anything."

"Cool. Sorry if that's not all that helpful."

"No, it is. I mean, that's the only bit of information we have at all right now. Anything's better than nothing."

"Man. We live in a world where someone's outdated phone is a clue. Technology, man. Gonna write a slam poem about that. Hey, I don't know if I'm out of line for asking—who's the girl you're with? A friend?"

I smiled despite myself. "It's…astronomically complicated," I said, even though it wasn't, really. I only wanted it to be more complicated.

He withdrew, blinked. "Oh. *Oh*. Okay. It *is* a bit of a cutesy thing. Sittin' on a roof, all cozy. Is she…you know, are you…"

"No. That's why it's complicated." Then I sighed. "I wish."

He froze, then thawed and shook his head knowingly. "*Aaahhh*. I feel that. Straight?"

I nodded, all big and exaggerated, even though, I realized, this had never actually been confirmed. "Mm. Pretty sure, anyway. She has a boyfriend. Like, some big-shot, objectively attractive boyfriend."

"Ah. My friend. The world has been cruel to us. What's her name?"

"June."

"June," he repeated, like he was seeing how it tasted. "Do you think it's significant at all that she's in the picture? Or was it a random, surreptitious creep shot?"

"Creep shot. No, if anything, it was to, I don't know, mock me. The general tone of their messages has been, uh, foreboding homophobia."

"And you think—do you think the person was *there*? At the party?"

"I don't know. If it was only to do with me, and just me? Then yeah, definitely. But Dad—if it has to do with my dad, then I don't know."

"They would have had to know there was a party."

I nodded. "And that I was going to be there."

"And, I mean, unless they had planned on going to the party themselves—they had to know you were going to be outside at some point."

"Well, I mean, I had to leave eventually. Maybe they were waiting for that and got lucky."

"Hm."

"Yeah. Thank you for doing this, by the way."

"What?"

"I don't know. Caring. Believing me."

"No worries, my friend."

"Like...why?" There I went. Wondering *why* anyone wanted anything to do with me when that wasn't actually a conscious decision people made. "Okay. That was a dumb question. Sorry. You don't have to have a reason. It's just that no one has really believed me so far."

"Listen. I don't wanna get all heavy on you, but Alex—he's gone, right? He's gone, and there's nothing that comes after that. And I have so many questions that'll never be answered. Like, there's some questions I probably don't even know to ask. But you've got something here. I believe there's something to this. And if there's even a chance you can find some answers? Find some *peace*? Some retribution? Then I don't know. I'm happy to see that through with you. If there was a chance for me to find those same answers... I guess I'd want someone else by me too."

I released a breath I'd been holding for four months.

"That means a lot."

"Bitch, I should have recorded that. 'Gerry, I got something for you!' Shit. Sorry. Are we friends enough for me to say *bitch*?"

I laughed. "Barely. But. Yeah. I mean, I don't know. For me, it's like, and I guess it's probably the same for you too—he kept this whole part of his life from me, and I feel like if he hadn't... It's like, none of this would be happening."

"Yeah. Exactly."

"Something else in common, then."

A small voice called for him in the background. "Coming, Mom! Okay, gotta go, but let me know if you get any more texts. Actually, would you mind sending all of 'em over? Not that I'll be able to figure anything out. But, you know. It'd be nice to have them on hand in case anything else comes up."

I did as he asked, secure in the decision and without any second thoughts. Even though I hadn't known him for long, Leo might as well have been a key out of a padded room.

He believed me. Because I bet he didn't want to think the universe was capable of this either, and he knew how helplessness felt.

He got it in the way Olivia didn't.

I wasn't sure if I could even trust Olivia at all. About anything. After what Heath had said about Olivia telling him about the messages—and she told people about what I'd said at the funeral—it was clear she no longer had my best interests in mind. I didn't think she cared about me at all. But the fucked-up part was that I didn't care. Was that really friendship, then? We had no reason to even be around each other anymore; it was one thing when we were younger, because everyone has something in common when they're younger, but now we were growing in entirely opposite directions, the void expanded by death, and there was so much doubt and uncertainty, and it was all death's fault. It was all death's fault. What hadn't death ruined? What was left?

Things were strained between Olivia and me, and there was nothing left to say. Clearly she didn't want to talk to me, and I didn't really want to talk to her. It was like holding on to a tooth that was only attached by the thinnest stringy bit of flesh and I wanted to *pop*.

In the second week of January, we were sitting at lunch while she was talking about some cast-member drama that'd happened at rehearsal for the spring musical, and to be fair, I wasn't listening, but she looked at me and said, "You don't want to be here, do you?"

I didn't know what to say, so I didn't say anything. Just looked at her face. I saw it as it had been when we were six, doing dumb stuff and playing Ghosts and kickball, and that time one of our neighbor's dogs got eaten by a coyote, so we took it upon ourselves to hunt them. Things were so simple then and so horrible now.

After that, I mostly ate lunch in the computer lab, slipping bits of sandwich out of my bag while scrolling mindlessly through Reddit.

But June was always a constant. June stayed.

Ten minutes there. Ten minutes back.

One night, I did the math—I'd spent thirty-three hours in her car. That seemed like a lot of hours to me, given that the additional seven hours between seeing her in the morning and in the afternoon were dedicated to her too. Sometimes I worried that I liked to think about her more than I liked to be with her. But then I'd spend those ten minutes with her again, and I realized nothing compared, nothing compared to June in control, eyes flickering, laughing. I couldn't get enough of her.

I became obsessed with her hands. How they were kind of perpetually moving, twitching, the knuckles on her skinny fingers popping every time she remembered to crack them, which was often. I liked to watch them when she spoke, when she curled them around the occasional vanilla latte, when she ran them through her hair. I loved June's hands. I loved June's collarbone. I loved June's hair. I loved her laugh and her nose and her purple varsity jacket. I loved June's everything.

I was beginning to think I loved without there needing to be a common noun to follow.

I had sort of convinced myself that us going to the River Styx— her taking me to the River Styx—was indicative of our relationship having blossomed, and that maybe we'd do things like that more often. Truthfully, though, it seemed like everything had sort of gone back to the way it was. Normal was fine, of course. Normal was more than I'd ever hoped for.

But I wanted more of her. I wanted all of her. And that was a problem.

Apart from that, for a time, I felt like I was actually getting better.

Not *actually* better. But a little. I'd settled into a comfortable sort of melancholy, watched the apocalypse reach its four-month anniversary, and then its fifth. I actually started to enjoy the support group sessions. Leo made them palatable at first, but the other kids weren't bad either. The ToD drifted farther and farther down my recently visited pages until it disappeared completely. The messages, weirdly, seemed to have stopped. Maybe they'd realized I talked to the police; maybe, if it was a bully, they realized they'd gone too far. Either way, I ended up sort of forgetting about it.

I don't want to make it seem like everything was fixed. Because it absolutely wasn't. When you tell a story, people tend to get bored of you repeating the same things over and over. And if I were to repeat myself, I'd tell you about all the nights when nothing helped. When Mom and I didn't speak. When I thought maybe if I was dead, then I wouldn't have to worry about dying anymore. When I went back to the ToD. When I missed Dad more than I could even say.

My life fragmented into biweekly support group sessions and ten-minute intervals. Like if you zoomed out on my life, there'd be these occasional snippets of joy, split up by vast emptiness, and nothing could bring them together. As if I wasn't really living the rest of the time. The truth was, I wasn't. I found it impossible to keep happy without stimulus.

But maybe that was how lives were. Wading through all the shit to get to the good stuff.

And sometimes, when I was really low, I fantasized about June ferrying me home after school and mentioning that she'd finally had enough of whatever plagued her, and then the two of us would decide, *you know what, let's just leave!* And we'd drive and drive and never have to go home like some Neverland Lost Girls, and that could be my new reality, and I'd say *but we have school tomorrow*, and she'd say *what's school*, and then I'd say *but I'm grieving*, and the universe would say *what's grief*, and then we'd spend the rest of forever in the woods, lying in bed and brushing each other's hair and skinny-dipping in the fresh water.

Gerry had mentioned journaling, or any kind of writing, as being a good way to keep my feelings in order. I guess what I wrote ended up being like a short story. Or a script. I wasn't really sure what it was. Gerry said that writing was the quickest path to the soul, which made sense, but I wasn't sure I actually wanted to get to my soul at all, for fear of what I'd find when I did. Still, it felt good to get the words out of me.

My story was about a girl who's walking through the woods and finds a metal pipe sticking up from the ground.

She puts an ear to the opening and hears something down there, like someone's muttering to themselves. She asks if there's anyone there, and a face—genderless, kind of ghostly—appears. Not all at once, because the opening is too narrow, but she makes out an eye, a nose, a mouth. And the person underground says *Oh, thank God you found me, I'm trapped down here. Buried alive.* Asks her to help.

The girl says of course she will.

The person underground says they're hungry and thirsty, so she drops down food and water.

The person underground says there's a lock keeping them down there, and maybe if they unlocked it, they could get out. The girl sends down a paper clip, a knife, a hairpin. Nothing works.

The person underground says a fingernail would do the trick.

She reluctantly agrees. Peels off the nail from her pointer finger and drops it down the hole.

The person underground says they need an extra finger to prop open the lid.

So she cuts off her finger.

The person underground says they could dig themselves out of there, if only they had one more hand.

So she cuts off her hand.

And the person underground keeps saying, *I need this, I need this, I need this*, and the girl keeps complying, slicing off little bits of herself until all of her has gone down the hole and there's nothing left.

Leo and I became makeshift detectives with no leads and barely anything to investigate, which was where the *makeshift* came from.

I went to his house for the first time toward the end of February. Mom was happy to drive me—she sensed I had fallen out with Olivia and was glad, I think, that I had a friend (besides, of course, the "girl who gives you rides," who she knew nothing about)—even though Leo lived a good half hour away. Though if she had known what we planned on doing, I don't think she would have agreed.

Leo: excited to see you. have all the info?

Me: Names, at least

Leo: cool. also cole's here, if that's OK.

Me: Gross. Turning around

Leo: k. bye bitch

Leo: jk

Leo: see you soon.

An uncharacteristic heat wave had been threatening to thaw the frozen expanse of northeastern Ohio for a couple of weeks, and now it seemed like it might have actually happened. Little splotches of yellow-green poked through the whiteness, and for the first time, I thought about a world without Dad in it that was warm. Spring would have to come eventually.

I convinced Mom to drop me off without coming to the door with me. Leo retrieved me, wearing an Adidas T-shirt under a denim jacket, and escorted me up to his room.

Cole was sprawled across the bed in Leo's bedroom, rapidly pressing buttons on his Nintendo DS. I had only seen him in pictures, so seeing him here was sort of weird. Even lying down, I could tell he was shorter than I'd imagined, and his style was almost the opposite of Leo's—he wore a plain black T-shirt and skinny jeans. "Hey," he said, hardly looking up from the screen; not necessarily in a rude way, but in the way you might greet someone you've known for a long time.

"That's Cole," Leo said, booting up his desktop. "He's bi and likes anime, and honestly that's all you need to know about him."

I smiled and looked at Cole, who didn't react. "I'm sure there are more facets to his personality than that."

Cole looked up and grinned. "Debatable."

Leo tapped at his keyboard. "Fucking anime," he mumbled to himself.

Leo's room looked plucked from a book you'd buy in Urban Outfitters about how having fewer possessions brings us closer to our spiritual selves, or something: white bedsheets and white furniture and white walls that were mostly bare, only home to a framed picture of himself and his brother that hung above the headboard. In it, they're both in nice pressed shirts in some green-looking place.

Leo caught me looking at it and I was intensely embarrassed, but he didn't seem to mind. "Yeah," he said, "that was the one thing I was allowed to keep up."

"What do you mean?"

"This place looked like—I mean, straight up, it was some John Nash shit. I put everything on the walls. Any pictures I could find. Pictures of us. Stuff from his room. Old schoolwork. To the point where I was hiding it because I knew it was fucking *weird*. Like, I tried to keep Mom out for as long as I could. Even Cole didn't know about it. Mom saw and had me take it down. Turned out, instead of grieving, I was building a shrine, which might sound not all that bad, but—"

"It was," Cole said.

Leo sighed, then looked toward me. "You know that feeling where, like, the world is spinning at a thousand miles an hour and there's nothing you can do to stop it and then you start to feel like there's nothing you can do about anything ever?"

"Yeah," I said, because I sort of did.

He shrugged. "I wanted something to do that was…tangible. Something that I could look at and say, hey, I have the power to impact this."

I found myself with an unwelcome curiosity: how he'd done it. His brother. Was it in the house? But for maybe the first time, that went away, because looking at Leo and this lone picture on his wall was enough to affirm for me that really, it didn't matter at all. I didn't need the gory details. I didn't want them. All that mattered was that he was gone, and Leo was alive to deal with it.

And then the subject of my visit came up: the list.

I'd made a list of all of Dad's patients based on the folders, and we were planning on doing a thorough search of each and seeing if anything incriminating came up. Leo had convinced me. I'd been hesitant at first, and still wasn't entirely comfortable with it, but he seemed confident we'd find something.

Leo and I began to sort through the names. He started from *A* and I worked backward from *Z*, and even though we had music playing and were joking occasionally, I was growing increasingly frustrated. There was almost nothing about anyone online, and even when there was, I felt strange—guilty, mostly, because we really shouldn't have been going through the names in the first place, but also annoyed because this felt completely pointless. Just because someone had driven drunk once didn't make them a serial killer.

But Leo insisted. Because we had to do something.

Doing something, though, wasn't really the same thing as accomplishing anything, and I grew disillusioned with the activity quickly. We weren't going to find anything. I continued looking only to appease him.

Eventually, he said what I'd been in equal parts anticipating and dreading: "June Copeland." Leo smirked at me.

I smiled, the way I did involuntarily when anyone so much as mentioned her name. "Yeah. She's there."

"Let's see what secrets I can uncover here."

"Good luck," I said. "I've tried."

Leo snorted beside me. He took a long sip of black coffee, then smacked his lips. "Yeah, I've been there."

Cole looked up from his DS. "Creep found my SoundCloud."

Leo continued clicking every so often, then said eventually, "There is seriously nothing about this girl anywhere."

"Are you actually looking? I think she can be skipped."

"Can she?" he said, then turned to me and raised his eyebrows.

I leaned in to look at his screen. He'd found the pictures of her on the Pleasant Hills website. "I've already looked at all of this stuff. This is all you'll find."

"So *you* certainly didn't skip her."

"I was looking more for...leisure."

"You're obsessed with her, aren't you?"

"Not obsessed," I said, lying.

Leo arrived at the picture of June and Heath being crowned king and queen at homecoming. "*Oof.* Who's this fucking alpha male? Blond preppy fantasy. Take me to your parents' charity function."

He tilted his screen so Cole could see, but Cole shrugged and said, "Eh."

"His name's Heath."

"Okay. What's the story on *Heath*?"

I slumped down, my hand keeping up my head and squishing my cheek. "He's loaded. His dad's the city attorney, him and June are madly in love, blah blah. And he has a dead mom, so I can't even say that I've, like, felt more worldly hurt than him. Him and June have been dating for, uh, like, three and a half years."

"No. Weird. That's weird. No one in high school who's normal dates someone for that long."

"You think?"

"Mm. What are they like together?"

"They seem happy." I thought of Heath in the darkened car after New Year's: *She's been happy.*

"What about you?"

"What about me?"

"Are *you* happy?"

"I-I mean—"

"Do you love her?"

I froze. Couldn't even keep myself from smiling. Someone had said it, and it wasn't me. "That's a jump…"

"You do. You love her."

I'd been pushing back the word so as not to even entertain the idea. I couldn't love this girl. Not here. Not now. So I said something else that I knew was true, at least: "She makes me feel like all this is worth it."

Leo and Cole looked at each other, then both at me at the same time, realizing, I think, that by *all this* I meant living. I worried I'd said something wrong. Leo spoke. "If that's not love, princess, then I don't know what is."

And if all of these things were a foundation, there was one pillar groaning under the weight: June had been growing distant.

Our car rides became quieter around that day with Leo, actually, as if speaking about her so freely had completely ruined everything. At first, I assumed it was a result of us being closer or more comfortable and not thinking of the silences as awkward—after all, she'd invited me to go to Spring Fling in a group with her and Heath—but then she was late for the first time one morning. She started to become harder to find after last period. And when I did spend time with her, she wasn't laughing at the same things—at anything, really. I worried I'd cursed it, or done something wrong, or maybe she'd finally grown bored of me.

On the last Monday of March, Greg made a point of finding me during lunch, huddled in the computer lab.

"Hey. I've been looking for you forever. What are you doing here?"

The truth was, I'd been coming here so regularly during lunch period the librarian didn't even make me sign in anymore. "I, uh... Don't worry. What's up?"

He pulled out a chair beside me, sat on it the wrong way with his arms draped over the back. "Oh, this is kind of out of the blue but honestly, I think you spend more time with her than any of us—has June seemed sort of off to you lately? Man, I don't know. They've both been kind of weird. Spending less time together. Acting cold."

I didn't know how to take this. Mainly, I felt a vague sort of flattery that *I* was the one he wanted to consult. Was I really who she spent most of her time with? I felt a sense of possession. Like I had been asked to speak for her.

But the truth was: No. I hadn't noticed anything weird about either of them. Mostly, I think, because I rarely saw them together—and June barely ever brought up Heath. This was a character trait of hers that I had appreciated so far, but now I was wondering why I hadn't seen there was something strange about that.

I told Greg all of this.

"Yeah," he said, "I haven't seen much of June lately and...eh. I'm sure it's fine, but, you know."

"Well...what do you think's wrong?"

He shrugged. "I don't really know."

The most selfish part of my brain whispered that maybe the deterioration of their relationship had something to do with my influence. Maybe she did feel something for me.

But when I went to meet her to go home later that day, that didn't seem to be the case.

The pair of them were standing outside June's car. I wouldn't have even known they were arguing had it not been for her hands—they were locked together in front of her stomach, and she pressed down each of her knuckles over and over, even after they'd stopped cracking. Her shoulders slumped forward, the small of her back resting against the car, like she'd been cornered. Heath was talking, but I was too far off to hear, and he was turned away, so I couldn't even read his lips.

When I approached, there was a lightning-quick swapping of looks: me at June, June at Heath, Heath at me.

Heath spun to face me. "Ah. This is embarrassing," he said, scratching the back of his head.

I decided to play dumb. "What?"

"Heath's gonna ride home with us," June said without looking at me, then pushed herself up, maneuvered past Heath, and went to open the driver's-side door. "Come on."

"Sorry," Heath said, his eyes pained, overly apologetic. "I hope that's all right."

"Yeah, that's—that's fine."

We climbed inside wordlessly, Heath in the front and me in the back, then pulled out into the sluggish current of two-thirty traffic.

Something was awkward, and I wasn't sure what.

Obviously, the fact that Heath was there at all was unnerving. This was mine and June's time, unfettered by the baggage we left outside the confines of this sacred place. The fact I considered him *baggage* at all was an issue, I knew, but still, I didn't like him there, in my seat—though I was getting a normally inaccessible view of the back of June's head.

"Is everything okay?" I offered to anyone who wished to answer.

Heath did. "Oh, everything's fine. Greg drove me this morning but had to stay late today, so I needed to hitch a ride back. No biggie."

"Oh. No, that's fine, I guess I meant..."

"It's all good, Whitaker," June said.

I wasn't sure how much I should share. "So, Greg asked me about you guys today, actually."

"Yeah," Heath said, "he'll do that."

"He said you guys have seemed off."

Heath strained against his seat belt to face me. "He did?"

"Yeah, he was asking if I knew anything, or, uh, noticed anything weird. Which I hadn't. Not really." *Until now.*

June repositioned herself in her seat.

"Don't worry about it," Heath said, apparently fighting to get the words out; he looked pleadingly to June, and then to me. "Sydney, to tell you the truth, we've been going through a rough patch."

June said nothing.

"Natural relationship peaks and valleys," he continued. "It happens to the best of us. We try not to clue anyone in because—well, you know how people are. They talk. Speculate. As you've experienced today. So clearly we're not doing a good enough job." I watched as he took June's limp hand and squeezed.

"Okay. I'm—I guess it's not really any of my business," I said.

"Yeah," Heath said. "I guess it's not."

"Hey, Whitaker," June said, all of a sudden a lot more chipper. "Since the weather's broken, are you fine to start taking your bike again?"

"I…" What was this? "I mean, yeah. Sure." Since Heath was there, I felt like it'd be too much to dissent.

June wouldn't even look at me in the rearview mirror—but she must have noticed the disappointment in my voice. "I thought you liked riding your bike."

"Yeah, I do." *But I like you more.*

"Exercise!" Heath chimed in. "It's good for you."

What was happening? Heath seemed blissfully unaware of the weight of what June had asked. *June* seemed unaware. I thought she liked these rides. I thought she liked *me*. Because without the ten minutes there and ten minutes back, I wouldn't see her at all. Nothing left to hold on to.

My chest clenched. Everything she left unsaid filled me up, and while we drifted quietly through downtown, I couldn't shake the thought that I was in some stranger's car, that I'd been hoodwinked, that all the signs of affection I'd worried I'd imagined really *had* been imagined, and this whole time I'd been completely delusional, obsessed with a girl who never thought about me at all. Why didn't she tell me anything?

Why didn't she tell me *anything*?

"Why don't you tell me anything?"

No one spoke.

But I had said it. And I wasn't sure why I was choosing this moment to do something about it. I guess I'd had enough: I realized I was losing her, my twenty minutes a day of sanity, and I felt I at least deserved to know why.

June actually looked at me now in the mirror. "What?"

Heath scratched the back of his head.

"You don't tell me anything. You *never* tell me anything. Everything is so vague and mysterious with you, like you're doing it on purpose."

"Sydney, I promise you, you don't want to—"

"Hey," Heath interjected, facing me. "I think you should calm down."

I was calm. "I am calm."

"You seem very antagonistic."

"What are you—"

"We're here!" June said, too loud. "We're here anyways, so. This conversation can end now."

We turned on to the cul-de-sac, then into my driveway.

I didn't move. None of us did.

And then I got out, said nothing, and slammed the door behind me.

I was very aware of the existence of her folder when I got to my room.

I could check it. Know everything. I could help, maybe. If I knew—maybe I could finish whatever Dad had started. I could *do* something. I was so sick of being left in the dark when I felt that June knew everything humanly possible to know about me. What could be in there that she was hiding? What was so important? What was so terrible?

And then something occurred to me.

First as a little almost-joke. A jab to my stomach. Something silly, horrible, pinching myself to see if it would hurt.

Maybe it had been June.

Ha.

I had trusted her almost instantaneously, after all. I had never even considered it.

Ha-ha. Imagine that.

But then the thought morphed into something real. Bea had refused to acknowledge me. Because she felt guilty. And the messages had stopped. But June, growing cold... Maybe *she* felt guilty.

Something happened between her and my dad. Something happened. What happened? What did that mean?

What would it say?

So many times I'd envisioned Anonymous typing out the messages, leaving the book, breaking in. I'd watched their hands as they cut Dad's brakes, then I'd followed the arm up to the face but there was never anything there. A clean, flabby surface where the guilty party should have been.

And now the face was June's.

No. That didn't make any sense at all.

It might have been more innocent than that. Who was I kidding? It probably was. It had to be.

Suddenly, I wasn't sure I wanted to open the folder anymore.

I wasn't sure I even wanted to remember it existed.

I tried to ground myself, but I had nothing to hold on to, and the wave swept over my head and dragged me out into a sea of ink.

Dad. Dead Dad. Dead Dad for no reason, no point, no purpose. Fuck domino effects. Fuck *everything happens for a reason*. Fuck it, fuck it, absolutely fuck all of it to hell.

I sobbed quietly into my hands so Mom wouldn't hear, and prayed for the first time since I was eight in Sunday school. That this could be solved. That this all could end. Dad. Mom. Olivia. Leo. June. Me. *Let's all melt. Let's all liquefy. Let's all forget any of this ever happened.*

13

I RODE MY BIKE TO and from school for the rest of the week, sort of begrudgingly. It was only the end of March, so it wasn't even like it was *that* warm, and the vestiges of cold seemed to sting even worse than usual because June had forced them upon me, and I wasn't sure what I'd done to deserve it. I was spoiled; this time the year before I would have happily ridden all the way through winter without complaint, but now I was rotten with the sense that I was owed something more than what I was receiving.

And that sense, even more so, was amplified when Olivia knocked on my door for the fourth time in two weeks; something this time compelled me to answer instead of getting Mom to say I wasn't feeling well.

It was the Wednesday before Spring Fling, and she was standing on my doorstep in her pajamas. Seeing her here felt odd, like she was somewhere she wasn't supposed to be.

We exchanged pleasantries.

"So," she said, "how are things?"

Was this an interrogation? I felt the urge to flee, but I was tied down. "Yeah. Things are—they're okay."

"How's *June*?"

"June's...fine."

"Good." Olivia shuffled her slippered feet. "Would you like to ask what I've been up to?"

Ah. This was going well. I could practically hear the creak of my fingernails being pulled. "Sorry. What have you been up to?"

"Well, opening night is in two weeks, so I've been pretty busy with that."

I blinked.

"For...the spring musical. *Guys and Dolls*. Did you not even know what—"

"Liv, I'm sorry—what are you doing here?"

She scoffed. "Oh. Okay. We're getting right into it, I guess."

"No, it's just that it's late, and—"

"Sure. It's late. Sorry to keep you from preparing to go to bed at, what, four in the morning?" I went to speak, but she stopped me. "Come on. Your bedroom lights are always on."

I didn't say anything.

"I wanted to know what you were doing for Spring Fling."

"I—I think I'm going in a group with June and Heath."

"You think?"

"I'm going in a group with June and Heath."

"Right. Are you…going *with* anyone?"

I nodded. "The kid from my support group who I told you about. Leo. He goes to Collins, but—"

"Listen. Miles broke up with me."

"Oh."

"Yeah."

"I'm sorry."

"Yeah, me too. It was pretty messy. Though I'm not sure you're *all* that sorry because this happened, like, seventeen days ago, and you'd think if you cared you would have, I don't know, mentioned it."

"How was I supposed to know if you didn't tell me?"

"Well, that was the thing. I wanted to. But you don't come to lunch anymore, and you always rush out of English, and I tried seeing if you were here a few times, but you were never in—or you were, and were pretending like you weren't, so—"

"*Liv.*" I ground my molars. "Did you come here to—I don't know. Be passive-aggressive?"

Olivia wrapped her arms over her stomach and fixed her eyes on her feet. "No. I wanted to ask you to do something that will probably cause me to reevaluate our relationship, based on your answer."

"What does that mean?"

"Skip Spring Fling. I can't go, because I'm sure as heck not going by myself, and I don't want to see Miles there, and I thought we could stay in and catch each other up, or whatever, because I honestly have *no* idea what's going on with you right now, and we can, I don't know. Watch YouTube and order pizza and...act...normal."

"Act normal," I repeated.

"Yeah," Olivia said.

"You know I can't." Act normal. Call off the dance. It really didn't even matter which one I was talking about.

Her face didn't change. She didn't even flinch. "Why do I *know* you can't?"

"Because you're only asking me now," I said, "and we already made plans. It's in three days. It wouldn't be fair to Leo, or—"

"To June, right? It wouldn't be fair to June?"

I frowned. "Yeah, I guess, I—is that why you're mad? Are you seriously mad about this? What am I supposed to do? It would be rude of me to—"

"We both know you're not worried about being *rude*. God. Sydney Whitaker worried about being *rude*. That's new. I'm really not an idiot, but you think I am, for some reason, even though I've gotten consistently higher grades than you since we were eight—"

"I don't think you're an idiot."

"It's about June. It's all about her, isn't it? It's all about her, and you're willing to go to some dance you and I both know you don't want to go to so you can buzz around her like some desperate little fly."

I didn't let her know how much that hurt. "I already said yes."

Olivia looked up at me, her eyes huge and imploring, bright even in the dark. "You seriously don't get it. You don't get that I would do anything for you. And I ask you to do *one* thing for me, and you just can't, and I get that you *love* her or whatever and she helps you and makes you feel something and okay, that's fine, but it's this one thing. One thing. I need you to say *Sorry, June, but my best friend of, like, eleven years, needs me for literally three hours of my existence—*"

"June needs me too," I said.

Olivia shook her head. "She doesn't."

"How would you know? You don't know anything about her."

"Neither do you."

My cheeks went red hot, but I wasn't embarrassed; I was angry. "You don't know what you're talking about."

"June's on another level. It's obvious. And"—she rolled her eyes— "you've been riding your bike again. She dumped you."

"That's not what happened—"

"Holy crap. You're totally delusional! About everything! You are actually delusional about everything."

"Are you done?"

"I get it. I get that you went through something awful, and you're still really struggling—like, obviously, you're still really struggling. But you're still going around like—like someone killed him. You still think that."

My stomach dropped. "What?"

Olivia took a step toward me. "No one killed your dad. It was an accident, Sydney. It was an *accident*. People die in car accidents all the freaking time. It's, like, in the top ten leading causes of death. I know at the beginning, I was maybe, like, not telling you that up front, or maybe I was playing along, but now I realize that was probably the worst thing I could have done because I was enabling you, or something…"

The corners of my vision went black and splotchy. "So you were making fun of me, right? From the beginning."

"God, I wasn't making fun of you, but—"

"But you saw everything. The messages, you—you threw the book in the fire. You know someone broke in. I told you everything."

"Yeah, all right, I don't know if you've noticed, but you're not exactly the most liked individual in the junior class. It's some persistent asshole messing with you. And I can see how you would think this is all some huge conspiracy against you, because, let's face it, you're not thinking straight—"

"But you were telling people about the messages. Heath—"

"I didn't tell anyone."

"You're lying."

"Great. Call me a liar. Perfect."

And then it clicked. I wasn't sure I believed it myself. But I knew it would rattle her, and I couldn't stand more lecturing about any and all of my human faults, so I said it: "You know, the cop said... After the person smashed the picture, he said there weren't any signs of forced entry."

"Okay. So?"

"You're the only person with a house key."

Olivia considered this, let the weight of the faux accusation settle over us. "You're *fucking* unbelievable," she finally said. She never swore. "You're, you're a *bitch*. You have been so mean, and so selfish, and I have no idea why everyone thinks helping you is so important because you *never* want to help anyone else. I get it about your dad, and like, even if I don't get it, I do, because I miss him too. And just because you're having a bad time doesn't mean everyone else isn't.

And I know that I'll never know you well enough to help you because you're so *deep*, I guess."

"You didn't even try to help me."

"Are you actually kidding me right now?"

"No. You didn't do shit. You came to the funeral, then gossiped about how fucked up I was, and then you linked me to some articles, and that was it. And you didn't believe me when I needed you to."

"I don't believe you because I'm not *insane*!"

"And then you throwing this on me, like, like some stupid *test* is so unfair. A friendship shouldn't be determined by some fucking ultimatum."

"You know what? You're right. This was never gonna work. You've obviously been checked out for months. This was pointless."

"Yeah. Maybe it was."

Olivia took a step backward. I wished she'd fall. "Yeah, okay, cool. Great. Have fun pining over some straight girl. That'll end well. Oh, and looking for a *murderer*. Sweet. Cool. Enjoy."

And then she turned on her heels and stormed away.

"By the way, I lost the freaking house key. It's for the best. I don't want anything more to do with you, anyway."

But I wasn't listening anymore. I shut the door too hard.

I wanted to scream.

I threw myself onto my bed, scrunched a pillow around my face like I was trying to suffocate myself, and absolutely wailed into it.

She doesn't need you. She doesn't need you.

Olivia was the sole messenger of everything I had feared was true, and hearing it aloud made me feel like I was choking, falling, dying.

I imagined myself stealing away to open June's folder in the middle of the night, but instead of answers, it was full of blood.

The day of the dance arrived without further incident.

Mostly. I still felt the hollowness in my stomach that let me know something bad was probably going to happen, though I felt that all the time, so it wasn't like it was very accurate. And anyway, the dance felt like an incident in itself. This wasn't how it was supposed to go. I was supposed to have a group of friends, like, eight of them, and we were supposed to all get ready together and then take pictures with our awkward dates, and even *my* version of normal, which was spending that time with Olivia, wasn't happening. Instead, my best friend hated me, I hated my best friend, and a girl I'd known for five months and a boy I'd known for even less than that were the center of my universe.

June. She'd make this all okay. Wouldn't she? Except after everything that happened, the thought of her wasn't even filling me up like it used to.

But maybe that could change. Maybe there'd be a marvelous shift in the air tonight and everything would feel okay and right. June. Cleaned-up June. June in a dress. June dancing. I so badly wanted to see June dancing.

Did I, though?

Because now, every time I thought of her, my mouth went acidic, and I felt the need to spit to clear the taste away.

So when she called at three that day while I was FaceTiming with Leo, after I'd already put on my tux because I was so excited, my gut splattered across the walls.

"It's June," I said to Leo. "Hold on."

Something was wrong. I knew it.

"Hey, Whitaker."

"Uh, hi. What's up?"

"So, there's been a development: I don't think I'm actually gonna be able to make it tonight."

There it was. Splat. "I…why? What's the matter?"

"Nothing's the matter."

"Why are you—lying, right now?"

A pause. "I'm not lying. Don't worry about it, okay?"

"How can I not worry about it when you—"

"I hope you have a good break, and I hope you and Leo have fun. All right? I'll see you…sometime."

I went to say goodbye, but she'd already hung up.

She didn't even sound upset. Her voice was completely monotone. Like it hadn't meant anything.

Leo's face appeared on the screen, and I think he was looking for a reaction from me, but I stared. "What was that about?" he asked.

I tried to keep the camera pointed at my face as best I could with my shaking hands. "June's not coming."

"Shit. Why? What happened?"

"I really, really don't know. She said she couldn't, and that nothing's wrong." And I wasn't even thinking about it, but I tugged at my bow tie with my free hand until it came loose, because I was angry and confused and could think of nothing else to do. Of course this had happened.

"Uh. What are you doing?"

I blinked back tears. "I don't know."

"Oh. I see what this is." Leo leaned back in his chair. "Don't tell me you're about to say: *Don't come*."

I didn't say anything.

"Do not *tell* me," he continued, "that you're gonna cancel because she's not going. Because that would be really, really stupid."

"No, I—"

"I have a beautiful rented tuxedo hanging over my door right now, and so help me, I'm wearing it. So here's the deal. I'm going to go put it on. I'm gonna lint roll it. And then I'm going to be at yours at"—he tapped the screen to check the time—"five thirty, when we are going to get a five-star meal at Ol-*eev* Gar-*dain*." He said it with a French accent.

"It's Italian," I said.

Then, in the flattest version of his usual accent, he said, "It's-a me, Olive Garden."

I laughed. I couldn't help it.

"And then—and then we're going to go to the dance and have a perfectly marvelous time, with or without the blessing of your special gal pal."

"Leo—"

"No. It's happening." And then, more seriously, quieter: "Your whole life can't revolve around this girl. It's not healthy. You can be happy without her, you know."

I couldn't even argue. No. It wasn't healthy. "She's all that helps."

"Yeah, in the same way a pacifier *helps* a baby who would prefer to spend half its existence sucking on a teat. Teats," he said, "are not forever."

"I know."

"Do you?"

"Mm."

"Repeat it."

"Teats are not forever."

"Put your tie back on. You look sloppy."

"Duly noted."

"Okay. Tell you what: I'm gonna shower. You can collect yourself in the meantime. See you in a bit."

"Bye, Leo. Thanks."

I did as he told me, because of course I did. Retied my bow tie, straightened my hair, stared at myself in the mirror for a really long time.

Mom started cooing and getting all teary and stuff when I came downstairs. She actually looked really, genuinely happy. "You look beautiful. Or handsome?"

"Either's fine."

She grabbed handfuls of my hair and draped them around the front of my shoulders, wound her hands through it, sort of shook it around my face. "You look just like your father," Mom said.

"You're only saying that because it's the thing people say in movies."

"No, you do. Your features are more from me. Well, more from your grandma. Same difference. But you and your dad have that same look in your eyes."

I smirked despite myself. "What look?"

She put a warm hand on my cheek and let it sit, looked through me instead of at me. "Like you know too much."

Leo arrived when he said he would, pulling up the driveway in his secondhand Buick. I met him there before he could even ring the doorbell.

"Look at you!" he said, clutching a little plastic container with my corsage.

He wrapped me in a hug that felt tighter than usual, and I breathed him in; he smelled like some generic dude cologne, but it was comforting regardless. "Thank you for everything," I said.

Mom made us take pictures in the front yard, which I wasn't happy about but Leo relished, positioning me like a mannequin into all manner of awkward prom positions.

We did go to Ol-*eev* Gar-*dain* two towns over, where we gorged ourselves on unlimited bread sticks, and when the waitress called us a lovely couple, we didn't correct her.

And by the time we got to the high school, I felt I had loosened up. I told Leo this.

"It was probably the bread sticks," he said.

We joined the horde of kids all funneling in, moving like a school of fish, like one sentient mass. "Where are all the Black people?" Leo asked after scrutinizing the crowd. "Am I in *Get Out*? Is this actually an auction?"

"Pleasant Hills, dude."

"Mmph. Pleasant, indeed."

We made our way through the entrance, past a parent-run bag check. Bea's mom said hello to me but gave both of us a double take.

Balloons dotted the floor and hovered above us; fairy lights flickered along the walls, whole strings of them strewn everywhere, across the ceiling, on the floor, along the tables.

I was looking for June at first. Of course I was. I kept thinking I saw her, but no one else had hair like her, so really I was kidding myself. Leo noticed I kept looking, so once we'd filed into the gym, which was packed and loud and full of black lights, he physically turned my head to face him and said, with no ounce of romance or misunderstanding or malice, and his hands on my face, "Hey. Be here with me, now."

At first it felt like a betrayal.

But then it became completely stupid and completely fun. We didn't know any of the words to the songs, but it didn't matter. The lights bounced from his face to mine, and his tie became looser, and I thought of how, if Gerry could see us, she would shout, "Oh, finding joy in the darkness! That's what life is all about!" My cynicism leaped from me in the form of sweat and belly-laughter and shrieks that came from deep in my throat. Leo spun me and twirled me, and the cringey DJ was about thirty-two, and we said, *What is he doing at a high school?* He kept playing these bad songs, and we laughed and laughed and laughed, fast-danced to the fast songs and slow-danced to the slow ones, and Leo was so much taller than me that my arms couldn't wrap around him so my hands sort of sat around his neck, as though I was very half-heartedly attempting to strangle him, and we laughed at that too.

And that was the world, for a bit. A world without June, without Dad, without death. Leo felt like the most important and wonderful thing.

It was the first time I'd felt like maybe Dad would've looked at me from above and thought, *Oh, thank God, she's not a total wreck.*

In a blink it was over. They played the last song, and the lights went up, and now it was bright enough to see what we'd done, bright enough to see the layer of sweat glistening on Leo's forehead and—he told me—the melted mascara underneath my eyes.

Everyone began to file out, laughing and talking loudly. I imagined their heads were still floating around near the ceiling. Leo and I hung back, waiting for people to leave first so we wouldn't have to squeeze through the too-small double doors. My cheeks hurt from smiling, my calves from jumping, and my head from the unexpected assurance that maybe, *maybe*, everything, someday, was going to be okay.

Then my phone buzzed.

fuck

fuck

fuck

fuck

My blood ran cold.

Leo noticed my face had changed, but I did my best to blink my expression away. "Could you do me a favor and grab our coats?"

"Yeah. What's…?"

I couldn't show him. It'd ruin the night. This wasn't supposed to be happening. "Please?" I practically begged, one moment away from kneeling and clasping my hands together: *Please, don't look.*

He nodded and shuffled away, but now, alone, I felt overwhelmingly as though I was being watched, and found a quiet spot behind the bleachers.

The texts wouldn't stop. *Buzz. Buzz.*

What had happened? Were they here? At my house? My mind spun, trying to keep up with my fears, trying to conceive of every possible worst-case scenario, trying to figure out what to do—

A tap on my shoulder.

"Hey, Whitaker."

14

JUNE.

I whipped around and almost shed my fucking skin, first from fear and then from confusion, and honestly there was too much stimulation, and my body had no idea how to process it, so I froze. She looked at me expectantly, mouth pursed in a weak smirk.

Her dress matched the bright red on her lips, straps wilting off the sharp drop of her shoulders. Her hair was coiled in its usual curls except she'd wrapped the pieces at the front away from her face, leaving room for the canopies of her eyelashes and the glitter she'd pressed on to her cheeks. She was beautiful—she was always beautiful—but her mascara was smudged, and her lipstick smeared, and broken red lines ran along the whites of her eyes.

I should have been happy to see her. I was, sort of. But something was wrong.

"What are you doing here?" I asked, because it had to be asked eventually so I figured I'd get it out of the way. I pocketed my phone nonchalantly, hoping she hadn't seen—or if she had seen, she wouldn't ask.

"So, it's a long story," June said. "What are *you* doing here?" I figured she was referring to the fact that I was behind the bleachers, conferring with some balled-up napkins and stray confetti. I would have been embarrassed had I not been so worried.

"It's a long story," I echoed. "Did you just get here?"

"A little bit ago, yeah."

"You came right as it ended?"

"Mm. But I'm here now. So."

I couldn't decide what she wanted me to say. "Well, you kind of… missed it."

"I didn't really come for the dancing. Also, your tie is coming off. How amateur." She grabbed hold of each end and looped it with her fingers, dancing while my body stiffened at the sudden closeness.

"You can tie bow ties?"

She shrugged. "Heath."

"Where is he? Is he here?"

"Nope. Just me."

I didn't know what else to say, so I said what I was thinking: "You look really nice."

"So do you," she said. My flesh rippled with goose bumps.

"I mean, do you want to go, I don't know—do you want to go do something? It sucks that you came all the way... Me and Leo were gonna go hang out at mine for a bit. You can come with us if you want. I mean, I'd also want you to come. I'm sure you'd get along with Leo. He, he goes to Collins and..."

June shook her head. "No, I don't think so."

"What do you mean? What's the matter?"

She shook her head again and looked at all of me, eyes big and pained and beautiful, then lowered her gaze to the floor. "I don't think that's a good idea. But I'm here for the time being, so..."

"Well, okay. That's fine. What do you want to do? We can sit, or... They're cleaning up, but I bet there's probably some pizza left, so maybe we could..."

"Honestly, I'm kinda bummed I didn't get to..." And then her right hand traveled upward, moved a little too swiftly along my bicep and then farther up, toward my collarbone, around my neck, then behind, and then her left hand followed and arrived beside the other. They linked together behind me.

I froze and melted, froze and melted, until my atoms drifted and split and died.

This was happening. This was happening here and now.

"Is this okay?" she asked.

"Yes," I murmured, intending the word to sound decisive, but it ended up being hardly more than a breath. *What do you do? What do you do, now, when you're me?* "But you said you didn't come for the dancing?" Images of Bea and I tucked away in the forest materialized

225

in my head; trees hid about as much as bleachers did, I thought. I wanted to check behind me to see if someone was watching, but I didn't want to scare her away. My arms dangled uselessly at my sides, my hands closed and opened. I was unsure of where they should be or why they were even there at all. It occurred to me then how many *parts* a human body has—how are we ever expected to coordinate everything at the same time? And how every part can feel, a billion little nerve endings... "Are you sure we should be..."

I didn't finish the thought. Neither did June, who led in the rhythmic foot-stepping, looking at me with such a heavy seriousness, such a terrible melancholy, that I sort of felt like crying. "I don't really know."

I laid my hands gently on her waist and held her to me.

Sweat from her neck and chest mingled with sweat from my palms and chest, and I decided I would never shower again, that I would vial up whatever Frankenstein concoction of my and June's liquids was being created and wear it as a necklace or a perfume or a crown.

Multiply it. Bathe in it.

From now on, when the death crept in, this memory was where I would live.

I wanted so badly for her hands to stay on me. I wanted to glue her to me. Actually, no. I was glad she could remove them whenever she wanted. Because she wanted to be here. She initiated. She pulled the strings. I was happy relinquishing control.

I imagined myself out of my body, splatted onto the ceiling, the wall, watching me, watching her, watching us. I'd drip, drip down.

Is this it?

For a moment, I floated. This was the first good float; the first

time it felt correct to be away from my body. One big release of everything pent up, everything validated. I hadn't misunderstood. I wasn't
imagining it. This was all June. It felt like a moment that existed
somewhere else, like this crawl space behind some bleachers was a
fucking rip in the timeline, and we were nestled inside it.

"You should probably sing something," she said.

"Should I?" I pinched the smallest bit of flesh on the inside of
my mouth with my teeth to make sure my senses were keeping up
with whatever, exactly, was happening. I wouldn't want to miss this.
The feeling of her hands on my neck was so foreign and wonderful;
she'd touched me before, exactly like this physically, but there was
something different and stirring about how she did now. "I can't sing."

"Neither can I," she said. She suddenly began belting lyrics to
Abba's "Dancing Queen," clutching my hands and sending the pair of
us lurching in a sort of ballroom dance fashion. She was right. She
couldn't sing. It was completely terrible. I don't think she hit one note.

"June." I laughed despite myself, with her still trying to sing,
as she pitched me around behind the bleachers after Spring Fling. I
wasn't sure why I'd said her name—not necessarily to get her to stop
or to get her attention, but it seemed like saying it would help me grab
hold of the situation. She laughed too. "June, someone's gonna—"

She screamed. "*Dancing queen—*"

"Someone's gonna hear—"

"Dancing queen, feel the—"

"*June.*"

"Okay!" We jolted to a stop. She grabbed my biceps, too hard this
time, and I pulled back, sort of from the shock. "Okay. That's fine."

My arms were sore where she'd squeezed them. "What do you mean, that's fine?"

June's face shifted, and she pulled me into her. I was holding her now, my whole world the smell of her neck and the frizz from her curls.

When she repositioned her head, her lips sort of brushed up against the side of my cheek; this was different. I was absolutely sure about it. There was something so intimate about this, from the way her hands pressed into my back with too much familiarity, to the way her breaths came out in shallow gusts. This was different. This was new and wonderful and everything I'd wanted—everything I'd wanted! June in the driver's seat! June pressed to me. June here. June now.

But it was all wrong.

This was all wrong.

It was all suspended in the air, hanging from the ceiling, limbs dangling—

The folder. June not telling me anything.

I felt myself stiffen. "What's happening?" I said.

"I wish I could..." She said that all dreamy, which only bothered me more. Was she crying?

I moved away, pushing her off my arms. Immediately there was a terrible, aching absence where her body had been. Her against me was wrong and her away from me was wrong.

June looked at me, shocked, scared, like she'd been sleepwalking and woke up here, or maybe like it was me who'd brought her here, but after considering it for a moment, I realized that no, my memory was completely intact and this was all her doing. "What's *happening?*"

June looked around. "That was bad," she said, brushing herself down, like I'd left some residue she wanted rid of. "That was so bad and stupid. I shouldn't even be here."

"What just happened?"

She dragged her hand down her face. "I don't know."

As the bliss left me, the anger arrived. She turned away; I heard the *click* of her knuckles. "No, June," I said, and she turned back, because she knew I was dead serious. "What just happened?"

Her eyes went filmy. "I don't know," she said again, shaky and uncertain this time.

"You can't—you can't do—I mean, Heath…" I was a hypocrite. I was the world's biggest hypocrite. I was actually defending his honor or whatever, even though I'd thought about his girlfriend in various states of intimacy a million times over the past five months.

June hardened. "Yeah," she said. "Heath. Yeah. Cool. Heath. I'm sorry. Okay? I don't know what to tell you." The *sorry* jumped out of her throat and crumpled awkwardly on the ground, lying between us like a corpse.

"Why are you crying?"

"I wish I could say more than that. I wish I could tell you more. I can't."

"Okay. I mean, is that it, then?" I asked. "Should I go?"

"You don't have to."

"Really? I think I do." I hated this. I got everything I ever wanted in one second, and it only made me angry. Didn't make me feel better at all. Surprise, surprise.

Behind June, Leo stepped forward, my coat in his hand.

June followed my gaze and jerked when she realized someone had seen us. So she was worried. "Don't worry. That's Leo," I said.

She nodded. "Okay."

Leo stood there with his mouth slightly agape and my coat dangling from his hooked arm.

I didn't say anything. Just left.

Everything was wrong.

Leo and I drove in silence.

What had that been? Bait? A trick? I felt like I had fallen for something, somehow. I wondered what June was doing, if she was still hiding in the gym, if she'd gone home to Heath. Pretended like nothing had happened. I took a secret pleasure in her having to deal with the aftermath.

It was more fun, I decided, to want than it was to get.

The nights I'd spent thinking of that exact thing happening had been exhilarating. I'd go through the details over and over, how her face would look and feel, and what she'd smell like, and the things she'd say. But now it had happened. And for some reason it was all only uncomfortable and sad.

Things would be different now. They had to be. I was hesitant to find out how they would be, because I feared I wouldn't like the answer.

But more than anything, I decided, there was something she wasn't telling me.

The messages. There was clearly something wrong. I hadn't gotten to ask. I was too flustered. I had her all to myself. I could have asked, and she could have explained everything—

And I was thinking about all this while Leo and I drove out of the parking lot, fighting against the post-dance traffic. We'd left ten minutes ago but were still in line to leave.

"You ready to talk?"

"Not particularly."

"Traffic is a perfect time to talk."

"Yeah, because we're *trapped.*"

"Okay, well, if you don't talk I'll talk for you. Blink once for yes and twice for no. Firstly—you got another text. Obviously. Right?"

I did a long, exaggerated blink. "What did it say?"

"That's not a yes or no question."

"Then blink in Morse code," Leo said. "Or, hey, here's an idea: tell me. With your mouth. And the sound that emerges."

"They kept texting me the word *fuck.*"

"What? That's the creepiest shit, I—Okay, wait, so, June? What happened?"

"It's complicated. It's complicated because I know if I tell you what happened you're gonna be like, *Oh, why's that a bad thing?* which I won't be able to explain besides that... It just. Felt. Bad."

"Okay."

"She—we danced, I guess. We danced. It was nice. Until it wasn't."

"What, because of...what's his name?"

"Heath. Yeah, I guess. And...I don't know. I don't know. She's so weird, dude. She's so weird. I don't—I don't know what she wants

231

me to do. And this whole time there's been the *file*, a literal fucking file containing probably everything about her in my dad's desk, and I could *open* it, I could see…"

"Okay, don't get mad at me, but I was thinking about this the other day, and I wasn't sure, but now it seems…ah. Is it possible that maybe she's the one that's—"

"Sending the texts." Leo looked at me. "Yeah. Yeah." I looked at the window. "I've thought about that."

"Based on the timeline you gave me… All the messages seem to coincide with her."

"With her doing what?"

"When you're around her. The funeral. The day you met her at the cemetery. And now this. You've gotten all the texts at milestones with her. I mean, Sydney…that folder, man. What if opening it solves all this?"

I willed the car to sink into the ground so I wouldn't have to talk about this any longer. "Because what if it's something bad, Leo?"

"Then you'll know. Then you'll know for sure that—"

"No. What if it's *bad*? She's…everything. Everything would fall apart."

Leo looked at me with this dumb gobsmacked expression. "Am I hearing this? You're saying you don't even want to know?"

"I don't know. I don't know what I'm saying. Okay?"

"You're thinking about what you want to be true. This isn't what I—"

"Of course I am. She's been there for months, and I'm not sure I'd be able to handle losing that too. Losing her too."

He thought about this for a moment. "If she was never actually there, or, if she wasn't there in the way you thought she was, then you can't really lose her."

"Oh, I can."

"I think you're being shortsighted."

"I think I'm acting in self-preservation. I know what will kill me. This will. And I don't think the truth is more important than that. Than my ability to fucking sleep at night."

"What if it does have something to do with your dad? Is June's—I don't know, sanctity—is she more important than that?"

"I don't know."

"If Alex—if I had known. Right? The extent of it. He told me... God, sorry, I fucking hate talking about this—"

"Then don't. I know what you're going to say."

"No. Let me have my spiel. He told me *some* things. Right? Enough to paint a picture. But a shitty picture. And if I'd had all the details? If I'd known? I don't know. I'm not sure I would have passed that up. Because I could have helped. I could have done something. Talked to him, or...gotten him talking to someone else. Maybe I could have—ah. It doesn't matter. That's all I'm saying. Maybe this is a chance to do something. Not for yourself. For her, maybe. And for your dad."

Then something outside the window caught my eye. A slice of red in the dark.

June was running.

Heels clutched in her hand, she hurried through the parking lot, dress trailing behind her. She wasn't looking back, so she wasn't running *from* something, she was just...running. Got into her car. Accelerated through the parking lot, up and over a curb, forcing herself past the traffic on to the main road in a flurry of shouts and horns.

Leo summed it up. "The fuck?"

I didn't even know what to say.

"What the fuck was that?" he asked.

I shook my head. What could I have done? Gone after her? Something was very wrong, and I didn't know what to do, except—

Open it. I had to open the folder.

I went straight to Dad's office alone, at my request and to Leo's dismay. But I didn't want to be around anyone. Not now. Mom was already asleep, thankfully.

I sat. Breathed. I kept stealing glances at the window June had knocked on, and thought of her in here, with me, remembering how exciting that first night had been, then realizing how far away it all felt now. I tried June's phone again and again, but she wouldn't answer. Tonight it felt like the office was watching me. It was sinister now, wondering, gossiping, taking bets on what I'd do next.

Open it. I had to.

I knelt next to the filing cabinet, key in hand, and turned.

I had to do this. It was for her own good. It was for Dad's own good. This was going to end, and I would know everything, and it wasn't because she was some girl I had a crush on, it was because something was truly deeply wrong, and I only hoped Dad would have approved.

Byers. Conley. Daniels. I froze.

What?

Byers. Conley. Daniels. Copeland. Copeland was missing.

I flicked through slowly at first, not really understanding. Then again, faster, and then through every single folder, thinking maybe I'd put it in the wrong spot or it had got misplaced somehow. But it wasn't there. There was no Copeland.

She was gone.

June was gone.

15

I THOUGHT BACK: I HADN'T moved her. Of course I hadn't. I'd made a point of keeping her there. So who could have taken it? Mom?

Then I remembered: New Year's. The smashed picture.

Someone had been in the office.

Someone had been in the files.

Someone had taken her. Someone must have. Whoever it was who smashed the picture, they knew her folder was in there, somehow, and didn't want anyone else to have it. Someone made sure nobody would read about June…

Or June made sure nobody would read about June.

I wasn't going to wait until the morning. This needed to happen now.

Me: Please text me or call me or come over. Please. I know you don't sleep either

Me: I need to know what's going on.

Me: Please

Me: Please?

Nothing. Total radio silence.

I texted Leo to tell him what was going on, but he didn't reply either. I assumed he had fallen asleep. And then I thought maybe June had fallen asleep too, as some last-ditch effort at optimism, but I knew almost for certain that wouldn't be true. She saw my texts. She saw my calls. And she wasn't responding—but *why*?

I didn't know what to do. What was I supposed to *do*?

The swarm of fears grew and pulsated, completely untamable. If they could *stop*, stand up straight, I could get a good look at them, but the only thing that made any sense was the thing maybe I should have known from the beginning, that June and Dad...

June. Dad.

In a gut punch, I knew what I'd been facing this entire time but had refused to really see—this was all the same thing. The mysteries weren't separate entities at all. They'd been the same this whole time, this incestuous amalgam of all my monsters, a rubber band ball, but instead of rubber bands, they were limbs and flesh and hair, and all of it could be traced back to either Dad or June. Why hadn't I seen?

I looked outside, and in the small hours the world looked sinister, like it was dark out and it'd never be light again.

I even contemplated waking up Mom, but what would she do?

Chastise me for looking for the folder at all, probably. She wouldn't understand. Even if she did, what would she do? There was nothing to do until June decided there was. This was all up to her now. Before, I'd felt a sick sort of pleasure at relinquishing the control of my entire existence to her, but now the thought enraged me.

I floated uselessly around in a half-dazed state through the night and into early morning, mind ticking, spinning—until my phone rang at 3:42.

June. It was June.

I answered, hands shaking, and I needed to get the words out, I needed to—

"June, I don't know what's going on, but God, I really—"

"I can't see you anymore." She blurted it out so loudly, so fast, that I thought she might have been saying it over and over to herself before she called. Like the words didn't actually mean anything. Like she didn't understand what that actually meant. "I can't see you. We can't talk. We can't be friends. Whatever. Anything. Nothing."

She didn't mean that. She couldn't. "June. Okay. Slow—slow down..."

"I'm sorry. That's all I had to say."

I sensed her phone shift—she was going to hang up. "June! I think I know what's happening," I said, a final bluff to keep her there. It worked; the line didn't go dead. I kept talking. "Please go off script. Okay? I—after the dance I wasn't sure, and, uh, I was talking to Leo—sorry—basically, your folder. There was a folder in my dad's desk. Yours. And I went to look for it a few hours ago, and it was gone, June."

She was quiet for a moment. I'd have thought she had actually

238

hung up were it not for her breathing. "What happened to it?" she spat. She was interrogating me. Like this was all my fault, somehow.

I thought about lying. "I thought maybe you would know."

"I don't. Why would I know?"

"Because—because it's *your* folder, June. Whoever broke in on New Year's... They must have taken it. June, you can tell me—was it you? Or, like, you must know if someone would..."

A pause. "What are you saying?"

"I have no idea! I don't know. But those texts or whatever I've been getting—it has to do with this, right? Just tell me that much."

"Listen to me. I promise, you don't know what you're talking about."

"Then tell me! Tell me what I'm talking about. You're right, I don't know, but I feel like I'm at least owed—I don't know, June. I care about you so much," I said. It felt like an admission. "I do. Okay? And I've been scared about this for...for months. Really fucking scared. About everything. I've been scared for me, and for you, and for what it could've meant about Dad, if something happened..."

I sensed June stiffen. "June?"

"I have to go."

"Oh my God, please. Please. I'm begging you not to go right now. Please."

Silence.

She was gone.

I debated calling again, texting again, but I knew that was it. That was my chance, and I'd completely ruined it. Now she was gone for certain.

Her and everyone else.

My trick no longer worked, the floodgates were completely, disgustingly open, and I had no other choice but to feel, feel, feel.

Sunday came and went in a blur, and I felt myself rotting from the inside out. Leo didn't know how to help, which wasn't his fault. It was like asking for help pushing tectonic plates back together after an earthquake. He did say he'd "look into things," but I couldn't imagine that actually consisted of much.

I didn't want to show my face at Olivia's after our argument. I didn't even have the ritual of school to distract me from anything. It was crushing, all-encompassing, and I felt myself petrifying in my bed, like the first week, when all I could think about was dying.

Dead. Maybe I was better off dead. Maybe it would be better if none of this had ever happened at all.

Breathe. Breathe.

June.

You don't have to think about dying if you're dead.

June.

June keeping secrets. June not telling me anything. Who even was she? Who was this June, and who was the June I imagined her to be? June. June decomposing in the driver's seat. There never was a driver's seat at all. The driver's seat had fallen into the Styx with the rest of it. Everything. I imagined a giant sinkhole opening up beneath me, dragging me down, and I didn't think I'd even try to keep myself above the ground. Sure, survival instincts would kick in eventually, but that wouldn't be me. That'd be my body. It was designed to survive. I couldn't fight that. But me? Sydney? She wouldn't do a damn thing.

And then, ten o'clock at night, I got a text.

surprise

If all of this was to do with everything else, then this was actually wonderful news—if June wouldn't tell me anything, then maybe this person might. This was the catalyst that could bring her back.

But...*surprise*? Did they know I'd discovered the folder was missing? Or that June and I had fought?

And then they sent a link.

A link that led, of all places, to the ToD.

The video had been uploaded that morning. Security camera footage. The time stamp on the bottom counted up steadily; it was forty past two in the afternoon.

Car crash. Pretty standard. Pretty boring, actually. It looked like the person had swerved to miss something barely out of frame, drove across the lane of oncoming traffic and hit a pole head-on. The car crumpled, easily as balling a napkin in your fist, like crushing sand, and there was zero movement afterward. From anywhere. You couldn't see anything inside the car, but based on how it folded, you probably wouldn't want to.

The realization came in pieces.

First was the thought that the car looked familiar.

Second was the thought that the street did too.

Third was the date next to the time stamp. September the fourteenth.

And then I played it back slowly. Read the license plate. The world spun. Somewhere outside the galaxy, a black hole devoured a supernova, and somewhere else a new star was born, and somewhere else, Sydney Whitaker watched her dad die over and over and over.

16

I WASN'T MYSELF. NOT THEN.

I was elsewhere. My body remained where it had been, but the *me* had left. My nerves melted away and my eyeballs plucked themselves from their stems and my brain cut its own cord, and eventually all that was left was the meat known as Sydney Whitaker.

And Sydney Whitaker convulses. Sydney Whitaker pinches the loose skin on the inside of her arm until it bleeds. Sydney Whitaker screams, implodes. Sydney Whitaker watches, over, and over, and over, until she convinces herself she was there, until she convinces herself it's someone else, until she convinces herself it's her in the car, gasping for more time while her lungs deflate.

While I watched this happen, all I could think of was how happy I was to reject the corporeal. How happy I was to float.

I watched while Sydney Whitaker flinched at Mom stomping up the stairs, watched as she pointed when Mom came in.

Mom didn't understand. She studied the me-that-wasn't-me for long enough to know it was bad, said: *You're not supposed to be on this; I told you.*

But then she realized what she was watching.

Mom went to leave, moving kind of unnaturally, like she was lagging, like the frame rate wasn't quite right, jerking like some Japanese horror monster.

It's Dad, Sydney and I said at the same time.

Mom already knew. She already knew.

In a blink I was back. I looked up at Mom from the bed with my own damn eyes, my own ringing ears, and my own mangled insides. Everything ached with an intensity I wasn't actually sure I'd experienced before, like this whole time I'd been pretending to grieve and pretending to hurt. But now it was here and pounding in my skull, and I didn't even think I could be free from the pain ever again.

Mom asked how I found the video.

I told her someone sent it to me.

She asked who.

I said the person. The same person it'd always been. That I should have known. That it was only a matter of time.

That did it for her, apparently. Mom left the room and called the police. I could hear most of the conversation, even from upstairs—Mom's half, anyway. She was saying things like "that's not good enough" and "why can't you just find the IP?" I heard her phone clatter down onto the table. Rustle of purse, jangle of keys.

I barreled down the stairs. "Where are you going?"

"To the police station," she said, eyes glazed, movements too erratic, too fast. "I'm sorry, baby. I need to talk to them in person. I won't be long. Well, actually, I might—it's entirely possible I might be long, but either way..."

I moved closer and wrapped her in a hug. Braced my body against her heaving chest, the fabric of her sweater, took one long uninterrupted breath in. This was the funeral. This was the body in the casket. I could practically feel her longing, her body coursing, raging, veins like tiny red rivers. We both knew in that moment that the two of us wanted him back more than anything, more than *anything*, and watching the accident made it all seem so futile, so indiscriminate in the worst possible way. Maybe if we stared long enough, we could reach in and pull him out. There was no reason for it. Not for any of it.

I sobbed into her chest. "Mom," I said, "I'm freaking out, Mom. I'm really, really freaking out."

"I love you," she said, over, over, over.

"I get why you were trying to...move on. I don't want to do this anymore. I don't want to think about this anymore. I hate it. I hate it. I want it to stop."

Mom pulled away with glazed eyes, and fluffed up my hair. I didn't think she knew what else to do. Her wedding ring clanked against my head, but I didn't flinch. "I'll be back," she said. She kissed me on the head. "How about you go and lie down, huh? Don't go anywhere, baby. Stay here."

Then she was gone and I was alone.

What do you do? Where do you go? I was being apprehended on all sides by something less than a ghost; there was nothing to fight. I considered standing in that same spot motionless until Mom came back. Nailing myself to the wall. Or maybe if I lay flat enough against the floor, I could mold into it.

I went back to my room, the adrenaline fading and a new terrible emptiness taking its place. *What do you do?* I couldn't even try to get the video taken down; the police would need to see it. It'd be evidence.

Evidence. Evidence that I was right. That something had happened to him. It couldn't have been random. It couldn't.

How would someone even have access to the footage?

Leo. I was too wired, but Leo would know what to do.

I FaceTimed him; he answered on the fifth ring. "Hey, man," I said, mainly in an unconvincing attempt to sound like I had my shit together, but my voice cracked on the *man.*

"Hey, hey, I've been meaning to talk to you—Wait, what's the matter?"

I wiped my nose with my sleeve. "I need to show you something. Okay? But only if you're okay with watching it. It—the person sent it to me. Anonymous. Whatever. It's a video of my dad."

"A video...of your dad? Of your dad doing what?" The urgency in his voice stoked up my adrenaline again. From this point, there'd be no stopping it.

"It's the crash," I said quickly. "The actual crash. And you can't see anything, like, anything bad, but I need you to know that's what it is before you watch it."

"Oh my God, Sydney. Oh my fucking God. How...?"

"I'm sort of, I don't know. Um. I think I need your help."

"Anything. Did you call the police?"

I ran a trembling hand through my hair. "We tried. They're not really understanding the situation. Mom's on her way to the station, and she said she's gonna actually show them or talk to them or whatever, but honestly, even if they do understand what's happening, would anything happen quick enough? Wait. I'm gonna text you the link now, okay?" I tapped off the chat for a moment and sent it.

"I got it. But what do you want me to do?"

"Do you remember that picture of me and June? And you looked at it, or whatever? All the information you got about it, somehow. Can you do that with videos?"

Leo exhaled. "I don't know, babe. That's tricky. Especially this—what's the ToD? Man, what the fuck is this place? It seems, uh, bootleg. I don't know if...I mean, yeah. I'll try. I can try."

We were quiet for a moment. I watched Leo click, watch, pause. He tried to hide the distress on his face, but I saw it. He glanced back up to me. "All right," he said, not really to me. I think he was calming himself down. "I'm gonna—man. Man. I'll try—I'm gonna look. I mean, it's surveillance footage, obviously. So firstly, this person needs to have access to surveillance footage—but it's a video *of* the surveillance footage, that, you know, they filmed on a phone, or something. So they got access, but they were too scared to download it, or weren't able to download it. Which..."

Who the hell would have access to surveillance footage? "I...
don't know anyone that could..." The pieces were there now, but I
couldn't join them.

"Okay, no, babe, wait. I was looking into this yesterday, after
Spring Fling—there were a couple of things that didn't make sense,
and I think I need to tell you—like, I think I might know—"

An engine rumbled below. A car had pulled into the driveway.

Leo heard it too. "What's happening?"

I pushed myself off the bed, flicked open the blinds. "That's
Heath's car." What was he doing here? Either way, the timing was
perfect. I had to talk to him. I had to tell him that June's folder was
gone—maybe he'd know. He'd *have* to know. If there was anyone on
the planet June actually talked to, it was him. "Leo, I gotta go."

"No! Shit, Sydney, wait, I think—" But the connection was bad
and Leo was pixelated and I couldn't understand him anyway, so I
hung up and rushed downstairs.

Don't go anywhere, baby. Stay here.

I took the stairs two at a time, then left through the front door
and shut it behind me.

It was raining that night, though it didn't register at first; the
blur in my vision and the chill shooting down my spine seemed more
internal than external. Leaves chattered in the wind and broke into
fits of applause whenever a gust hurtled past. Drops plopped against
the concrete and the roof and my brain, quick enough to be indistin-
guishable from one another, fuzzy and constant, like TV static.

Heath.

I had to squint to get a good view of him through the headlights and the rain, and even then, it was barely more than a silhouette. He stood with the driver's-side door open, him behind it with his hands on the top, as if it were a shield. "Sydney! How are you? Sorry to show up so late, but I didn't want this to drag on any longer. I think we need to talk. The three of us."

My stomach dropped.

He knew. He knew how I felt. June must have told him what happened at the dance. "The three of us? Is June here?"

He nodded toward the car. "She's with me."

"I mean, we can talk here, if—"

He shook his head. "No can do. I've been thinking about this for a while—don't worry, I'm not mad, but I've got a whole evening set up for us at mine. Drinks, et cetera. And I'd hate to disturb your mom."

"She's at the...police station."

Heath blinked. "Did something happen? Oh, tell us on the way. This weather's absolutely horrible. Come on. Why don't you sit in front?" He got back inside before I could answer.

My gut flipped and I wasn't sure why.

But June was in there. And I needed to talk to her. I needed answers.

So I moved forward, rain splattering into my eyes, pulled the handle of the passenger door, and lowered myself into the seat.

June was there. In the back seat. She wouldn't even look at me, just faced forward with her shoulders hunched and her eyes closed. "Why did you do that?" she asked so quietly that I wasn't even sure she had asked at all.

"What? What do you mean?" We pulled out of the driveway, rain battering the roof.

What *did* she mean? Why did I get in the car?

My phone buzzed. I slid it from my pocket.

Leo: was trying to tell you. did research. Heath lied to you. mom's not dead?

Who was the only other person who knew about the ToD? My mouth went dry.

Leo: and didn't you say his dad was the city attorney?

The red wrapping paper in the picture June sent. It was the same as the paper around *Healing Homosexuality.*

Leo: he'd have access to the cameras

New Year's. The picture. June's phone.

Olivia wasn't lying. She hadn't told anybody. And the house key—she hadn't lost it. It was stolen.

Heath didn't look at me when he spoke. "Sydney, if you're thinking about calling the police or anything, I'll ask that you don't," he said. "Because if you do, I'll have to crash the fucking car."

17

HEATH ALDERMAN STILL LOOKED PRETTY much the same.

Eyes narrowed, intense, looking at all of you, everything. This was Heath as he'd always been, but now it was different, now it wasn't charming, now it was ugly and putrid and charred.

"Could you put your phone down, please?" he said to me. His gaze didn't waver from the road, and mine didn't from him. His jaw clenched, and the tendons in his hands flexed like he was trying to choke the life out of the steering wheel. "It would make things easier."

That took me a moment to process. When faced with the answers, I'd envisioned myself going red hot, accosting the perpetrator, completely confident in the knowledge that I was correct and this was happening now. But I didn't *want* to believe it. *Nothing's wrong. Filter it out. Avoid chaos.* And that was why I'd gotten in the car. And that was why, when I looked at him now, I still wasn't even sure I hated him. I couldn't process any of it. My brain was not interested in concluding that the person behind everything was at the wheel, had been in my life, had been there all along, and there was nothing, nothing I could do about it.

"Okay," I said, because I didn't know what else to say, because based on the malice in his voice I believed him, because even if he was bluffing, I didn't want to call him on it. "Okay. I'm putting it down." And I did. Slowly. I set it at my feet and left it there—but not before managing to flick open the camera and press *record*, somehow, with my fingers trembling.

He wasn't looking at me when I sat up again. He hadn't seen.

I twisted so I could look at June, but there wasn't much to look at—she was only a heap. Hands clasped together in her lap. Tear tracks on her face glistened in the glow of the streetlights. I tried to get her to look at me, tried to screw my face into some expression pained enough to convey everything I wanted to say to her: *What's happening? What did he do?*

What did he do?

"What's going on?" I tried.

Heath grunted. "I'm still trying to figure that out myself."

June's voice was barely hers. It was smaller than I'd ever heard it, the edges shaky and blurred. "Please just drop us off somewhere. Anywhere. Please. If not me, then Sydney. She has nothing to do with this."

251

He scoffed. "She has everything to do with this."

"We can't do this now, baby. It's not a good time—"

He adjusted the rearview mirror to get a look at her. "Not a good time? What the fuck does that mean? What's a good time for you, then? Clearly what matters is what *you* find convenient. No. When you instigate a relationship's demise, June, you don't get a say anymore. You have *none.*"

I had never heard him speak like this, to her, to us, some sort of evil villain garbage. My body hung uselessly from me, unfamiliar and heavy and clenching, my brain trying to reconcile all the memories with this new face behind them. I had told myself that *knowing* was going to make all of this easier. A name and a face were supposed to make me less afraid. But all the unknowns had been limited by my imagination, and the answer was scarier than I could ever have conceived.

"Why am I here?" I asked, in a futile attempt to exert some amount of influence over the situation.

"We needed to talk. Obviously."

What life June's voice had lost, Heath's seemed to have gained; there was something wired about it, too much of it, irrational and unpredictable and hooked.

"Okay. I'm listening."

"God. Where do I start?" Heath tapped his fingers against the wheel impatiently. "I just—I take *issue* with the emotional cheating. You know? Of course I do. It's not a compassionate thing to do. It's dishonest, and almost worse than physical cheating—actually, strike that, it *is* worse, because sex doesn't necessarily mean emotions have to be involved, but that's definitely what's happened between the two of you. *Emotions*. Right? It's not compassionate. But neither is June wanting to call off a relationship when her partner is at his lowest point. It's very selfish."

Call off a relationship.

She'd broken up with him.

"You're wrong," June said.

Everything shook. Everything pulsed. The world flew past, all streetlights and raindrops, the wipers squealing. It seemed like it was all moving faster and faster and faster, and it hit me all at once, everything fitting together.

The air around Heath's body seemed to go red. He'd sent the first text after the funeral, then after the cemetery. He stole her folder. Everything was too bright and too much, and I had to say the words: "You did everything," I said. "It was all you."

Heath didn't even flinch. "Well, yes."

With nowhere to go, the fear became almost claustrophobic; I felt like I'd been trapped in this car for a million years. Where even were we? I'd lived here my whole life, but as the residential streets rushed past, I couldn't place us. Where were we going? "What do you want, then?" I said, purposely speaking from the back of my throat so the sound wouldn't waver.

His grip tightened again. "I wanted to ask how it feels to know you've singlehandedly ruined *everything*. Because you have. None of this would be happening if it weren't for you. Oh. And your fucking faggot of a dad."

I clenched my teeth so hard, I thought they might shatter.

Dad.

Dad.

The fear turned to anger and the anger to rage. "What did you do to him?"

Heath laughed. He actually laughed. I couldn't move.

"Nothing, you fucking moron. I didn't do anything to him. Can't say I was upset when I heard the news, though, but that's not a crime."

I dove. June stopped me before I could make contact, threw herself between me and him from the back seat. I wanted to beat that smug little smirk off his face. Everyone I'd ever watched die on the ToD now looked like Heath. It was Heath, getting hit by a train. Heath, leaping off a building, jump, gasp, *splat.* Heath, beheaded by ISIS. I didn't even understand. I didn't understand why he was saying any of this, so I replied with the only thing I knew: "You're lying."

June grabbed my arm, and I knew the pressure was too tight, too much, but the pain didn't register. "Sydney." Her eyes caught mine and kept them in place. *Relax,* she mouthed.

Dad. Heath was lying. He had to be. "You're fucking lying!"

"Do not raise your voice."

God, no, Dad. No, no, no, no. Someone had to be responsible. It *was* Heath, and he had to admit it. Liar, liar, liar. This was the solution. It had to be, because if it wasn't, then it was nothing; it was a completely senseless death orchestrated by nothing at all, that happened for no reason at all, dumb fucking luck and fate and wrong-place-wrong-time, and I wouldn't believe it, I couldn't, because he wasn't like the people on the ToD. He was Dad, and he was too good for that. He was too fucking good to die in a heap of metal for no reason at all. I choked on the knot in my throat, pushed it down, down, down. "What does that even mean?" I asked. "What did he do to you?"

"Firstly, what did he do to *June*," Heath said. "He put fucking ludicrous ideas in her head. And it worked! Obviously it worked, and we're all here now because you finished the job."

"I have no idea what you're talking about," I said.

He looked at June in the rearview mirror. "Sweetie, I genuinely don't understand how you could have put up with someone so useless for so long. Christ, you didn't just put up with her, you think she's *attractive*."

"Stop it," she said.

"Just admit it!" He smacked the wheel with the palm of his hand. "Holy shit!"

"I *don't*!" I didn't move. My shoulders were fixed forward. I dug my nails into my thighs to keep my hands from trembling. June went on, "I don't. That's what I've been trying to tell you."

I tried to look at her out of the corner of my eye.

"I was wrong. Okay? About all this. You're right. You've done so much for me, and I never appreciated it. I'm ungrateful. Didn't realize how good I had it. And Sydney, she's, she's nothing. She's nothing to me at all."

I knew what she was doing, but fuck, I wished she'd stop.

"Stop. Drop Sydney off wherever. Throw her—throw her out, for all I care. Let's go back to yours. I can spend the night, baby, we can do whatever you..."

Heath took his eyes off the road for a moment to look at June. "You're a fucking horrible liar."

June's face warped. She knew she'd lost. "I'm not lying—"

Heath gripped the wheel, hard, and jerked, sending us careering to the right and then back again. My heart groaned as I dug my nails into the seat for some stability.

In that moment, I realized somebody could actually die. I realized *I* could actually die.

This wasn't going to end with a slow stop. It would be too hard and too fast, and Heath was too far gone to be reasoned with, and the pitching in the pit of my gut told me this was last-moment material. I'd spent the majority of my time since Dad left wondering what this would look like. Sort of fitting. It occurred to me that maybe we'd be caught on surveillance footage, swerving, smashing, leaving, and in a couple of months the comments on ToD would pile up, and a girl somewhere else who'd lost her dad would be thinking, watching, trying to piece together the lives of the people who died, wondering who they were or how this could have happened...

"Heath!" June screamed. She really did scream this, shrill on the vowels. I had never heard her so afraid. The sound tore into every part of me. "Stop!"

"You stop! You fucking stop!"

"There's no mass conspiracy," June said. "Sydney didn't do anything wrong. She did *nothing*. Neither did her dad. You did this. You did all of this to yourself."

Heath choked on a sob; was it real? I couldn't tell, and I guess it didn't matter. "I love you. That's not wrong."

"It is. Because it's impossible to love someone and treat them the way you treated me. It's impossible."

Fast. We were going too fast.

"I have given you every good thing you have," Heath said.

"You've given me shit," June said. "Sydney's dad talked to fucking *Child Protective Services*, Heath. That's real-world stuff, okay? That's real-world stuff that you can't wave away. You can't just get out of that."

"It was *bullshit*! All of it. This, Sydney, the fucking therapy—it was all deliberate sabotage, and you know it. Everyone tries to take everything I have. I'm a victim, June. We're both victims. Why can't you see that?"

"I wanted to help you. You took advantage of that. Of me."

Heath sobbed again. "I begged you. I reminded you of everything, of how volatile this whole fucking thing is, and how *delicate*, really, truly delicate, and you didn't even care. You didn't even care that it was gonna hurt me, and that I was gonna hurt myself. And now, look. We all have to fucking care."

We took a turn then, and I tried to get my bearings.

The street sign: River Styx Road.

He was driving toward the river.

"Holy shit, I can't believe I've lost you to some *dyke*!" He slammed the steering wheel. "I can't believe it. I can't believe it, June. Were you that desperate?"

By now, we were barely staying within the lines of the road. The earth shook beneath us, intermittently left us as we shifted up and on to curbs. A bright, white light tore toward us at an impossible speed, and Heath barely jerked the wheel to miss it. June shrieked.

She was crying now too. "Stop!"

"June—"

"Sydney, he's not okay, he's gonna—"

"Oh my God, shut up!" Heath pounded on the brakes, then immediately back on the gas. Screeching of tires. The sudden stop and start meant the dashboard got closer, then too close, and my face made contact.

I recoiled, my hand shooting up to the warm, wet spot on my cheekbone. My ears rang. Everything slowed. I rested my head against the cool glass of the window while behind me June said something I couldn't make out. I watched the rain fall, a million tiny comets...

The rain. The River Styx.

The quicksand.

The quicksand. It was on this side of the river. And with the rain, the mud would be loose enough to hold the car, easy.

Synapses fired and words and thoughts and phrases all came from nowhere, and I settled.

Beside me, June grabbed at her hair in handfuls. Begged.

June in the driver's seat. June in a beanie. June at the River Styx. June. June decomposing in the driver's seat.

Too fast.

"I don't want to do this anymore, June."

My mind spiraled. Absolute chaos. The world hurtled past, none of it really making any sense. You don't understand what it's like to be in a situation like this until you're in it, I think. You can watch movies, but there is nothing comparable to a sense of imminent death. Of primal fear. A million years of evolution had led up to this, a million years of searing, primitive fight-or-flight instinct with no way to fight and nowhere to go.

Nowhere to go.

We were halfway down the road.

"We can't do this here," June said. But her voice was hopeless. She'd realized what I'd realized: there was no way out. June in the back seat. June more frightened than I'd ever seen anyone. June resigned after her options had run out. June without a plan. Did *I* have a plan?

"We can't do this anywhere anymore. I'm done, June. I'm done. I'm done. I'm done."

Heath. Heath in the driver's seat. Dad. Swerve, *smash*, gone. Lungs popped like balloons. Popped like balloons.

The accelerator whined; we were nearly there now. In ten seconds we'd reach the sign on the left that said RIVER STYX, and two seconds after that we'd be at the drop.

I would not fear death.

Do it. I had to do it.

And once I realized that, an inexplicable sense of calm fell over me.

"June," I said, "can you just talk to me?"

"Sydney…"

"Please."

Heath shouted something, but I wasn't listening anymore because I didn't fucking care. All that stood between me and eternity was the tree line, and I at least wanted her to talk to me. "Okay," she said, "so, everything is gonna be fine. Right?"

Seven months since. Seven months since. A million months since. A million years since. *Where am I? Where is he?*

"And I want you to know that I'm so grateful for everything you've done for me—"

June grabbed for me.

"—and that I'm so, so sorry."

We were at the tree line.

I will not go gentle into that—

It was so funny; I had never said it to myself before. I'd never said the words. But God, I loved June Copeland. I didn't love her unselfishly. I didn't love her healthily. But I loved her so badly, it hurt.

I will go gentle into that—

"Sydney, you are so wonderful, and I know what you're thinking, and you need to do it now."

Find me somewhere in the ether; I don't want to lose you. I don't want to lose you for good.

I lunged, grabbed the wheel, and heaved.

We barreled past the tree line. No vision. No sound. Just tumbling, and throbbing, and crashing, flesh and bones and muscle, no up or down or sideways. There were screams, but I had no earthly idea which one of us they'd come from. But I would not take my hands off the wheel. Even as Heath's body crashed against mine, I would not.

Trees reached and scraped and tried to stop us, and the world exploded in perfect incandescent symmetry.

And then we slowed. Rolled. Rocked backward.

Stopped. We had stopped.

Breathe.

Breathe.

I assessed.

Alive. I was distinctly alive.

Heath was trying frantically to get the car to move, flooring the gas, but it wouldn't; the tires sputtered uselessly below us, no traction to propel us forward.

Quicksand.

We'd made it to the quicksand.

My vision returned, barely, because all I could see was the glow of the headlights and the steady rain falling within it.

It was so quiet. Where were the screams? The back seat was quiet.

June.

The window beside her head was smashed, tiny sparkling shards of glass clinging to her hair. Her forehead glistened red. She didn't move.

"June," I said once, but no sound came out, so I said it again.

She stirred. Moaned.

I gasped for air. "June, come on..."

Heath groaned beside me. "You fucker. You *fucking...*" I leaned over to unlock the doors, but before I could do anything to stop him, he grabbed me by my throat. A searing pain rocked me, and I could do nothing to stop the cry that billowed out. I clawed helplessly at his grip—until I caught a glimpse of June as she reached through the gap in the seat and dug her nails into the nape of his neck. He shrieked, and his hands shot away.

June barely had enough strength to get her own door open, and once it was, she didn't move, so I leaned back and practically pushed her out of the car. "Go. Go," I told her. She fell into the mud with a soft *splat.*

That was when I remembered the phone. My phone.

Heath and I seemed to realize at the same time.

We both lunged, but he was too fast, and my back was in white-hot agony. He got there before I did, grabbed the phone, and smashed it against the dashboard.

Once. Again. Again.

That didn't matter now. I had to get to June.

I leaped from the car and went to her, making sure to move fast, to keep my feet up so I wouldn't get stuck. It wasn't easy; the rain was beating down and each step threatened to pull me under. There wasn't time for that. Not anymore. I tore through the sodden earth, around the back of the car, and made it to June, anchoring myself on an elevated bit of dirt.

"Give me your arms," I told her.

"I can't. This one—" It was pitch-black, but even with the traces of moonlight crawling through the trees I could make out June's arm hanging limp and unnatural.

"Okay, just…" I grabbed her underneath her arms, got the best grip I could, and yanked.

June hollered, and I groaned with exertion, but I continued, pulling and pulling until the earth beneath her popped, releasing her. I hauled her to the side of the pit, far enough out that she couldn't be dragged under again.

The car continued to disobey Heath, and he waited, but then shifted his attention to us. His eyes flickered; he wasn't finished.

"You have to get up," I said to June. She didn't even try to move, her eyes struggling to focus on anything, so I dragged her up while she tripped over her feet. "You gotta. Come on. Come on."

"June, let me help you," Heath said behind us.

Thunder boomed somewhere far away.

June and I scrambled, and we tried to run—I hated it, didn't want to run, but we had no choice.

It didn't even matter, though. June was too slow, and Heath was too fast, and we had barely gotten into the forest before she screamed. The most awful, animalistic sound, the sort of sound that reminds you that we're no different from mice, that we're not gods, just mammals, that when we scream, it all sounds the same, and pain is pain, and Heath had June's left arm clenched in his fist and he squeezed and tugged and ripped.

That's when I heard the sirens.

Heath did too, because he dropped June like she was nothing, climbed back into the car and tried to start it again, but the tires had now disappeared up to halfway, and hardly even turned when he floored the accelerator.

Maybe this was the endorphin rush that comes with pain, that says *Hush, it's okay*, but I was almost reveling in Heath's panic. The sirens were closer now, and I had June in my arms, and it occurred to me I was watching him lose everything.

I looked down at June, her eyes screwed shut; never before this had I noticed how human she was, how breakable.

The police emerged from the tree line.

There were two of them, both carrying flashlights; one illuminated the car, the other June and me. I thought of how pitiful we must look to them, these two girls huddled together, soaked with mud and rainwater and blood. For the first time, I assessed myself, put a hand up again to the warm spot on my cheek, followed the trail down, down...

Once the officer had looked us over, he craned his neck to speak into the walkie-talkie on his chest.

Where do I start? That was the only thing I remember thinking, the only thing I thought that wasn't red, but a series of words: *Where do I start?*

I remember sitting with June, her head propped up on my shoulder, rain lashing at us while the lights grew brighter and brighter.

Shouting.

More sirens. Not police—ambulances.

Heath, being told to get out of the sinking car.

I remember: *You'll be all right, girls. We'll get you fixed up.* Mom. She was there. She'd come with the cops from the station. Sobbed. Held me gently. Didn't even worry about getting mud on her clothes. "You're okay, baby."

Heath, being taken away.

He'd scared the whole neighborhood, they said. Got calls from everywhere, all about some lunatic driver. Even folks a mile away had heard a crash.

The sky was so bright over the river. Like fireflies.

The stars were close, but not close enough to take sides, I realized, as I stepped over the fallen tree at the fork in the trail, the splinters of our names cast aside and buried in wreckage.

18

THEY SEPARATED US WHEN WE got to the hospital.

I'd asked to stay with June, but she was in worse shape than I was, and they were sort of rushing her around, a towel draped over her shoulders—to warm her up, sure, but I think also to conceal the failure of human anatomy that her lower left arm had become. We said a hurried goodbye, and a nurse, probably noticing the way my face fell, said, "Don't worry. You'll see her soon." She didn't know anything that had happened. She had no idea that I'd already mentally lost June, and that I worried if she slipped out of the hospital doors without me, I might never see her again, that if we weren't pressed shoulder to shoulder, something could worm its way between us. But something about the easiness of her words calmed me.

She led Mom and me to a cramped examination room that smelled like alcohol and flu.

And once the door shut, Mom held my face in her hands and scrutinized me. Her eyes flicked back and forth, trying to find something in my face, something in me, and I wasn't sure what, so I looked at her as gently and as honestly as I could.

"I'm sorry," I said. For making her worry. For being unfair. For the fact that any of this had happened to us at all.

"*I'm* sorry," she said. "I'm sorry this has been so difficult. I would—God, Sydney, if I could take this all from you, I'd do it in a second. Those"—she rubbed my cheeks—"bags under your eyes..."

"A parting gift." We both laughed—less laughs and more quick exhales, but the moment was significant in that it existed at all, despite everything, despite the tears pooling on her face that suggested the last thing she wanted to do now was laugh.

Mom picked a dry clump of mud out of my hair. "I can't even tell you how afraid I was when the police told me. I can't even begin."

"I'm okay, Mom."

"I know. But my mind had already gone to that place, and that takes a toll on you. When it's about your daughter—"

"I know." I lowered myself on to the examination table and tried to lean back, the paper crinkling underneath me. My back screamed. I managed to lay my head down and looked at the ceiling. There was a sort of mural taped to it of a night sky, stars and planets and galaxies all swirling against navy blue.

This was the hospital Dad had died in.

Did his ceiling have stars? I couldn't remember. I couldn't remember.

"So much," she said, then lowered her voice. "I'm so sorry this has been so hard."

"I didn't mean to make it seem like—like, I don't know." My throat clenched. "Like you didn't care, or. Obviously you care. You were trying to make it easier."

She nodded. "You like that June," Mom said. "A lot."

My body tensed, but I didn't look away from the ceiling, partly because it would've been too much effort to get back up and partly because after she had said that, I didn't want to face her. It felt like an accusation. "I do."

"Does she care about you in the same way?"

"I think so. I hope so."

"Is it...romantic?"

"I don't really know anymore. Maybe. On my end, anyway."

Mom's feet shuffled against the tile. "Well. Then I care about her too."

I went to chew my thumb to keep from crying, but clenching my jaw made the cut on my cheek open, so I lay there expressionless while my vision blurred and thought about all the things that would come next.

The doctor saw me. Stitched me up, confirmed I had whiplash, and sent me home.

I'd asked her if she'd seen June. The doctor had sort of straightened her back, frowned, said, "She's getting X-rayed at the moment. We're hoping she won't need surgery. But the main thing was that cut on her head, to get to it..." She winced. "We had to shave a patch."

Afterward, Mom and I were led to a side room where one of the police officers who'd found me and June was waiting for us.

My stomach lurched at the sight of him, as if I was back in the worst of it, as if I still needed to be saved from something.

But I swallowed and breathed, and when he asked, I told him everything. I told him about my dad and June and Heath and the messages and what he'd done. What happened in the car. I told him I grabbed the steering wheel. I told him everything, anything I could think of, but disconnected, factual, because I wasn't entirely sure I'd be able to get through all of it otherwise. He asked questions intermittently, prompted me to elaborate, but nothing was pointed or accusatory—he believed me, I could tell. He was sympathetic. He believed me. He was going to do something.

I mentioned that I'd taken a video while we were in the car, but Heath had destroyed my phone.

"What happens now?" Mom asked when I was finished. "What's going to happen to him?"

The officer flipped his notebook shut and put his pen in his breast pocket. "We're going to do our best."

I froze. "What does that mean?"

"Personally—I don't know if I should be telling you this, but personally—there's no doubt in my mind that boy should see jail time. Not a doubt."

I knew what he was implying. "So why won't he?"

"It's a very complicated situation."

Mom gestured at me, all of me, living, breathing proof of what Heath Alderman was capable of. "That didn't sound very complicated to me."

The officer bent in closer to us and lowered his voice. "That family has this town in a choke hold. We liaise with the district's benefactors, the local government, the schools—and not a single one of those bodies will be interested in seeing that boy in handcuffs." He leaned back and brushed down his trouser legs with his palms. "Unfortunately there's no way to corroborate any of this, especially without the documentation, like you said. *This* incident especially is the most compelling—and even then, it's your girls' word against his. There's little we can do." He got up to leave. "I'm sorry, ladies. I realize this has been a stressful time for you. We'll let you know first if anything changes. Get some rest, now."

The officer left, and with him, the entirety of my faith in the justice system.

Mom and I seethed. We talked about what to do in a situation where nothing could be done. She said we'd keep trying. She said she was sorry.

But mainly, we pulled out a board game from a sad-looking pile of them in the corner—Chutes and Ladders—and it was actually fun. We kept talking, and the words came effortlessly now—but still, I found it hard to relax without actually seeing June in person. I worried that maybe she'd slipped through a crack in time and space. I thought of her, looking back at California, worried it would crumble if she wasn't there to watch it—I felt the same way about her now. But she was fine. And I didn't have to think about Dad constantly for him to continue existing in some form. That wasn't fair. Not to me. Not to him. He was my dad, and I was his daughter, and that was enough; that was imprinted somewhere, either in me or somewhere else I couldn't conceive of. And I looked at Mom, really looked at her face, and I realized that I was her daughter—and this was important too.

Mom had told me months before that I still had a life to live. And now, having stared into oblivion, playing some game with her in a hospital waiting room, waiting for the girl who was everything, I actually felt like it was true.

I was okay. And June was okay.

But she had questions to answer.

Two hours later, there was a knock on the door. June's face lit up when she saw me, and at first, I didn't even register anything different about her. It was June, and she was here, and that was all I needed to know.

We hugged too hard, and it hurt like hell, but I didn't care. I buried my head in the space between her neck and shoulder as all the fear I had felt about her, about what she could have been, purged from me. She was here. She was now.

I couldn't even keep myself from crying, and from the way she heaved against me, she couldn't either.

Only when she pulled back did I notice the brick of a cast on her arm and the shaved bit of hair on the right side of her head.

I realized the woman behind June had to be her mom. She had June's wide-set eyes and tight curls, bunched up on the top of her head. They were about the same height. It was funny; even given the couple of times June had mentioned her mom, I'd never imagined what she'd looked like. Maybe I'd thought June actually just appeared one day, perfectly formed.

I smiled as much as my wound would allow, and let her hug me. "I'm so glad you're both all right," she said.

"Mom," June said, "is it okay if I go back with Sydney?"

Our moms exchanged a look. June's mom went to speak, seemingly apologetic, but mine stopped her. "It's no problem. They should be together tonight, I think."

So we drove. We sat in the back seat, not saying much; neither of us wanted to talk about anything. Not yet. There were too many tragedies, so many that I didn't even know which one to focus on. None of us did. We were experiencing the full body-and-mind equivalent of not knowing what to do with your hands.

June spoke in a strangely casual way to Mom about how she'd never broken a bone before and how badly it hurt when it happened. I felt the jagged texture on my right cheek, dragged my middle finger up and down the stitches. Likely, I think we were still in shock.

And then a hand on mine.

June wrapped her fingers around and squeezed. There wasn't anything romantic about it, I didn't think. It seemed more like necessary contact, like holding a baby after it's born.

June wasn't looking at me. She was staring out of the car window, the streetlamps silhouetting and dancing and playing along her profile, the long shadows appearing, skewing and disappearing like lifetimes one after the other. I squeezed back.

June next to me. June in a bed.

Mom had graciously left us to our own devices. It took approximately a thousand years to get comfortable. My head was pounding, and June didn't seem much better off, and I think we were both so struck by the novelty of being together like this that it was difficult to decide what we should do or how this should look. We finally settled on lying next to each other, heads propped up with pillows, looking up at the ceiling.

She had answers, and I wasn't sure I'd be able to look her in the eye.

I wasn't sure she'd be able to look me in the eye.

So this was fine for now.

"Okay," June said, and exhaled. "Hi."

"Hi," I said back, then laughed at the ridiculousness of it all. Because there were no words. There were no words for a lot of different reasons, so, really, it seemed there should be negative words. We had been given too much, and now it felt like we should take something away. I couldn't comprehend the fact that she was finally here, that this would all end, that everything she'd kept buried was going to be dug up, reanimated. I think we were both nervous to find out what that would look like.

"You look like Frankenstein," she said.

"Frankenstein's monster, thanks. You—I can't think of anything known for having a cast and an edgy haircut."

"Here's one: June Copeland."

I laughed. "Then you look like June Copeland."

"Are you okay?" she asked.

"I don't really know. I think I'm feeling less okay by the second," I said, because it was true. At the hospital I'd felt relief that it was over, but now there was panic that it'd happened at all. Anxiety slithered near the bottom of my belly, threatening to sink its teeth into me.

And June still had some talking to do. "Are *you* okay?" I asked.

"I think I feel...great," she said. "Maybe it was the drugs they gave me. I'm sure the trauma will hit in the morning. But right now I'm okay. Yeah. I'm okay."

We both considered that for a moment. Outside, the rain had stopped, and there was no sound besides our staggered breaths—until a dog barking made me flinch.

"I need to know everything," I said.

"I know," she said immediately after, like she was waiting for me to ask. "Now?"

"Yeah."

"What do you already know?"

I wasn't actually sure. I was sure Heath had sent the messages. He had broken in, had uploaded the video. I was sure he had hurt June. And Dad—well, I wasn't sure about anything. But I didn't want to assume. And I wanted to hear her say it. "Nothing. I need to know, first: Did you have anything to do with this? Any of it?"

"No," she said, the syllable low and punchy. "I'll explain, but...no. You gotta believe me, Whitaker."

I did.

"Well." She took a breath. "God. I don't even know how to do this. You know I've thought about this moment happening probably hundreds of times? Literally, hundreds? And even then, I never knew what to start with. There's so much that I...don't know where to start."

This wasn't going to be easy, I realized. Not only in the sense that it wasn't as simple as going down a line of questions, ticking them off, moving on—for June, this was a catharsis, and for me...well, I wasn't really sure what it was yet. That depended on what she had to say.

"I don't know," she said. "If we go chronologically—I already told you some of the *very* beginning stuff. Moving kind of sucked. This place was totally foreign to me. I met him, Heath—I met him at cheer tryouts at the beginning of summer. He was at the school for some student council thing, and it was right after tryouts, and I felt like I'd done terribly, and I was so worried that, like, all the girls were looking at me, and I was so homesick... So afterward I found this stairwell to go cry in. I felt so pathetic. He found me there. Brushed me down. Made me *laugh*. And oh my God, Whitaker, I know based on what just happened this probably seems too awful to say, but he was *so* charming. Seemed so mature. Even when we were, like, what, fourteen? We were dating three weeks later. I was obsessed with him—I felt like I owed him everything after what he'd done for me."

Her words were already stilted, wavering, and I thought I should touch her, so I reached over and took her hand, the way she had in the car, and squeezed. "You're okay," I said.

"He did *everything* right. He was so sweet. Considerate. My mom loved him. *I* loved him."

She stopped, so I asked, "What happened?" to help spur her along.

June took a shaky breath. I dragged my thumb along the back of her hand, and it didn't make me nervous. "It was a year of being, you know, a 'power couple,' and having all these friends and this new life and stuff, and I think that was all so exciting to me, and that…that was why I didn't notice there was anything wrong. He, um… It was evident pretty early on that he struggled with stuff. He'd have these, sort of…breakdowns, I guess? I don't even know what to call them besides that. They'd come out of absolutely nowhere and go on for hours, him telling me how I didn't love him anymore, or how he saw me talking to somebody else, or just *looking* at somebody else. But stupidly, so, so stupidly, I felt…bad for him."

"That's not stupid. It's your empathy."

"No, it was stupid, because it was selfish. Because afterward he'd always sob, like, full-on sob, and apologize, and in my head I was like, *I'm gonna fix this poor, broken boy.* He was always so in control of everything, I guess, that having this one thing, having him, like, beg me to forgive him, even after he'd… I felt like I was gonna be the one to mend him. Obviously that didn't happen."

"You couldn't have."

"I know." She rubbed her forehead. "I know that now. And even then, a lot of the time, I felt guilty for setting him off, even though… I don't know. I know now it was never my fault. It was never my fault."

I felt her body change beside me, her stomach sucking in and out too quickly. June was trying not to cry. Fuck my whiplash, I decided, and rolled over on my side to face her, wincing to brace myself from the pain that shot down my spine. I held her hand tighter to make up for the absence of any words; her palm was sweating. "It wasn't your fault," I finally echoed.

"He basically started pulling me away from everyone. Friends. He made me quit cheer. All this was, like, under the guise of 'helping' him. He said he worried so much about me, that he was so nervous that he always wanted to make sure he was around. Because he didn't want anything bad to happen to me. He had me get rid of all my social media because it worried him too. I was being caged in, and it was so gradual that I didn't even notice, like, one bar, and then another, and I *did* it because I wanted him to be okay. And, um…" June couldn't even get the words out.

"What?"

"Uh, sex stuff too. He…like, I was never trying to fight him off me, or anything…"

"But did you say yes?"

She shook her head. "Sometimes. But other times…I mean, no. No. I didn't."

"Then it doesn't matter that you weren't fighting him off. That wasn't consensual, June. You need to have said yes."

"Then…"

I pinched my bottom lip between my teeth until I broke skin. "I fucking hate him."

She sighed this sigh that told me everything I needed to know. "I'm learning to."

God. I wanted to bottle her up and steal her away somewhere safe and beautiful so she'd never be hurt ever again. "By the beginning of junior year, I felt like I was actually losing it. I was crying all the time. Hated myself. My self-esteem basically shriveled and died over two years. I didn't even…recognize myself. And I had nobody to tell me any of this, you know? Because Heath had isolated me from everyone. So by that point, I was like, well, me and him should break up, which was hilarious, because it wasn't even because of anything he'd done—it was a, like, *I need to work on myself* sort of thing. It was like my body was *telling* me, you know, *we need to get you the hell out of here*…I wasn't making that connection. So, anyways, beginning of junior year, I did the whole breakup song and dance, like, *it's not you, it's me*, and he *freaked out*. Cried. Yelled." June gnawed on her thumb. "And he told me he was going to kill himself. So I dropped it."

We looked at each other.

"I dropped it," she said again. "I believed him. And then I tried to break it off *again*. A couple of months later. And I almost did it too. I drove away, the whole thing. Five minutes later, he texted me a picture of an empty bottle of pills. So I went back. He was bluffing, obviously. But he spun it like, *See, you came back, so you do care about me.*" June stopped and rolled over as best she could manage. She tried to read my face. "I know you think I'm crazy."

"Why would I think that?"

"Because"—she fought back tears again—"because for the past few months, I've envisioned myself telling someone this story, and, like, trying to figure out how to phrase it in a way that doesn't make it sound like I'm a bad person for not doing something, or, you know, for not standing up for myself. I thought I was being strong, and sticking it out, because I'm busy fixing him, and you think, like, it's not like he's *hitting* me, or anything, so you feel like maybe you're making a big deal out of nothing, or that you're a bitch, or something—"

"I don't think you're a bad person," I said, and meant it. "He would *want* you to think that. Right? You're not. You're not a bitch. It's his fault."

"I know." She exhaled. "I know. And when it was good, it was *good*. There'd be, God, like *months* at a time where things would be fine. Perfect. He'd be loving and gentle, but then it'd all go to shit again and I had to deal with it. And the best way I can explain it is… that you forget what normal is. You forget how people are supposed to treat you and talk to you and…touch you. You forget what that's like. And with everyone else gone, there's no one to show you or to tell you. So slowly you start living in this fucking upside-down world except there is no rabbit hole, no, like, point of entry, it just *happens* around you, and you never stop to think, *Well, shit, what the fuck is happening here?*" She took a breath. "Until you, I guess."

My stomach leaped.

"So, all this was happening, and I was like, okay, a breakup can't happen, and I felt like shit all the time, so, yeah, that's when I started to see your dad. Middle of junior year, I think."

"What did you tell him?"

She shrugged. "Everything I knew, at the time. Like I said, I thought there was something wrong with *me*. And I wasn't withholding anything from him—honestly, I didn't realize. So, Ben—ha. Sorry."

I grinned, a foreign pressure on my cheekbones.

"He diagnosed me, I guess, and I—I had a deadly amalgamation of shit going on. I was depressed and anxious, but I think I already knew that. But then he was like"—she mimicked Dad's voice—"'it seems like you have symptoms of PTSD.' And I was like...*what*? PTSD? What trauma am I *post*? And then, I...yeah. I kind of realized.

"Because your dad was smart, and even though I never explicitly told him, he clued in to what was going on. He basically pieced it together from me having mentioned Heath in passing a couple of times. Figured everything out. Our sessions became exclusively *about* abusive relationships. And at the time, I was like...abusive relationship? That term seemed too extreme. Way too extreme. And it terrified me. Like, that didn't happen to people like *me*. I was too smart for that. Too strong for that. Right? But I'd spent years rationalizing away the whole thing. Heath made me think this was all normal. Your dad confidently told me it wasn't. Ben was the reason I finally figured it out, how I remembered that this wasn't the way one human is supposed to treat another. And, you know, I realized it had nothing to do with being smart or strong. Nothing at all.

"I confronted Heath about everything when senior year started. And we—God, I don't even remember what I said. We fought. It escalated. And escalated. So, yeah. He, uh, grabbed me. Hard. You know, like, around my arms?"

My chest bubbled with rage. Suddenly I felt like we were back in the car, and I wanted to crash it again, except this time we're two degrees more to the right or left, and a rogue branch decapitates the driver.

"It bruised really bad," she continued. "And I knew if your dad knew, he'd do *something*. And I didn't want...God. I can barely even put myself back in my headspace from that time because it's all so ludicrous, but I guess some of me still wanted to protect Heath, and I don't know. I wasn't even planning on telling your dad at first. But he could tell something was the matter, and I needed to tell *somebody*, so I spilled everything that had happened. He said he was going to—that he had to—file a CPS report, because I still wasn't eighteen."

"Oh, God."

June nodded gravely. "And I told Heath after, obviously. That your dad knew. He was...livid. That was the beginning of September. And then a couple of weeks later—"

"He was dead." We both understood who *he* was.

Dad. Everything—all of this—was about him. I wished so badly that he were here. To tuck my hair behind my ear and put his hand on my ankle, not because the girl broke my heart but because she broke all of me, and I broke all of her too, and now we were here trying to put each other back together without any more bloodshed.

"June," I said, not a clue how to phrase what I was about to ask. "Did he do something to my dad?"

"No. I mean, I don't think he—"

"Remember that website I told you about? Where I was watching people die?"

June nodded.

"Heath sent me the video. Of...my dad's accident. He'd gotten it, somehow. Maybe from his dad, or, I don't know, but..."

"I'm so sorry."

"You don't have to apologize for him."

"I was with him. That whole day. And if he *had* done something, I can't even begin to conceive how or when or what he would have done it. Is that what you thought all this was?"

I nodded, as if to say: *Of course—what else could it have been?* I felt almost combative, but June was so gentle and honest that I had no choice but to believe her. Of course I felt combative, because this whole thing was about looking for a fight. A fight. And here she was, saying there was none to be had. That it wasn't Heath. That it wasn't anybody. I'd been holding on to the last thread of hope that horrible things had to happen as a consequence of something else, that Dad wasn't subject to the same unfair odds as everyone else—but they didn't, and he was.

"In the video," I said, "it looks like Dad sort of swerved, and I guess...I guess it could have been anything. An animal or some debris in the road or something..."

"It could have been anything," June echoed. "I'm sorry, Sydney."

"It's okay," I said, because there was nothing else for it to be. "So, what happened to the report?"

"I don't know. Maybe he never got to it, or he did send it but it was dropped because of what happened... I really don't know. But I never heard from anyone. And I turned eighteen pretty soon after, anyways. So nothing even came from it."

"But what did I have to do with this? With any of this?"

June looked me in the eye. Her head was backlit by the glow from my desk lamp, illuminating a sort of angelic haze around her, while the weight from her cast made her whole body slump. "He wanted... revenge, I guess. He thought you'd been in on it, somehow, and had convinced himself that you two were in cahoots trying to convince me to leave him. Making up stories, whatever. He thought you were spying for your dad at school or something."

"I—I never even knew you were—"

"Whitaker, I know that. Heath is... He's paranoid, and he sees things that aren't there. That can't be there."

"Is he—like, unwell mentally?"

"I think. I mean, I know. He has to be. I tried to get him help. Gently, I mean, because overtly suggesting anything like that would have...but, I mean, yeah. He is. So, I don't know.

"Some of the stuff he did because he's entitled and narcissistic and has a superiority complex, sure. But some of the other stuff, maybe he wouldn't have done it if he was, you know, well, but... Lots of people are mentally ill," she said, "and they don't do these things to other people. Manipulate them and stalk them and, oh my God, almost fucking *kill* them. I totally believe he would have crashed the car or driven us off a cliff or whatever. I'd never seen him so crazed. And no one who's okay would have gotten to that point."

Cogs turned in my brain. "When you offered to drive me, did he—"

She exhaled. "Don't hate me."

"I won't."

She snorted. "I told him I was keeping an eye on you."

"Oh my God."

"Yeah."

"But then, why would you even want to offer in the first place?" June was quiet. "Did you feel guilty? And that's why you...?"

"What do you want me to say? Maybe a little, I guess. Sure.

Whatever. But that's not what it was, really. I got the sense that—that we both—that we were both losing the plot a little bit."

I laughed under my breath. "And you liked that?"

"And I liked you." I stiffened. "I liked you. I liked your sense of humor, and how you treated me, and how when I spoke to you, it always seemed like you were really listening. Your dad told me that I wasn't supposed to be treated the way Heath treated me. You showed me."

My cheeks went red hot.

"Heath noticed how I...was. With you. He knew. Or maybe it was his paranoia, but if so, maybe it was the first time his paranoia was right. And then that became *why*. I'd placated him for the first couple of months, but I didn't realize that until after...that he was doing that stuff to you, sending you the... I didn't know. I didn't realize how bad it was. I would have never dragged you into any of this if I had known."

"Why didn't you tell me what was happening? I mean, I can't believe I never picked up on it... I could have helped. I could have—"

She shook her head slowly. "There was nothing you could have done. There was nothing you could have noticed. No one ever would have known. It's not your fault that you didn't recognize someone wearing a mask. Whitaker, there were *so* many times I wanted to tell you. Everything. But I was terrified of you confronting him, and something *happening*, or...or something happening to me."

"What about your mom?"

She started crying again. "She didn't know either. Can you believe it? She didn't even know. She loved him. And I didn't want to tell her

283

because—I didn't want her to worry, and my dad—he, a lot of the same stuff, and I—"

"Why didn't you end it?"

June swallowed hard. "I was so scared of what that meant. I had it in my head, like, I just had to make it until the summer. I would think that every single morning. Wait until the summer. Because then we'd break up, he'd be at Yale, or whatever... In retrospect, yeah, I'm not sure that was the best thing to do. I'm not sure. I'm sorry. I should have told you everything. And I think I hate myself for that. When you're in it, it's like—it's like you can't even see yourself without it. At that point, he was this gangrenous limb I didn't have the luxury of lopping off. I was petrified. And you helped me forget. About all of it."

I shifted my weight, the bed creaking beneath me. "Is that why you started being...I don't know, you were kind of...cold."

"I'm so sorry," she said. "It honestly...*kills* me to think that you could have thought...ugh. I was always scared he was watching. I thought maybe if I acted like that, I'd start to believe that was actually how I felt, and I wouldn't have had to worry about you or this anymore."

"But then...Spring Fling?"

June nodded, understanding what I was asking. "Heath had changed his mind at the last minute. Decided that *we* wouldn't be going. That appearances were less important than keeping me away from you. And I was so mad, I—we were at his place, and all I could think was that it wasn't fair. It wasn't fair that I had to live like this. He'd already taken most of my teenage years, and then you came, and you were someone who actually made me happy—and now I couldn't even have that. It all came to a head. I managed to leave as soon as I could, like, with the dance almost over so he wouldn't be suspicious, and I was so worried I wouldn't make it, but I did and...dude, I'm so sorry. I'm so sorry I did that."

"Why? No, it—"

"I made you uncomfortable. I know I did."

I shook my head. "It wasn't *you*. I knew it was wrong. I knew something was wrong, and that tainted the whole thing."

"He found out I went."

"How?"

June swallowed. "He was tracking my phone."

"Yeah, he was texting me."

"Of course he fucking was. Afterward, he forced me to make that horrible phone call. I felt awful. I'm not sure I've ever felt more awful. He said he'd hurt you. He said he'd hurt you if I ever spoke to you again."

"So then...why tonight? What happened?"

"I ended it. For good. And he *knew* I was serious. He knew I was so *done*, so completely, entirely done, and he knew I had you, but he convinced me to—I'm so sorry, I didn't know he was going to try to get you too, and I would have said something, but I was so afraid he'd hurt you."

I shook my head. "Don't worry. It's okay." I looked at her and smirked. "In one piece."

That made her cry.

"Oh God, I'm sorry, I didn't mean to—"

She smiled. "No. I...thank you."

"For what?"

"I don't know what would have happened if you hadn't done what you did. That's what I was most afraid of. At the time, yeah, the immediate threat of what was happening was terrifying, but it was the thought of what could've happened that scared me more. What could have happened if I hadn't ended it. If we hadn't met. I don't know. Maybe we're still in shock. But honestly, I just feel kind of happy. I'm happy that we're okay. And I'm happy that I'm here with you right now." June repositioned herself, nestled in the crook of my arm, the weight of her welcome and comforting. From above, it must have looked silly because of how much taller she was than me, but lying there, feeling it, having it happen—it didn't feel silly at all. I felt myself stiffen, then relax. Put my arm round her neck and rested my hand on her bicep.

She was here. I was here. We were okay.

But I wasn't finished. "Did you talk to that police officer?"

She nodded. "Mm-hmm."

"What did you tell him?"

"Anything. Whatever I could."

"And what did he tell you?"

"That they couldn't do shit."

"Same."

She sighed, loud and long. "It's such bullshit. There's no proof. Can you believe it? There's no proof of anything."

"Heath took your folder. Right?"

"He said he burned it."

I swore. "I was taking a video. In the car. Heath hadn't seen, but while I was trying to help you… Fuck. He smashed my phone. I don't get it. How can the police do *nothing*? Like, bare minimum, that was reckless fucking driving. Right? How can nothing happen?"

"His dad's gotten him out of worse."

"There has to be something we can do. Mess up his Yale admission? Send out—I don't know, letters?"

June shrugged.

"I don't know. Something. Anything."

She shook her head. "Like I said, he's leaving for Connecticut right after the school year is finished. Some pre-semester class or something. So I—we—only have to worry about him until then. His admission— that's the only thing that guarantees he'll be away from me."

"I don't think that's right," I said. "He shouldn't get away with it."

"I know you're right. I'm scared, I guess."

"And what about in the meantime? Are you sure he won't try anything?"

"He'll get off the hook for this—for everything—but barely. Barely. His dad's gonna be pissed off, because this is the worst he's been, and even if he's messed up right now, he's too smart to try anything else. I'm not sure he's convinced he can pull this shit anymore." She paused. "Because of you, I guess."

"What do you mean?"

"He knew he had me. That I wouldn't do anything about it. But now that he knows *you* know everything, that you saw what he's like… He's too smart. He won't. I'd be surprised if he even looked at me over the next month."

It broke my heart to think that Dad knew. Dad knew all this was happening, and knowing him, I bet it ate him up there was nothing he could do. I wondered if he'd ever imagined this happening. "I don't understand how somebody could do this to you in the first place."

"I don't think that boy has ever seen a happy, loving relationship in his whole entire life. His dad was horrible to his mom, and is still horrible to him."

"Heath told me his mom died."

She scoffed. "No. They had a messy divorce when he was in middle school. Heath... He gets off on control. I won't even give you that *I don't even think he realizes it* line, because he *totally* realizes it. He knows exactly what he's done. And, like, looking back now, I know he liked me *because* of that—that I was lost and vulnerable and would have been alone had it not been for him. He always tried to make me feel like I was still that scared little girl in the stairwell."

"I hate him, June," I said. One of the understatements of the century. "I fucking hate him."

"Honestly, I don't want to think about him right now."

"What do you want to think about instead?"

"I don't know. Something happier," June said, a new tenderness to her voice. "That it's over. But also this. And you. And what we're going to do about all of that."

What was she saying? For the first time, it felt like this door I'd been imagining for months had been opened, and the universe was asking me if I'd like to step through it—and for some reason, that was harder than I'd imagined. As if I feared taking one step toward it would force it shut. But maybe I had an obligation to force it shut, so I said aloud the one thing that scared me most.

I'd envisioned this conversation happening so many times, but there was one thing that could ruin it all. "I'm worried that I've made you out in my head to be something that you're not."

June was silent for a moment, then said, in a small voice, "I'm worried I did the same thing for you." I think she could tell, based on the way my body tensed, that her words surprised me. "Like looking out of a window of a house I was locked inside."

My breath hitched in my chest. If that was what I was for her, then what was she for me? Like the last thing you see before falling into a black hole. This was the first moment—the first beautiful, unrestrained moment—where I thought about June and myself as *us* without any trepidation. June and Sydney. Now it wasn't trying to cover up something else. Now it just *was*. I wanted to touch her, hold her, put my forehead against hers and leave it there. "So what do we do?" I asked.

"I don't really know."

"You're going to college."

June nodded. "Even if I wasn't, I still wouldn't know. I think this is... I think we need to be careful." She craned her head to look at me. "Are we damaged goods?" she asked. Even with the mischievous grin, and the way she was squinting at me, I was pretty sure there was a part of her that was genuinely asking.

"No," I said, confident. "I think... I don't know. I think we've felt a pain that most people don't have to feel until later."

"Yeah. So, actually, it's kind of like a club."

"Right. Very exclusive."

June squirmed upward and sat, cross-legged, facing me. "I don't know if this is okay," she said, "but I care about you a lot, and even if we're not sure what that means right now…I'm happy to spend the summer learning."

I didn't know what to say to any of this. It was a lifetime's worth of thoughts and feelings and fantasies, and they were all here, all now, and I didn't know what to do with any of them, didn't know what to say to this beautiful girl, this beautiful girl who found me while I was busy burying myself alive, and dug me out.

I thought I should touch her.

I hoisted myself up to meet her and mirrored her position, my legs crisscrossed. And then we looked at each other, and I took in all the things that I couldn't before, for fear of being caught staring. "That sounds nice," I said. Then, maybe because the weight of the situation was starting to become uncomfortable, or to take the attention off me, "Let me feel your head."

June scoffed, but leaned forward.

"It does look good," I said. I dragged my fingertip along the patch, careful not to touch the stitches.

"I don't know. I'm not sure it goes with my aesthetic."

"There's this joke: What do you call a straight girl with an undercut?" June blinked. "A liar."

She snorted. "Well, maybe it goes fine, then."

That was when we kissed, hard.

Her hands wrapped round my biceps and squeezed as we did, and I felt all of her; her hair on my face and her nose smushed against mine and the softness of her lips and everything, everything, and I wanted to melt into her, and I wanted to live tucked in her eyelids. One kiss, then her mouth contorted and there was another, and another, and she smelled like sweat and the hospital and it was wonderful, and I'd never kissed someone like this, it went on forever, and for a millisecond and a Big Bang and an entropy and it was so much more than I ever could have wanted even though it was nothing like I had imagined.

She stirred against me in a way that felt encouraging, so I continued, exploring everything previously untouchable. At one point I accidentally brushed against her cast, and she unlocked from me for a moment, and said, laughing, "Oh God, that's probably the least sexy thing ever," but it wasn't really, not even close, and I pulled her to me again.

We were here now. A billion years had led to this and there'd be a billion years to come, but right now we were here, and with my lips on hers I was trying to tell her *thank you, thank you, thank you*, in the smallest way, in this small moment, and I think maybe she was doing the same thing. For both of us, this was our first act of freedom.

When we finally pulled apart, her eyes crinkled at the corners and she threw herself back onto the bed. I followed, engulfed by a pain that was no longer pain but pure intensity of feeling. "I feel so light," she breathed into my ear.

"Me too."

I got the inexplicable sense of being underwater, or in space—of a weightlessness that required you to hold your breath.

And there we were, the two of us, clutching my duvet while the world spun underneath us, and we were there for no reason, no reason at all; the same random events that had killed Dad had jolted us awake and brought us here. I thought back to the first week after he died, thinking then there was no feeling quite so strong as misery, but here, there was something greater, greater than ecstasy and misery and not on the scale. It wasn't neutral, not nothing, not a compromise between the two—it was separate and hollering and lovely.

Peace, peace, peace.

"Whitaker," she said, "how did we get here?"

I did not have an answer for her besides my hands in her hair and the moonlight on her face.

19

A MONTH LATER, I BARRELED through the front doors of Pleasant Hills High with a scar on my cheek, a skip in my step, and a USB stick clutched firmly in my left fist.

Leo and I had a plan.

We weren't sure it was a *good* plan, or even a viable plan, but it was nonetheless *a* plan. And we only had one shot to get it right.

His footsteps echoed beside mine on the vinyl floor as we shot through the empty hallways. I could tell he was nervous because he wasn't really speaking; he was worried about getting caught. That hadn't really been a concern of mine, because the one person

I'd worried about finding out already had. Mom found Leo and me scheming a couple of days after he'd managed to pull the file from my phone's mangled hard drive. I'd pleaded with her, expecting her to put on some big song and dance, but she just stood and listened, sipping her coffee. "I don't know what you're talking about," she said.

It made sense, though. She was pissed off when we took the file to the police, and they'd taken it, but sort of half-heartedly, like nothing would come of it. So we decided some vigilante justice was in order.

The graduation ceremony had already begun.

It wasn't really the sort of plan that required Excel spreadsheets or precise timing. All we needed to know was that we had the file, and that Olivia would be there to open the door.

A week after the night of the crash, she'd slipped a piece of notebook paper into my mailbox, folded into a triangle:

sydney,

your mom told my mom what happened and then my mom told me. you might not believe me when i say it but i'm glad you're okay. june too. like, really glad.

i think maybe stuff has gotten a bit too complicated and that our friendship was becoming more work than a good friendship should. and i don't really think it was anyone's fault, which honestly might be the worst part. it's just sad, you know? so. i don't really know what the answer is. idk if there is an answer. we can talk about it, if you want. regardless of what happens between us i

propose one last hurrah so we can nail this clown for good.
idk the whole story obviously but i guess i wanna help you
make things right.

So we did talk. It was ridiculously awkward at first, but eventually we settled into it, made old jokes, and decided that maybe we'd try again. Take it slow and all that. No obligations. Because we weren't sure we wanted to lose each other for good. And as we were talking about what we could do, I told her about the video Leo had managed to retrieve from that night, and she realized the ring of keys she had for all her theatre tech stuff included the projection booth.

Leo and I entered the gym at the tail end of the alma mater. The standing crowd faced a stage a couple of feet off the ground; behind the stage, Pleasant Hills' pennants, sports championships, and a massive tapestry depicting a purple panther, yellow eyes staring down. When the song ended, the bleachers groaned as everyone sat down. *Everyone.* People in Pleasant Hills came to graduation even if they didn't have a kid who was graduating; it was a sign of town unity, community spirit—and it was exactly what we wanted. Everyone in one room.

I bet a lot of them came because they were looking forward to Heath Alderman's speech.

Thankfully, no heads turned toward us as we snuck inside. All the graduating seniors were sitting facing the opposite way, and the sound of the doors opening was masked by the commotion. We scurried to the left, where there was a hallway that led to a set of stairs.

Which led to the projection booth.

"You still have it?" Leo whispered sharply from ahead as we made it to the staircase.

"Ye of little faith."

"Just checking."

The ceremony continued as we ascended, quickly enough not to waste time but slowly enough not to make too much noise. The principal had gone up to the microphone to introduce the next speaker. "Typically at this point in the ceremony," he began, "a speech would be given by the valedictorian of the graduating class, followed by the class president, but this year, we are lucky enough to have a student who has earned both honors. A very exciting time for Pleasant Hills High, and for our community. Truly, this kid's a go-getter, and we all can't wait to see what he does next. It's my pleasure to invite Heath Alderman to the microphone."

Gross.

We'd made it to the door of the projection booth, where Olivia was waiting, wringing her hands.

Leo muttered a *thanks* and zoomed past her, while I stood there, not really sure what to say, until Olivia wrapped me in a quick hug. "Go, go," she said. "Do the thing. Go." Then she disappeared down the stairs.

I followed Leo and jammed the USB stick into his hand.

"Principal Stevens," Heath began below, "trustees, faculty members, family, friends, and fellow graduates, today is truly a day of celebration. It is an honor to be here—"

Leo booted up the computer connected to the projector and stuck in the thumb drive, then cursed it for taking too long.

"—to speak to the community, absolutely, but especially to address the incredible group of friends, peers, and scholars with whom I've shared these halls for the past four years."

Leo clicked his tongue while the monitor came to life.

"Even though I stand before you today, I, believe it or not, do not know it all." This got a laugh from the audience. "Surprising, I know. So I'd like to avoid giving advice—"

I cautiously raised my head to the window, looked down at the graduates clad in bright purple robes below, then up past Heath, to where June was, salutatorian, sitting in her rightful spot on the stage. She deserved more. We locked gazes, and she gave me the faintest nod.

"Okay," Leo said. "Ready, ready, ready. Go."

I pressed a switch on the control panel. The screen would only keep physically rolling down if the switch was held in place, so I positioned a stapler on top to weigh it down.

We fled. Rushed back downstairs to absolve ourselves of responsibility and to witness the chaos.

It worked. The video was running. But we needed the sound.

Heath's speech faltered, and he craned his neck up to watch the descending screen. He flashed a smile at the audience. "I promise I wasn't going to bore you with a presentation!" The audience laughed in that nervous way audiences did when something happened that wasn't supposed to. Heath gestured up to the booth we'd vacated. "Sorry, folks, not sure what's wrong. Can someone, please...?" A random administrator nodded and made their way to the back of the crowd, toward the stairs we'd come down.

The video itself was mainly darkness, and seeing it projected, my stomach sank. Nobody would understand what they were looking at. This was a complete waste of time.

But then I heard it.

"I wanted to ask how it feels to know you've single-handedly ruined *everything*," said Heath's voice over the speakers. "Because you have. None of this would be happening if it weren't for you. Oh, and your fucking faggot of a dad."

Everyone froze.

Heath looked up at the screen in disbelief, then back to the audience, then back to the screen. He truly had no idea what to do, floundering, his arms at his sides and then up to his head and then back down, like he was short-circuiting—it was the most delicious thing I'd ever seen. "Everyone, there's clearly some sort of technical..." he said, as if that weren't very obviously him. His car. His voice. *His* June.

The thud of my head bouncing off the dashboard.

"You stop! You fucking stop! Holy shit, I can't believe I've lost you to some *dyke*!"

The audience was in a state of disarray. They were one moving person, one collective being, twisting and revolting and shouting.

Heath wailed over the sound of his sins. "Folks, I'm sorry, I have no idea what this is!"

And behind him was June. Everyone by now had understood the connection, that June was a part of this too, and the crowd, in between watching Heath melt after being doused with water, was looking to her for guidance: what to do, where to look, how to feel. She gave them nothing except a small, closed-mouth smile that, if considered, would probably have told them everything they needed to know.

She'd won.

Heath looked pleadingly at the audience. "Does anyone know what this is?" he asked, like an idiot.

The district superintendent, who was standing on the stage ready to shake hands, touched Heath lightly on the shoulder and gestured toward the stage stairs.

"No," Heath said, close enough to the microphone for it to pick up his words. "I have a speech. This isn't right."

The audience jeered. Dumb old Heath.

The principal made his way back to the microphone while the superintendent gingerly took Heath's arm and led him offstage. "Listen, I think we're going to get on with things, I, uh—the next speaker? Who? Oh, yes, we have a Pleasant Hills alumnus here to, eh—"

Leo and I slipped out of the door. We'd seen enough. "We did it," he said, and wrapped me in a hug. "Done. How do you feel?"

The truth was, I didn't know how I felt. It absolutely sucked that this was pretty much all we could do, and the feeling that maybe I'd failed June hadn't gone away.

I turned the question back to Leo; this was probably as important to him as it was to me.

He smiled, and that was when I realized his eyes had gone filmy. "Yeah," he said. "I think we've done something here, my love. Something good."

And honestly, I think that was all he wanted.

We really didn't know if anything would come of it.

But we knew Heath sure as hell couldn't show his face back here again.

It was the first really warm day of the year, leaving all of Pleasant Hills a sort of sweet-smelling oven of warm earth and concrete and sky. Heat distortion wobbled up from the parking lot, and the emerald oaks behind melted and trembled.

The cemetery glistened in the light.

June parked the car and looked over to me. "All righty," she said.

It was the second week of June. It had been nine months, I realized, as we stepped through the plots together, weeds and too-tall grass clawing at my exposed shins, making them itch. Nine months.

And we were here to say our goodbyes.

We'd decided it would be fitting, after everything that had happened.

I'd been found out following the graduation fiasco. Of course I had. The school had caught us on the camera inside the projection booth. They were trying to figure out who Leo was, and obviously I wouldn't snitch, so they threatened to charge me with trespassing. Called me into some "disciplinary meeting" and everything. But when I got there, it'd been the same officer from the night of the crash. He'd looked at me, shook his head, and let me leave without any questions.

But it had become one of the biggest scandals in town history. I'd been worried people wouldn't really *get* it, or if they did, they wouldn't know what to do about it, but I was pleasantly surprised. There were Facebook posts. A petition to the local government. Granted, there were as many posts in disagreement, calling Heath things like *responsible* and *stand-up* and berating people for potentially ruining the kid's life *over one mistake*. The usual. Nobody was sure if anything would come of it—if anything *could* come of it—but generally, it seemed like people cared. The police definitely felt the pressure, I think. And because of it, Heath left for Connecticut two weeks earlier than he was supposed to—despite rumors that admissions at Yale had caught wind of the situation. Another rumor: the big brick house on Longbrook was going to be put up for sale.

Now the two girls who had been trying to peel the shadow of what had happened from their lives were going to cleanse themselves for good.

I realized I had never actually said the words. Not when he died. Not at the funeral. But that was the thing—I wasn't sure they were actually words. *Goodbye* was a feeling I'd been avoiding, Band-Aiding, trying to ignore. Now I was here to kiss *goodbye* on the mouth and send it on its way.

June and I stood there for a moment, not really certain how to make that happen.

We stared at the stone. The grass had grown back over his plot, which was difficult and welcome in equal measure. Difficult to see the earth getting on without him. Welcome to see that something had grown.

Male shouting echoed in the distance. It wasn't directed at us, it was a sort of general happy commotion, but June's head shot in that direction anyway. "Sorry. I thought..."

"It's okay." I didn't really say what I meant. *You're okay.*

Everything had changed in barely any time—although I should have been used to that by now. Weirdly, I'd been sleeping better since. Probably not what most people say after a near-death experience. I'd vowed never to go on the ToD again. But that wasn't too hard; instead of thinking about June, I could be with her instead.

She looked at me expectantly. "Do we say something?"

"I don't know. I don't think so."

So we didn't. We sat by the headstone, which looked like a headboard, and I dug my fingernails into the earth, imagining that everything below was Dad and in a way this was like holding his hand. It was all like holding his hand. I could go on and live a life and the whole thing would be like holding his hand.

A warm breeze drifted past us. I thought of the mindfulness techniques Gerry had taught us at the last session:

I'm here. I'm warm. I feel the sun on my shoulders, hear the robins, smell the sweat from her neck. I'm lucky. I'm alive. I am not alone.

And when eternity comes for me, I will not rage.

But I don't have to worry about that for now. There's still so much to do.

Now, it's summer. I'm spending it with her.

We go to the county fair, and I wipe the unnoticed powdered sugar from the corner of her mouth, and that does not remind me of death.

We grab the edges of the world with our fingertips in the early morning, we laugh at constellations, and that does not remind me of death.

We walk the same path Dad and I walked at the River Styx, and some days even that does not remind me of death.

I am still very afraid. I don't think I'll ever not be.

Dad never goes away. He's in the trees, and the inside of my eyelids, and sewn into my flesh. This isn't something I can change. And I know that she'll be gone too, probably sooner than I think; it's only a matter of time before I sew her in too. I worry about not having enough time—and about not being present enough here to spend the time I do have with her fully. And sometimes when I think about that for too long, about Dad for too long, about ends for too long, the fear comes back as fresh and itchy as when it first arrived. But when it does, we talk softly under blankets. June and me.

This will not last forever. I know.

But for now, if you need us, we'll be here, eking out meaning from the rest of the beautiful days until the lights go out.

If you are affected by anything you have read in
The Truth about Keeping Secrets, or are worried about
anyone in your life, these are some of the organizations
that can offer support.

elunanetwork.org

avp.org

suicidepreventionlifeline.org

nami.org

thetrevorproject.org

loveisrespect.org

A Conversation with the Author

Why did you want to tell this story?

A couple of years ago, I developed a fear of death that was beginning to affect my everyday life—a lot like Sydney's. Mine wasn't initiated by the same event as hers, but the fear was the same, so I wanted to write a story about a girl overcoming that fear (because therapy is expensive). From there, June appeared, and Heath and Olivia and Leo, and then it became about a lot of other things that I thought were important: sexuality and truth and grief and abuse and all kinds of death, not just capital-D *Death*.

There's also the whole other dynamic of Sydney not even being able to grieve properly because she's convinced there's a killer on the loose, which offered a fun challenge: writing a story where the thriller elements serve as a backdrop to something more grounded in reality.

Were there any parts of the book you particularly loved to write, or scenes that were particularly challenging?

I loved writing Sydney and June's interactions, to the point where I would sometimes write scenes of them talking to each other about whatever, knowing they wouldn't make the final cut. The second chapter, when Sydney is really in the depths of her grief, was difficult to write because of how dark of a place that is to inhabit for long stretches of time.

Did any particular books, writers, or other art forms influence or inspire you while writing *The Truth about Keeping Secrets*?

I read a lot of YA while I was writing. A foolproof way of unsticking myself whenever I felt stuck was to escape into someone else's work: Jandy Nelson, particularly in *I'll Give You the Sun*, writes with such control and purpose that you can't help but take notes; Nina LaCour's *We Are Okay*, for similar reasons; Alice Oseman, for when my teenagers started to sound like themes dressed as teenagers; E. Lockhart for taut, sophisticated storytelling. Additionally, I'm not sure *The Truth about Keeping Secrets* would have been written had I not read *Looking for Alaska* by John Green in middle school. For bite-size inspiration, I liked to read poetry—mainly Fernando Pessoa and Sylvia Plath.

Do you have any particular writing habits? Are there times or places where you write best?

I usually write in bursts; I'll have, for example, twenty minutes of uninterrupted "on" time, when I'll write without stopping, and then ten minutes of "off" time, when I can do whatever I want. I'll do that for a few hours every day.

I get fidgety when I'm in the same environment for too long, so I don't have one particular spot that I like—there's five different places in my flat that I cycle among—and I think I write best in the very early morning/very late night. There's something about feeling like the only person on earth that helps the words flow.

Is there anything you've learned through the novel-writing process that you wish you'd known when you started out writing this book?

I really wish I hadn't self-edited while writing the first draft! I'd always go back and edit scenes despite the knowledge that they could be moved or changed or cut—and, what d'you know, they often were. I wasted a lot of time that could have been spent finishing the thing.

In 2016, you published your poetry collection *Graffiti*. How does writing your novel compare to your experiences writing poetry? Have you been writing poetry while working on *The Truth about Keeping Secrets*?

I love writing both poetry and prose, but for the exact opposite reasons. Poetry renounces structure and can really be anything at all, whereas a novel relies on structure. I really enjoyed mulling over the anatomy of the story until everything finally clicked into place.

Writing a novel is sort of like being in a really intense relationship where you can't imagine devoting any of your time or energy or waking thoughts to anything that isn't *it*, so any scraps of ideas I had while writing that I'd normally turn into poems were whisked away to be incorporated into the book somehow.

Do you have advice for other young writers starting out on their writing journeys?

I have no original advice, so here's some unoriginal advice: Read like a writer (so, like a thief), make a habit of it (maybe aim for a daily page or word count goal), and don't let the fear of failure discourage you from writing completely (you can edit a crappy page, but you can't edit a blank one). And keep everything you write, so you can laugh at yourself later.

Turn the page for two never-before-seen poems
by Savannah Brown

today i've decided to speak to the trees

maidenhair dogwood and buckeye
wing-tipped seraphim spread-
speak quiet, for them to talk back you must
make some admissions, like catholic confession,

so i tell them i often feel like i am looking at life
in the profile instead of straight on or
like all the world lies behind a keyhole and the vignette
of my vision is all the things i don't know.

i tell them i asked too many questions
in sunday school and look where that got me
and that sometimes i hold my breath for too
long to remind myself what i stand to lose.

i tell them considering these things with any conviction
is like binding magnets of the same polarity;
my mind would rather be flung to the corner of
the room than consider itself disposable.

sometimes i am thankful for my hot animal flesh.
sometimes i am so deeply distressed
by my hot animal flesh that i write poems
to try and transcend the biological —

maybe my heart instead of i am
ought to be bragging i matter —

and the trees say we don't bury,
we plant.

the trees say reality is a story told
by the winners, the loving and beating and conscious,
and nestled in between the cracks we don't step on
lives the seams that keep the cosmos from splitting,

and at the end of the endless day
i curl myself against them,
the jagged roots like a womb,
and the trees remind me that being human
was the hardest thing they ever had to do.

for no reason

rot lies with me in bed

clumsy, stinking beast who

threads forever through my lips

and pulls, mouths

there's no place for me here;

prove me wrong

i should fear my heart both beating and still;

prove me wrong

(here, i shoot

up with a rasping gasp)

only pain;

prove me wrong —

the sky does when, through a yawning

wound it sends

a baptism, then flecks

of sunlight,

which glint off the canal like diamonds,

for no

reason

Acknowledgments

To my agent, Richard Pike: You championed *The Truth about Keeping Secrets* from the beginning. Thank you for taking a chance on me, for shepherding me into this wonderful world, and assuring me that there was room for my voice within it.

To my editor, Holly Harris: I cannot imagine what this experience would have been like were it not for your commitment to scraping chunks of my brain from the walls and gluing them back together, repeatedly. Thank you endlessly for your enthusiasm, your guidance, and your patience. *The Truth about Keeping Secrets* and I are so grateful for you.

With that said, a massive thank-you to the entire team at Penguin UK: Stephanie Barrett and Anna Bowles, for such studious and thoughtful copy edits; proofreaders Petra Bryce and Mary O'Riordan, for your meticulousness and care; Emily Smyth, for turning "can it be, like, classy?" into a cover more beautiful than I could've dreamed; and my brilliant publicist Harriet Venn.

Thank you to my beta readers—Patrick, Kate, Delen, Charity, Jessie, Jordan, Robyn, Anne, and Anya—for providing incredibly helpful feedback on an early draft of TTAKS.

Thanks to General Elijah Wadsworth for founding Wadsworth, Ohio, in 1814 so I could grow up there two centuries later and subsequently write this book about it.

To my parents: I'm not sure why you've both tirelessly supported me in all my ridiculous schemes, but I am so thankful you have, and I think, somehow, it's worked out. And to my partner, Bert: It's very funny of you to say that you've contributed nothing, and even funnier to say that this is the first actual book you've read, but I'm not sure that's true (about your contribution, not your reading habits). You are my closest confidant and greatest friend.

Thank you for everything.

About the Author

Savannah Brown is the author of *The Truth about Keeping Secrets* and *Graffiti*, a self-published poetry collection, which was a finalist in the Goodreads Choice Awards. Savannah grew up in Wadsworth, Ohio, and currently resides in London, England. When she isn't writing, she can usually be found watching conspiracy theory documentaries, making faces at her cat, or worrying.

FIREreads